THE FABER CARIBBEAN SERIES

Editor: Caryl Phillips

The aim of this series is to publish the finest work being produced in the Caribbean and the Caribbean diaspora, in the four major languages of the region: English, French, Spanish and Dutch. It contains original work, including classic texts, much of which is published for the first time in English. It also aims to give anglophone readers in particular a broader and more profound sense of the literary culture that has evolved in the area over five hundred years of history. While the emphasis is on fiction, it is open to all literary forms.

A View from the Mangrove

ANTONIO BENÍTEZ-ROJO

Translated from the Spanish
James Maraniss

faber and faber
LONDON · BOSTON

First published in 1998
by Faber and Faber Limited
3 Queen Square London WC1N 3AU

Typeset by Faber and Faber Ltd
Printed in England by Mackays of Chatham plc, Chatham, Kent

© Antonio Benítez-Rojo, 1998
Translation © James Maraniss, 1998

Antonio Benítez-Rojo is hereby identified as author of this
work in accordance with Section 77 of the Copyright,
Designs and Patents Act 1988

A CIP record for this book
is available from the British Library
ISBN 0–571–19325–0

2 4 6 8 10 9 7 5 3 1

for Julio, wherever he is

CONTENTS

AUTHOR'S NOTE

With this collection of stories, I am finishing an old effort:
to write a trilogy of works on the Caribbean using three
different genres. The present book is preceded by the
novel *Sea of Lentils* and the essays in *The Repeating Island*,
which were published in English in 1990 and 1992
respectively.

Most of these eleven stories have not been published in
either English or Spanish. The only exceptions are
"Heaven and Earth" and "Gentlemen's Agreement,"
which first appeared in *New England Review and Bread Loaf
Quarterly* (1984 and 1985, respectively) and were included
in *The Magic Dog and Other Stories* (Hanover, N.H.:
Ediciones del Norte, 1990), © Antonio Benítez-Rojo;
"Incident in the Cordillera," published in *Review: Latin
American Literature and Arts* (1996); parts of "Marina 1936"
first appeared in *Conjunctions* (1996). With the exception
of the translation of "Heaven and Earth," which was done
by Marta Siberio, all of the translations were done by
James Maraniss, my friend and colleague at Amherst
College.

As will be seen, the scenes, characters, conflicts, effects,
and narrative styles that I use here change radically from
one story to another. I did this for two reasons. The first
one lies in the historical complexity and ethnic and linguistic diversity of the Caribbean, which seemed to me to

need reflecting within the book in some way. The second has to do with me myself, with my Caribbean nature, which inclines me irremediably toward the heterogeneous and the polyrhythmic. And so "Gentlemen's Agreement" is constructed upon a strictly historical incident; "The Broken Flute," on a tragic anthropological reflection; "Incident in the Cordillera," upon the obsessive description of a landscape; "Veracruz," on a desire to demystify history through humor; "St. Martin's Cape," upon an imaginary dialogue concerning an economic subject; "Windward Passage," on the confessions of a guilty priest stationed in Hispaniola; "Summer Island," on events surrounding the colonization of St. Kitts; "A View from the Mangrove," on the troubled days of a soldier during Cuba's War of Independence; "Heaven and Earth," on my own political and cultural experiences; and "Marina 1936," on an experimental model that combines the poetry of nostalgia with extreme forms of the baroque and magic realism. I don't pretend to be entirely original: the human conflicts that I put into "Full Moon in Le Cap" have their points of origin in a forgotten drama of Derek Walcott and an unforgettable film by Milcho Manchevski.

PART I

GENTLEMEN'S AGREEMENT

The cabin that serves as John Hawkins's quarters in the ship *Jesus of Lubeck* is airy and spacious, though rather low at the ceiling. A gilded light comes into the room through the starboard windows, burnishing the painted planks, the wax on the furniture, and the silver of the candlesticks, vessels, and coffers. Tapestries hang from the bulkheads, instruments of navigation from the overhead beams. Most apparent among these instruments – for their size as well as their visible swaying – are the yellow brass astrolabe, whose ciphered rim is a bit worn from fixing latitudes, and two large globes, probably of Dutch or German manufacture, one featuring the constellations, the other the outline of the known world. There is something unsettling about these cosmic orbicles, perhaps their continual oscillation, perhaps the thinness of the cord that holds them. In any event, their engraved surfaces show fiery-tailed comets and prophesies of Melancthon and Nostradamus.

The bunk is in a corner; beneath it a pile of notebooks and three trunks in a row; beyond it a cupboard, deep and solid, from which a shelf protrudes, holding a compass case, a wide navigator's chart that curls to within an inch of the floor, and a set of hourglasses with very white sand. The room is dominated fore and aft by a culverin, an eighteen-pounder, as well as a rectangular table with stools set about it. Mounted on a strong, heavy carriage, the culverin has been placed in firing position, so that a third of its shapely muzzle disappears through the open porthole. The table, clutching the planks with its clawed feet, is set with two large oval baskets in which papayas, pineapples, and guavas ripen. Facing the table, as he leans back upon the culverin, George Fitzwilliam laughs, slapping his thigh with his cap of scarlet cloth. At the head of the table, seated in a high-backed chair, Hawkins smiles, more with his sparkling grey eyes than with his tightly compressed lips.

The subject is Africa. Hawkins hazards a new venture, one sure to interest the queen. He hopes that she will again assume most of the loan and the cost of provisioning the *Minion* and the *Jesus of Lubeck*. Of course, he will have to sail earlier, risking the dog days, with their fevers and calms, to get a jump on the Portuguese. With enough time he will be able, for one thing, to try his luck with the Waloffs. He had been assured that they were very tall and hardy Negroes, used to the rigors of Senegal's desert backlands, although he had also heard that they were exceedingly vigilant, light footed and long winded, as difficult to bag as deer. Moving to the table to pick up a piece of fruit, Fitzwilliam suggests that they take on horses at the Canary Islands after enlisting good horsemen from among London's idle gentlemen. Hawkins, however, holds that the dunes of northwest Africa are quite far from resembling the Midlands meadows. He has considered the matter, and the best idea is to build a fort, modest but strong, on the coast south of Cap Blanc. There he might deal with the Bedouin sheiks, and surely one of them would swallow his bait of pistols, harquebuses, and leather cuirasses. No one to match them at running after and catching Waloffs, for they were a race of horsemen schooled in war, in eternal combat with rival breeds; further, they were ancient enemies of the Spaniards and the Portuguese, an incalculable advantage. Within a couple of years the fort will be like another Elmina, and then it's just a matter of collecting four or five hundred healthy Waloffs every autumn and dispatching them to the Spanish Main. He would also route part of the squadron to Sierra Leone on the high seas, stopping nowhere. It wouldn't do to have to face again the arrows of the Cape Verde Negroes, whose poison would shut the jaws as though with locks and could polish off the strongest Plymouth lad in under a week; nor would the squadron penetrate the San Domingo's swampy mouth, where you had to move with poles, and the Negroes, baptized by the Portuguese, were particularly hostile: he remembered a swimmer with a back like a hippopotamus who, his neck pierced by a crossbow's dart, had yet the spirit to knock down an oar from the last boat, return with it to the shore, and wave it at the ship like a trophy until falling dead at his chieftain's feet. No, there could be no landing at all until they had passed the Bijouga Islands, for their only decent objective to the south of Cap Blanc was Sierra Leone: on the banks of its rivers there were great bands of clashing Negroes, teeming villages like Conga, and petty monarchs like Zambulo, Yhoma, Sheri, Sacina, and Setecama, all desperately greedy, drunk on women and palm wine, and ready to sell each other out for a trifle. There they would board another five hundred Negroes and head to sea with the first favorable wind, after taking on yams and rice, which, together with the sharks they might catch and lentils they bought in Gomera, would feed their cargo through the fifty-day voyage.

Fitzwilliam, rolling a guava from hand to hand upon the table, feels honored once again at Hawkins's confidence. He might think himself lucky to have joined his destiny to that of this circumspect man with high forehead and foxlike beard, who in just a few years had become a partner of the queen. Besides good money, Hawkins had gained for himself a coat of arms – its motto, *Advancement by Diligence* – whose crest bore a Negro in chains above a lion rampant on the waves.

Hawkins removes his glance from the bronze globe of the constellations and tries to gauge the effect his words have made upon the young gentleman's face. Practiced in reading the minds of his interlocutors, he senses enthusiasm and admiration in Fitzwilliam. Satisfied that this nephew of Lady Jane Dormer – she who had married the Spanish ambassador to the queen – has been won over to his plan, he smiles with approbation and begins to talk of America. His gray pupils brighten as he retakes the oscillating globes, suddenly incarnadined by the strange light brought in the window from the setting sun.

On his first triangular crossing he had reached Hispaniola, a green, velvety island with high sierras and a very healthy coast. There he had seen those marvelous hides, broad and thick, which folded with the gentle stubbornness of sheeted steel. He had also seen the powerful machines costing twenty thousand ducats that harnessed the river's current to move wheels and complicated gears to crush armful upon armful of sugarcane; the frothy juice cooked quickly in large copper pans until changed, through miraculous transitions, to golden granules of sugar. He had seen the groves of cassia trees, the forests of mahogany and palobrasil, the cotton plantations, and the hedges of sarsaparilla, ah, those exquisite bits of handcrafted tortoiseshell. He recalled that his old *Salomon* had been taken by the wind to a great bay, wide and deep, shaped like a horseshoe, from which he could see the roofs of a settlement: it was Puerto Plata, at the foot of Monte de Plata, the Silver Mountain, whose peak was wrapped in a veil of argent mist; those exotic gleams were said to issue from the waters of a vaporous lagoon, but how was one to know? In any event that was what a Dominican friar, caretaker of a stone monastery near the village, had told him. By the way, in that particular monastery a priest named Casas had lived and written many books: he was a man who had stirred himself on the Indians' behalf throughout his life; he had tried to lighten their ordeal in the mines and the fields, but he did not succeed, and now this weak race, diminutive and beardless, had sunk into the earth never to return. When the ships dropped anchor in Puerto Plata and the cargo was brought out, there was not a colonist who did not dream of acquiring at least a dozen slaves, especially Sapies from Sierra Leone, who because they were the last to be captured were in excellent condition. The villagers' excitement was such that the mayor had had to beg him the favor of withdrawing his ships toward a deserted cove that had turned out to be the port of the abandoned Isabela, a damned village, a town laid waste by hunger and disease, by conspiracy, by the plague, by crime and execution, yes, the half-built town that Christopher Columbus had been unable to complete. Its ruins stood upon a flat elevation, slightly inclined, near a stagnant river; the blackened stone columns and arcades, now hidden by vegetation, gave out mournful exhalations, as if the huddle of streets and walls were a solitary and vast tomb. Before he left Puerto Plata someone had whispered in his ear that there were ghosts in Isabela, the tormented souls of the ones who had died there unconfessed. But that was just idle talk, since no matter how much you might wander through the place you weren't going to see even one of those imagined damned souls, nor anything that might resemble one. It was true that once, when he had slipped through a curtain of dense growth, he had found himself in an enclosure – perhaps the nave of a church or even a hospital or a barracks. There he had been overtaken by a vision of ten or twelve knights in old-fashioned armors, stretched out upon the grass, swords between their legs and fists clenched over the hilts. Then, as if they had felt his presence in some way, they opened their eyes, and with hollow, resonant voices began to sing a sombre requiem. When they had finished, he politely asked them if they would like to buy Negroes, for he had brought some vigorous and hardworking ones. But the Spaniards' flesh grew paler until it faded out entirely, and beneath the coats of rusty mail there remained but bare and whitened bones . . . And Hawkins settles back into his chair, lets out a little cough, and winks repeatedly at the gaping Fitzwilliam, who finally explodes in laughter as he slaps his thigh with his cap of scarlet cloth.

He had sold nearly three hundred Negroes in Isabela, as well as many yards of cloth and an unforeseen number of metal and earthenware utensils. The colonists came out gaily to buy. They came from Puerto Plata, Montecristi, and Santiago de los Caballeros, an important city wedged within the mountains. There were so many of them that he had stalls set up along the shorefront, and his musicians, cooks, and pages couldn't meet the demands of the dusty, happy throngs that came out one after another. Never had an Englishman been seen there before, and the children had touched their clothes, and the young girls looked at them entranced, and the men fought for the pitchers of ale and learned to bowl at skittles. When he unloaded the first Negroes, the shouting and enthusiasm terrified the poor devils, who thought they were going to be roasted for dinner. A frenetic planter, pointing right and left, pressed his demand for twenty slaves to restart his stopped sugar mill; another, with a hot, furtive look, pointed out two trumpet-lipped girls, because I want them for domestic service, fifty gold pieces for each. Naturally there is always some difficulty, and one night a man named Bernáldez had shown up with a captain's commission written at the General Court of Santo Domingo and tried to intimidate him with pistol shots and a grandee's airs. He had even had the nerve to capture two sentries who had been posted on the hill. Of course they had been ransomed for a handful of Negroes, and the matter had ended there: Captain Bernáldez was so grateful to him that he gave him a safe conduct certificate and allowed his own men to trade their purses, jewels, and gold chains for slaves at a rate of ninety ducats each. As it turned out, Negroes were also traded for goods, and after a few days the load of hides and sugar exceeded the capacity of his ships. As he still had a certain number of sick Negroes, he had offered them as rental payment for a rotten-timbered merchantman whose owner had used it to ship products to the port of Santo Domingo. That sorry hulk could never have made the long passage to England, so he had resolved to send it to Seville, consigned to Hugh Tipton, agent for Hickman and Castlyn. He did the same with the caravel taken from the Portuguese on the upper Mitombi, too ridden with wormholes to make it around Cape Finisterre. But here there were some serious difficulties: the merchantman, for reasons that he still did not know, had stopped in Lisbon, where the anger of the slave traders, unused to foreign competition, had forced the authorities to confiscate her. Meanwhile Tommy Hampton managed to get the caravel to Seville, though it had no better fate than the merchantman, and the merchandise got locked up in the warehouses of the Board of Trade. More dead than alive, poor Tommy had had to leave for the Canary Islands disguised as a monk to escape the dungeons of the Holy Office. In spite of these calamities, the venture was thought an excellent piece of business in London: after expenses, there had been a profit of . . . well, business is business, and it wouldn't do to divulge every detail, especially with the queen involved. And as for the queen, it was then that she and the royal council began to consider him a man for great undertakings.

Coche, Cubagua, Margarita, three minuscule islands north of Venezuela, their pearl banks the finest of the New World . . . On his previous journey he had seen those fabulous pearls, grave and translucent, which could burn the hand with their brilliance. In Cubagua he had met an old Indian, dry as a husk, who was a survivor of the early divers. He was sold there when pearls were weighed like flour in the squares of Nueva Cadiz, the main town of the island. In those times its streets had swarmed with taverns with gaming tables and young whores from the coast whose small breasts, pointed like canoes, were smeared with the red dye of the bija plant to repel mosquitoes; there, in those haunts, the men killed one another with knife thrusts, or perhaps, sored and stinking, lay dying in some hammock as they begged vainly for confession, their crotches stuffed with pearls and worms. Bad living, the burnings and sackings of the French corsairs, and the lack of water and the abundance of hurricanes had turned Nueva Cadiz into a ghost ship, her gunwales eroded and her masts decrepit; over her quarterdeck, blackened by oblivion, the sea birds went to die . . . Thus Cubagua and Coche had gone to hell. And the isle of Margarita must have suffered the same, since her church and fortress were now just hollow stones, enormous spider webs figured with towers, arches, and portals. In the dockside huts there lived six or seven pigheaded Spaniards who, naked, with daggers in their teeth, went diving every day beside the last remaining Indians. It was then that the man from Flanders arrived with the Negresses. They were bluish, big-hipped, and very woolly; when made to kneel they looked like merino ewes, when they dived, like sea cows. One night they decided to die together, and it's said that their pregnant bellies, until the breakers destroyed them, floated on the surface like wineskins. But soon a Portuguese brought a hundred Negroes, and many of the Spaniards of Terra Firma abandoned their unproductive mines and flocked, with their barefoot Indian women, to the pearl banks that beckoned from Margarita . . . A man could dive to a depth of five fathoms, an Indian seven, but a Negro trained well by the Portuguese could go down to nine or ten. The Negro divers were not allowed to eat any soup or potatoes, nor juicy fruits, nor fried foods, salads, barbecued meats, or stews; to make them descend to such depths in their cages without bursting it was essential not to fill their bellies and to keep them alive with strips of jerked meat and no more liquid than a quart of water per day; nor were they allowed the pleasure of Negro or Indian women, or animals; the disobedient had their members sliced off, for continual squirting weakened the lungs . . . Nobody like the Portuguese at handling Negroes and getting good things from them. The Spaniards, on the other hand, had a knack with the Indians, except, naturally, the Caribs. He had not been too cautious in keeping his men from going ashore at Dominica, since the Caribs would fight until they dropped dead on the spot. Some said that they couldn't be counted as Indians, but rather as an exterminating plague, the Black Death itself made flesh and fang. They were taller than the Arawaks, slender and man eating; their females fought beside the males and, puckering their lips, screamed and yelled like the monkeys of Sierra Leone when their young are captured, and they delivered tremendous blows with their clubs and javelins; it was not true, however, that they were born with tails. The Spaniards had ceased trying to conquer their islands, which, curving like a palm leaf, stretched from the Gulf of Paria to the Virgin Islands Passage. To console themselves they called them the "useless islands," though it was well known that many were rich in freshwater springs, nor did they lack inlets and anchorages, nor forests with good stands of timber, nor delicate white beaches sown with turtle eggs. God only knows what will happen to them in the years to come. The Spaniards, anyway, stuck to the larger islands and the coasts of the New World. He knew of dozens of towns whose inhabitants fought with swords in hand over just a few Negroes. Thanks to this dearth of muscle, more than one Englishman would get rich from the slave trade.

Followed closely by Fitzwilliam's look, Hawkins walks to the cupboard, stops before the chart that curls over the shelf, and points a finger at the paper. "God willing, tomorrow we shall be in Riohacha," he murmurs. "There we will fish for more pearls."

Beyond the stockade half of Riohacha has been converted into ash and ember, mud walls smoking from wooden ribs. In the village square a hundred men, armed and uproarious, gamble at skittles and knucklebones, roast suckling pigs on a spit, and guzzle wine at a depot improvised from scorched planks and a roof of palm leaves. The small church is intact, and in its cramped atrium two halberdiers amuse themselves by sticking the haunches of the cattle that a corpulent man drives by amid the incessant barking of a black dog. The other stone building is a combined house and redoubt on whose flat roof are flags bearing the cross of St. George and the Tudor coat of arms, four cannons, and a score of harquebusiers, almost all leaning on the rail that overlooks the courtyard. Below, among the rosebushes, Hawkins, Fitzwilliam, and two young captains pace in unison together with the important men of Riohacha. With a courtly gesture, Hawkins invites all to follow him down a hall at his right, at the end of which a linen-covered table gleams with the silver that travels with him on the *Jesus of Lubeck*; on it are small loaves made from the flour of his own storeroom, figs and dates taken on in Senegal, and claret provided by the Huguenot corsairs of Cabo Roxo; with another gesture, haughty and imperative, he signals to his musicians, and at once a Devonshire air leaps through the hall, grazes the whitewash, plays among the crossbeams, and enlivens the wine and the appetites of the Spaniards, who nudge one another and whisper that you might say what you will about Juan Haquines, but not that he is not a grand *señor*.

The noble gentlemen could see – Fitzwilliam translates – that his intentions were the best, and no one regretted what had happened more than he. He had ordered twenty lashes for the idiot who started the fire. If it had been intentional, the wretch would now be swinging from a yardarm. But in spite of this, what kind of reception had his emissary been given? None other, to be sure, than a humiliating tongue-lashing from Don Miguel de Castellanos, who was trying to frighten him with absurd threats, and who boasted that King Philip would send him enough gold to finance the town's reconstruction ten times over. This meant that Don Miguel thought he could get along on money from the king, as if his owning that house, the only stone house in many leagues of coastline, were not enough for him. What harm had he done to be received in such a way? Here was Francis Drake, the youngest and brightest of his captains, whose attempt to fill his fresh water casks had earned him nine cannonades ordered by Don Miguel; here was Robert Barrett, his first mate, incomparably serious and diligent, who when he had approached the stockade to buy a bit of meat had been rebuffed by a fusillade from Don Miguel; he himself, whose tranquil and serviceable nature had been amply proved from Nueva Cadiz to Cartagena, had had no recourse but to take the town and rescue his men from Don Miguel's abuses. His only wish was to sell a few Negroes, some linens and trinkets, and all at prices much lower than those set in Seville. Did not the gentlemen think it would be better for them if trade were free, not wholly dependent on the leeches at the Board of Trade?

The faraway report of an harquebus at the forest's edge silences the Spaniards. Tending toward miserliness and apriorism, a fashion of the time, one of them may remember the stiff royal fines levied at those who flout the commercial monopoly, another may perceive a divine plan in that loud noise: the soul is endangered; the English serve a heretical queen, and one should not deal with them.

All together, stunned and stumbling, the men flee through the miserable gate of Riohacha.

In the square there are, approximately, three hundred naked men. There are also over fifty naked women, some of them with children in their arms or on their backs. With the exception of these last, who wear a kind of halter, and, bunched and weeping, wander to and fro like domestic birds, the rest are yoked by iron manacles to a long cable. One end of the cable is tied to a ring stuck into a corner of the church, the other is wrapped around one of the pillars of Don Miguel de Castellanos's house. By the church stands a youth, dressed in red hose and a Coventry blue doublet, who plays with the crack of a cord whip upon the bodies of those at hand. To avoid this punishment, the naked men and women slide in a row toward the center of the cable, which smokes with the friction of the manacles. Just a few paces from the stone house, a sailor in a dirty cowl repeats the action of the red-stockinged youth opposite, so that those who flee the lash of each are going to collide in the middle of the square. This painful mass of bodies, writhing in sweat and supplication, stays together for only a minute, as burly young men in leather jerkins thrash the great tangle of flesh with guava-wood clubs, dividing it, diffusing it in groaning flight to the cable ends. Then the scene is repeated again and again.

The onlookers to this event, Hawkins, Barrett, and Drake, do not seem touched by any sort of feeling, say of approbation, enthusiasm, disgust, compassion. Their movements, the words they exchange, are of a businesslike nature, the jargon of their trade. Hawkins, for example, has begun signaling repeatedly to even the blows' intensity: neither too much nor too little, just the amount needed to make the captives keep their limbs in motion, since the prolonged crowding within the ships now demands exercise in the open air. Afterwards, each captive gets a squirt of water on his head from a sponge and a bit of rice with shark meat.

Fitzwilliam's appearance at the gate of the town, the tip of his sword at a runaway's nape, interrupts Hawkins's signaling. It is apparent that Fitzwilliam has been overcome with joy, his cheerful shouts and gestures show it. The Negro, nonetheless, though he regards the sailors in the little square with indifference, is taken every now and again with fleeting tremors that draw his unease out to the surface of his skin; face to face with Hawkins, he lowers his head to his ragged shirt and mumbles a few words. Hawkins shrugs and turns to the triumphant Fitzwilliam who, educated at the court of King Philip, is able to understand the Spanish or Portuguese that some slaves manage to stammer out.

"This bird is an escaped slave of Don Miguel's," Fitzwilliam says. "He knows where the town treasure has been hidden. He will give away the secret if guaranteed his freedom and released upon the Guinea Coast."

"Sierra Leone, Sierra Leone," the Negro interjects.

Hawkins frowns and peers deep into the Negro's eyes. The man has dared to raise his head and is making rigid motions of assent. Half absorbed and half perplexed, as if something mysterious about that race had been revealed, Hawkins glances at the wretched string of prisoners, who, their meal now over, are being loaded in the longboats to be taken back into the ships' holds. Then he rests his hand on the Negro's shoulder.

"*Negro bueno*," he says in his meager Spanish as he smiles with curiosity. "*Negro bueno*," he repeats.

Barrett is to undertake the mission, and Drake will be his lieutenant. During the first nightwatch, the two will penetrate the forest with one hundred chosen men. The Negro, well guarded, will guide them to the treasure. Barrett will surround and subdue the encampment; Drake will stay in reserve, to cover Barrett's retreat once the silver and pearls have been taken. Life will be taken only in self-defense; he who kills for this reason need fear nothing, but he who causes needless injury will be hanged. These are the instructions.

Hawkins, now seated at the solitary table of Don Miguel, hears the drumbeat that signals his men's departure and which is to roll again at their return if the action is successful. Then, with a certain hesitation, he flips the hourglass that sits beside the candlestick. His hand remains upon the table, upside down, wrapped around the base of the hourglass, as if it were a dice cup hiding a decisive roll. Still without moving his arm, he watches the sand as it falls from one hemisphere to the other, passing from time controlled to time untamed. He does this every time he weighs anchor in these waters. And so, elbows on the table, he listens to the whispering passage of the seconds, the minutes . . . His thought conjures first a blurry, flat image; later, bit by bit, this becomes a lively canvas, a nocturnal landscape not wholly illuminated by the waning yellow moon that floats above the beach. Coils of foam, one after another, spin and stretch upon the sand like fleecy rugs; before their murmuring departure, they leave burbling jellyfish, snails, ribbons of slime, and branches of seaweed on the sand. Along the beach the men walk in silence; they are many and they go quickly. Trampling shells and seaweed, they seek a firm foothold in the wet sand. Among the marchers are one-eyed men with felt eyepatches, amputees with sinister hooks, toothless men whose mouths have sunk; others there are whose faces have been eaten out by scrofula, or stippled with the pox, or riven by some terrible scar. These are trusted men, men tempered by shipboard illness, by Portuguese gunpowder, by the arrows and lances of the Negroes of Senegal, Cape Verde, Guinea, and Sierra Leone; they carry broadswords, quivers, crossbows, horns, straps, pikes, knapsacks, harquebuses, and pistols. And the clash of so much leather and iron sounds a somber drone of cowbells and aching backs. At the point are two fine youths in steel breastplates. They could be brothers, as both are of medium height and sturdy, with saffron beards. Between them, manacled, walks a Negro. The men change course, leave the beach and head toward a mass of vegetation on the left. One of the captains waves his handkerchief, and the column stops; then, without letting go of the cord that holds the Negro's hands, he hugs his companion and says something in his ear: the other smiles and goes to the rear.

Hawkins sighs, lifts his eyes from the hourglass, and claps loudly twice. Their faces flustered and still dull with sleep, two blond, lanky youths enter pell-mell to serve their commander an austere collation of cheese, meat, bread, and wine. One of the pages is Hawkins's own nephew; the other, a bit taller and more agile, is a Devonshire lad named Miles Phillips. Hawkins, as he takes little sips from his silver goblet, comments that the malvesie grape of the Canary Islands is dry and sweet at once, a cheerful, lucky wine; there are those who to abbreviate call it *sack*, but he has always known it as *canary*, as his father had done. In the times of good King Harry, when his brother and he had berthed at the wharf to lead into the city the carts that carried barrels from Tenerife, the old men who sunned themselves on the rock at the crossroads had shouted to him: "Westward ho, John Canary!" And so in Plymouth many had known him as John Canary. Now, thanks to the Negro in chains on his escutcheon, they called him John Moor . . . What was the name of the Negro who had escaped from Don Miguel? Diego? Pedro? Whatever his name, he was one of a kind. Fitzwilliam had said that before Don Miguel bought him he had belonged to the butcher Lope de Aguirre, and before that to one of his victims, a captain named Ursúa, a rich and learned man who had caught him in Panama. Barrett said that he spoke Spanish pretty well and that he even knew some English and French, which was unusual, since the Spaniards did not bother to learn other languages. Yes, he was a singular Negro, a Negro with secrets, one who understood whites. What tricks must he have learned from the runaways in Panama; what crimes must he have committed at the word of Lope de Aguirre! And if by chance he were not a murderer, he had at least been witness to that tale of madness, highlighted with slit throats, dismemberings, and burnings: "Lope's Search for Eldorado: A Bloody Affair," he had entitled it when writing it down in one of his notebooks, still affected by the account of the mayor of Asuncion. Yes, after all that, not even a Negro could be an ordinary man. That Negro had learned to think, to calculate, even to negotiate, since he had offered the treasure of Riohacha for his freedom and his passage to Sierra Leone. Could he know something about Eldorado? No, if he did, he would not have asked to be taken home. Could Eldorado exist? Maybe, but finding it was not a task for John Hawkins, sailor, privateer, and merchant with agents in Tenerife and on the Barbary Coast, owner of shares in the Merchant Adventurer, married to the daughter of the Royal Navy's treasurer, and associate of the queen and of London's most powerful investors. No sir, the chimera of Eldorado was rather for cavaliers like Fitzwilliam, or poor devils like Barrett or Drake. No, not Drake: he was not at all foolish, and if his religious passion against Catholics did not lose him his head, he would go far. But Drake did not believe in trade with the Indies, and in fact he did not believe in commerce at all. He had a soldier's mentality, not a merchant's; he preferred the easy conquest of the spoils of war to the elegantly worked out gains of buying and selling. Of course, one should not overlook the fact that Spain had ceased to be the proverbial enemy of France and had turned against England like a rampaging dragon. If the two nations should ever conceive a serious enmity, the time of Francis Drake would have come. But no, that wouldn't happen, thank God: King Philip did not like wars, unlike his father, and Cecil was too able and sensible a man to lead Queen Bess to certain catastrophe. For that matter, both kingdoms depended on trade, above all England, which did not have the riches that Spain could draw from the Indies. There was nothing to fear from Drake. In any event, nobody could say that he had not tried to set him out on the best of all possible courses: first he had promoted him to captain of the Portuguese caravel, then he had given him command of the *Judith,* and now he had sent him along with Barrett to seize Don Miguel's treasure. This was more than enough for a distant cousin. What more could he do for him?

Hawkins kept reflecting as he sipped his wine and nibbled at his meat and cheese. Now and then he would squirm restlessly in his chair: maybe the jungle would swallow Barrett, who was brave but superstitious; maybe right now he was stopping to take the Negro's rope with his right hand and wipe the sweat from his other hand on his Spanish pantaloons; maybe he would decide to wad his handkerchief in his hand, maybe not, maybe he'd worry that this might impede his drawing quickly the two-shot pistol that he carried in his waistband . . . And suddenly Hawkins's imagination was again with his men, and phosphorescent flashes, ephemeral as sparks, would jump out on either side of the path which the Negro seemed to be inventing with each step. Toward the thicket would slide the snakes, repugnantly on their bellies, and the fat, arching spiders. Occasionally a particularly malignant hiss would paralyze the Negro's foot upon the underbrush, for beyond his naked toes there might lie in ambush an agony of vomiting and dreadful convulsions: there were those coiled serpents with two heads and inky blood, whose movements were perverse; there were the ones whose throats were wide as hunting pouches, and the ones who before biting shook the rattle that they carried on their tails; there were, above all, those skinny bright red ones, oily as eels, whose poison, according to the Spaniards, turned the blood to putrid water before you could say "amen." Barrett would think about all that and a chill would set him shivering beneath his breastplate. Perhaps he would remember the jaguar which a few days before, almost at the edge of the forest, had disemboweled the gentle snouted beast who licks the anthills; or the butterfly that fluttered like a spellbound shroud and showed a death's head on its wings; or those huge birds, probably the souls of Indians, who mocked with laughter, whispers, whistles, coughs, and even bells; or the toads who croaked misfortune, or the bats as big as rabbits who drank the life from those who slept outdoors. No, Barrett would feel no unease at recognizing Drake's voice at his shoulder. He would not answer his salute, but neither would he order him back to his place in the column. And thus, united by one's misgiving and the other's boldness, both would follow the Negro, losing themselves progressively within the enigma of shadow and miasma . . . When the now dying fires on the Spanish encampment appeared floating in the mist, Barrett would take them for spirits of the forest. Then, avid and impulsive, Drake would shout the order to attack. The men, howling like wolves to exorcise their fear, would fall upon the sleepy sentinels, upon the tents, upon the hammocks, upon the sacks, chests, and coffers of money hidden beneath mountains of sheets. Barrett would react too late to turn crime into moderation, and Don Miguel's head would already be fixed on the end of a pike. With trembling lips Barrett would reproach Drake for the blood unnecessarily spilled, for disobeying orders: "Do you think the queen will reward you for a killing that could well cause a war with Spain, or at least an embargo?" But Drake would shrug in his impudent way and, smiling, he would turn toward the pile of coins, the bags of pearls, the stamped bars of silver, the sacks of gold dust spilling out upon the trampled earth of Don Miguel's tent.

Hawkins stares at the string of sand which seems to bore through the hourglass. Why hadn't he gone for the treasure? Would it not have been better had he taken Barrett's place, and Barrett taken Drake's, with Drake, for example, left to guard the ships? Could the Negro have something to do with this? For some reason that Negro offended him. Yes, of course, how could he, John Hawkins, trader in Negroes, come to put himself in the hands of a runaway slave, to follow him everywhere through the trackless forest in order to obtain what he had never got through all his cleverness, all his skills as merchant? This was to upset the natural order of things. Besides, that brazen Negro had the mark of one who brought bad luck, for it was a fact that there were people who attracted misfortune; even clothes, houses, and ships could do this. Without going any further, there was the *Minion*, of his own squadron, three hundred tons of cursed planking. It had cost Tommy Hampton some work to put her crew together, since from Lizard Point to Dover there was nobody who didn't know that this rigged coffin had already murdered three crews. He remembered the first one well, the one erased by the plague, and then next summer's, blown up by gunpowder in Plymouth Sound, and the last, sucked to the bone by the African calms. The

scarce dozen men who in each case had been able to survive swore that the ship knew the way back to England,
that certain canvases furled and unfurled by themselves.
But the *Minion*'s curse ended at her own rail and jib; the
Negro's was different. His evil effect flourished all around
him, thus, in Panama his hideout had been annihilated by
Ursúa, and then Ursúa and his beautiful wife had been
beheaded by Lope, and Lope had been quartered after
killing his own daughter, and now Don Miguel had lost
Riohacha, the king's treasure, and perhaps his life. What
would he do with the Negro? He certainly couldn't take
him along to Plymouth, keep him in his own house and
then let him off at Sierra Leone in the coming year. The
best idea would be to sell him in Cartagena.

Clearly relieved by his decision, Hawkins sighs, rubs
his hands, and turns toward his pages, who look at him as
they yawn and rub their eyes in a corner barely illumined
by the flickering candle: "You should go to sleep now, I do
not need you." And crossing his arms on the table, he lays
down his head.

The drumroll, a bit disheveled by the morning breeze,
enters the house like a whirl of cranes. Hawkins blinks,
clears his throat, and putting his hands behind his neck,
straightens his spine. Then he passes a benevolent look
over his pages' bodies, bound together in sleep over one
of Don Miguel's capes, and he pours himself a glass of
wine. He takes a sip, but this time he doesn't seem to
savor the malvesie with the usual pleasure, as if that hazy
night of apprehension had diminished its flavor. But upon
hearing the drum again, now inside the village without a
doubt, he smiles, kneels, and with his hands together like
a child gives thanks to God for the success of his venture.

Don Miguel de Castellanos and John Hawkins, armed

cap-a-pie, walk together in the afternoon along the river wharf. Between them walks Fitzwilliam, his head turning from side to side, interpreting as his commander and the Spaniard expound opinions, complaints, and demands. Although the three men's gestures are restrained, their faces are red and sweating under their helmets. Don Miguel shows more age than Hawkins, his figure bends rather heavily beneath his cuirass, his beard has whitened, and the skin of his eyelids and cheeks has begun to droop around his eyes. Nevertheless, there is a vigorous air to his gait, and his gloved hand, placed delicately upon the hilt of his blade, gives him a certain gallantry and softens his step. First Hawkins's attention and then Don Miguel's is drawn by a distant hubbub coming from an English pinnace. The boat cuts through the rapid current by means of oars, and Hawkins thinks he recognizes, standing at the poop, the corpulent figure of Job Hortop, the *Angel*'s gunner who, egged on by his joking comrades, is trying to toss something overboard, something that struggles and hinders him. The stifled barking tells Hawkins that it's the black dog that Hortop, as his only booty, had taken from the village church and which he had baptized "Slave" in a comic ceremony of lifted cassocks and tavern songs. After the plunge, the animal's head emerges as a dark spot and moves away downstream. On reaching a cable's distance it stops and then begins to trail along against the current, indicating that the dog does not swim freely, that it is towed by the pinnace as live bait.

"*Pescan caimanes,*" Don Miguel says.

"They're fishing for alligators," Fitzwilliam translates.

"*Pescan caimanes,*" Don Miguel repeats with irritation, turning his back on the river to make Hawkins understand that there are still some matters to settle and that the

– 24 –

sun is beating down too fiercely to waste time in foolishness.

There is, for example, the question of the six thousand pesos that Hawkins wants for himself from the king's account in exchange for ceding sixty Negroes. Don Miguel thinks this sum excessive – Fitzwilliam translates – three thousand pesos is the most he can take from the till, and even that is risking jail. Hawkins makes it understood that, from Don Miguel's current position, he could not stop anyone from taking the whole treasure. Furthermore, was he going to overlook the fact that the operation had not spilled a single drop of Spanish blood, that his captains Drake and Barrett as well as the most hotheaded of his men had proceeded at all times with absolute correctness? But, well, enough said: four thousand pesos for the sixty Negroes and license to sell his merchandise there. In the morning he would leave town, replacing all that had been taken, and the next day he would hand over the treasure in a public ceremony, which would inaugurate a week of healthy commerce. He would also appreciate letters sent to Cartagena announcing his arrival and at the same time praising him for his good conduct and scrupulousness, since he knew that some ill-intentioned people put out the word that he was a pirate when in truth he had always behaved as the most honorable and serious merchant. What had he to do with those French devils like Sores and Letelier, who stole even the nails from the towns and hanged or beheaded whomever they wanted? What did Don Miguel have to say to all that?

Don Miguel sighs, assents, and with a slightly ostentatious gesture of goodwill, opens his arms to Hawkins. Then, when Hawkins and Fitzwilliam are about to leave the wharf, he says impulsively:

"El negro."

Stopping on the blackened planks of the wharf, Hawkins lifts his head haughtily and concentrates his look upon the scornful eyes of Don Miguel, whose tawny spots remind him, for a moment, of the bronze globes that hang in his cabin on the *Jesus of Lubeck*.

"Quiero el negro," Don Miguel says somberly. *"Lo haré descuartizar para escarmiento."*

Fitzwilliam turns pale, and with a trembling voice translates Don Miguel's demand: "He wants the Negro. He wants to have him quartered as an example."

Hawkins frowns and sticks out his lower lip in a pout, as he has heard it said that Queen Bess does when something, no matter how insignificant, is asked for after a deal has been settled. *"Sí,"* he answers after a moment of feigned resistance, and he looks askance at Fitzwilliam, brushing off his display of protest.

Don Miguel, removing his helmet and carrying it at his chest, bows gravely, and spinning on the heels of his high boots, returns to his men at the other end of the wharf.

Hawkins stays at the wharf for a while, and just before Don Miguel's boat disappears around the point, he lifts his hand in a cordial gesture of farewell. Then he turns toward Fitzwilliam, who in a low voice has been begging him not to hand over the Negro, since he had given him his word of honor that under no circumstances would he be given back to the Spaniards. With an impatient gesture, Hawkins answers that the word of a gentleman is not on trial when given to a Negro. Furthermore, Don Miguel had more than enough reason to reclaim his former slave and to do whatever he would with him. That crafty and ill-omened Negro had dared to play with the weakness and ambition of his natural masters, and such dangerous disloyalty should be dearly paid for.

From the pinnace, scarcely visible through the fading light of the evening, comes a sudden burst of shouting. To judge from the uproar, the most extraordinary of alligators is about to be caught.

INCIDENT IN THE CORDILLERA

It is a narrow pass. Plants are growing here and there, meager, creeping, gnarled. The road winding through it is a colonial highway, a poor, ungraded road snaking its way through the mountains, detouring around the volcanos and rushing streams. This particular highway, turned white by the two-way traffic of mules and donkeys on the pumice, runs west to east through old Guatemala. It seems to exhale a vapor in the midday sun, because a sudden gust of wind squeezes in between the granite bluffs that flank the road, picks up the dust, and swirls it toward a distant forest, which from this narrow prospect looks like a minimal green eyebrow. The mule train, driven by slaves and guarded by Spanish soldiers, creeps through this parched slot. Above the wind the animals' bells are audible, but the sound, like the dust, rushes forward: to the file of Indian bearers, *tamemes*, and the Spanish rearguard about to enter the pass, the tinkling of copper must be inaudible. A big lizard, crusty and loose-skinned, crosses the road and darts into a thorn bush. One of the soldiers, a young man marching with the Indian messenger at the head of the train, shifts his crossbow to his left hand and hurriedly crosses himself with his right. Suddenly, a thick flock of birds of all sizes and colors flies over the pass: they screech and caw as they desperately flap their wings. Beneath them, the mules come to a dead

stop and tremble, rattling the objects inside their packs –
silver for the king. The slaves tug on the halters, raise
harsh voices that the wind instantly drowns out, beat the
mule's flanks furiously, but cannot get the animals to
budge.

The *tamemes* break the line and gather in a mass, gesturing and staring. On their backs they carry bundles, chests,
and baskets held fast by straps wound tightly across their
foreheads. With their burdens wobbling in the wind, hud-
dled together and bent over by the weight, the bearers
look like a flock of chickens before a storm. Suddenly the
wind stops, along with the mad flapping of wings. The
dust stops whirling and falls straight down, like flour
sprinkled over the mule train, turning the bundles,
manes, haunches, helmets, and capes white. Now the
very air itself has become dazzling whiteness, silence,
endless time. The *tamemes* stop their talking; the slaves
drop their staffs, shield their eyes with their hands, and
look up at the blazing sky.

A thick sulfurous steam, escaped from God knows
where, settles in the pass. The air becomes dim and green,
like a flood of putrid water. The faces of the Spaniards
seem to crumple and hang limply from their helmets; the
skin of the slaves softens and oozes a rank sweat, while
the *tamemes* pant in the calm, bent over their arched, but-
tery legs, swollen ankles, miserable and split toenails.
One of the youngest bearers lets his bundle slip off his
back: the rolled blankets embroidered with quetzal feathers unfurl matter-of-factly along the road; another spills a
cascade of glittering doubloons, a dozen silver goblets.
Every load is shed, and together with finely wrought silver, loaves of brown sugar, bricks of indigo dye, *achiote*
cakes, and chunks of oily chocolate tumble out. Now the
chests and saddle packs disgorge pineapple and guava

preserves, clumps of *mesasuchil* flowers, and sarsaparilla roots; the spices of the Indies season the chalky stones. The *tamemes* pay no attention to the threat of the soldiers and gingerly step backward, bent, as if they were trying to avoid a stalking enemy.

The slaves still stand at the head of the procession, leaning on their mules. They have yet to notice the *tamemes'* silent revolt and, not knowing what else to do, begin singing to lull the animals and get them moving again. The rough chorus breaks off, withering in the stinking vapor that has invaded the pass. All eyes look up, and the stupefied slaves then hear the last echo between the granite walls. The young soldier who'd been startled by the lizard who crossed his path sets his crossbow on a rock, pulls out a dagger, and hamstrings the lead mule. The animal falls heavily, and then, with cool deliberation, the soldier stabs it despite its desperate neighs.

Stiff, covered with blood, the young man walks over to the Indian messenger, a skinny, one-eyed man who has stretched out on the road with his ear pressed to the ground. With the sinister calm of a man bewitched, the Spaniard kneels down and lays the blade of his knife on the Indian's throat. The scout fixes his round, birdlike eye on the soldier, then turns his head to study the overhanging stone. With nothing said, he then gets up and sets off, running down the road. An instant later, a steady rumble resounds in the pass and now the road itself begins to tremble, swing, sway, and split into spluttering ditches. A fissure shaped like a lighting bolt traces a line from the top to the bottom of the wall: the mountain shudders and crumbles over man and beast.

"Are you coming with us?" asks the most corpulent *tameme* as he knots a dirty rag over his head to cover a still-bleeding cut. The slave shakes his head, and with haughty indifference starts to survey the distant forest. The four surviving Indians, each one hurt, gather together everything they've salvaged from the cave-in. They turn away from the slave, tug the mule into motion, and climb the steep mound that has buried the pass. This battered group – the slave follows them with his eyes – makes its difficult way back. When they reach the top of the mound, the *tamemes* pause to catch their breath. To make their climb easier, they have slung their baskets over their backs: their silhouettes, etched into the evening light, are as still and gloomy as crosses in a cemetery.

The slave, after examining the bruise on his shoulder, tries to stuff his bushy head, white with dust, into the dead soldier's helmet. He tosses it away in disgust, and the noise of the metal on the stones has a timbre of sandy desolation. Now he bends over the soldier's body: with both hands he pulls on something half-hidden in the dust. One hard tug that knots his muscles yields a crossbow. Then he kicks the dead man over on his face, strips him quickly of his quiver, crossbow bolts, sword, leather pouch, and water bottle. A distant shout spins him around. One of the *tamemes* comes bounding down the rubble, raising a cloud of dust. "*Negro! Negro!* Wait! I'm going with you!"

The slave waits with downcast eyes. He digs his toe in the dust, his face now sullen and shut.

"Where are you going?" the *tameme* asks, wheezing and clutching the splint on his right arm. Judging by the looks of his hand – attached to his wrist by a bloody tatter – it is not now and may never be of any use to him. A big rock must have fallen on it. "Where are you going? Do you think you can get through here by yourself? If the Spaniards find you, they'll feed you to the dogs. The dogs

are bad. And so many of them. Three, four, five dogs."
The slave shrugs, glancing toward the distant forest.
"Come with me, *negro*, come on. Two heads are better
than one," the Indian says, shaking the dust from his *ayate*
with his good hand. "You don't know these roads. Do you
really think you can walk around here with a sword and a
crossbow? Hell, who the hell do you think you are? You're
no *capitán*. Get rid of them, *negro*. For your own sake, man.
Come on, say something."

The slave tilts his head back and points his finger to his
throat. The curly bristles of his beard conceal a terrible
scar.

"Christ, *negro*, you're lucky! A dog got you. If it had
been a jaguar, you wouldn't be standing here. You
escaped, right?" The slave frowns and answers with a
grunt. "Lucky you're with me, too. I've been down this
road to the coast and back to Quetzaltenango three times.
In four or five days, I'll show you where the runaway
slaves, the *cimarrones*, live," he adds, pointing east.

"They'll make a bandit out of you. You're young and
ready for anything. A five-day walk from here. The Mico
mountains." The slave, his filed teeth shining in a broad
grin, raises his hand to his chest and nods in assent. "But
you'd better get rid of those weapons," the Indian says,
trying to take the crossbow away from the slave. The man
lifts it over his head, out of the *tameme*'s reach. "All right,
negro, whatever you like. When we get to the forest we
leave the road. The messenger, one-eyed Felipe, must be
on the loose over there. You can bet he went to
Acazabastlan to see the mayor, who pays good money for
bad news."

The men walk side by side, avoiding the crevices in the
road left by the earthquake. The Indian glances back at the
now distant mound and crosses himself without breaking

his stride. "May God have mercy on their souls," he murmurs.

They leave the pass behind. Now the road leaves the cordillera and drops sharply down to a sea of pine trees, many knocked down in a north-to-south direction. The dust here is the color of terra cotta, and the vegetation, though still sparse, freshens the air a little with a hint of wildflower and resin. "Look," says the *tameme*, pointing to a stone ruin on a crag. "The Quiché warriors got as far as this when they fought the Tzutuhiles." He proudly adds: "My mother's uncle was the lord of Huehuetenango. The Spaniards burned him at the stake, along with the lords of Atitlan and Solola because they refused to stop worshiping the old gods, Tepeu, Gugumatz, and . . . Shit!" he shouts in fear. They hear a muffled thunder, and the earth trembles a second time. Instinctively, the two men run as quickly as they can toward a patch of grass until the Indian, after a savage tremor, falls forward in the dust.

"Son of a bitch!" the Indian howls as he gets to his feet, the pain etching on his face. "This goddamned hand is bleeding again," settling his arm back into the rag hanging from his neck. The slave examines the *tameme*'s bloody, limp, dislocated hand and tightens the sling around the Indian's wrist until the bleeding stops. Then he ties the Indian's pouch to his own and slings both over his back beside the weapons. "It's like a squashed rat," the *tameme* says, staring sadly and incredulously at his hand. "Oh, Christ, *negro*," he laments, "how will I pay Don Esteban's tribute with this shitty hand? It's no good anymore, *negro*. I'm not worth shit. I'm a cripple. My wife will end up a whore, and my children will turn into thieves. I know it. I'd be better off dead."

The slave unstops the water bottle, hands it to the *tameme*, and walks on ahead. The Indian takes a long swallow and catches up to his companion. "Know what I'll do? I'll go down into the jungle with the Lacandones over beyond Vera Paz. They're wild, pagans. People say they run around as naked as monkeys, and you can't trust them at all. Who knows? Maybe they'll take me in because of all the things I know about. I'm not just a bearer, I can do other things." After a pause, he adds, bitterly: "Even if they kill me, shit, what am I going to do when I'm as good as dead as far as my family is concerned. *Sí señor*. They'll believe the rocks flattened me, and I'd just as soon be dead as be a beggar at the church door."

The slave nods understandingly and takes the *tameme* by the shoulder. They walk on for a short while, until the Indian stops and pulls a curved, silver-handled knife from his *ayate*. "Do me a favor, *negro*," he says, looking into the man's eyes. "Cut this hand off. And I know how to heal a cut." The slave takes the knife and runs his finger down the blade. "Look, if you don't do it, the hand will rot in two days. That's how it went with poor Anselmo, my brother. First the hand, then the arm, then he died screaming and shaking, not wanting to see anybody, God's mercy on him."

From the parapet of the Quiché lookout tower, you can see the road to Acazabastlan and the broad, forested ravine it skirts. Eaten away by time and weather, the tower walls jut out of the underbrush like huge, blackened stone teeth. One cranny has been cleared. In it, the *tameme* dozes while his companion barbecues a small animal, perhaps a puma cub. A dubious awning improvised from their ragged blankets shields them from the sun. The Indian, sitting in a cushion of cut grass, has his back against the wall, his head hanging down on his chest. His arm is still in a sling, but this one is not made from his *ayate*. This sling is made of woven tree bark, and the stump of his arm is packed in dark green leaves. The slave, hunkered down, his torso bare, stares thoughtfully into the pale wood fire. His thoughts entwine, uncoil, fold over with the flame; images, word-sounds, and desires crackle briskly, falling one on top of another, adding luster to his quiet eyes.

A single scene, long enough to be described, does take place. Beside a sleeping river with low banks there is a circular stockade made of strong, sharpened posts. A dusty path leads up to the gate, which opens suddenly. Visible inside is a village of huts with cone-shaped roofs. Inside one of them is a tall woman, singing seriously as she mashes something in a mortar. Her shaven head is oiled and gleaming. She flaunts a copper bracelet on her arm. Now a child starts to howl; the woman stops singing, turns her body toward the darkest corner of the hut, and stretches out her arms in a gathering, maternal way. The scene, or rather the imagined picture formed in memory, begins to tremble, to fold over at the edges like a leaf fallen into the fire. The shapes and colors quickly fade, turn to smoke, and two tears well up in the man's eyes.

In the dream of the *tameme*, or perhaps in a memory he understands to be not entirely his own, there is, first, darkness. Not the darkness of a moonless night, not even a night of star-obliterating cloudiness. It is the darkness of an era without seasons, weeks, or calendars. There is water in this primeval darkness: it's not visible, of course, but you can feel it, like a frozen, still embrace beneath a sky that's black and empty. There is also land here, submerged, a loam that supports the *tameme*'s naked feet. Still within this mythic dream, the man starts walking, wandering, cold and worn-out through the silence and lost time. Somewhere – impossible to tell if it's near or distant – there is a burst of pale light, almost like the glow of smoldering ashes from which emerge murmurings, deep muffled voices that fill this measureless seashore void and make it vibrate. Heartened, the *tameme* walks toward the luminous pulsation with careful, muddy footsteps. Somehow, he knows that hidden under blue and green plumed mantles lie Tepeu and Gugamatz, the Creator and the Shaper. In his dream, he hopes they will restore his right hand.

At daybreak the spectacle of the pine trees growing in the ravine makes a pitiful landscape. The trees have all been knocked down north-to-south and form streets or gutters of uneven ground, some of which are marked by long, toothed cracks. At the edge of the crevices there are often uprooted trees, their roots huge, wormlike knots. This may have been the epicenter because there are thousands of torn, battered pines, and one slope is carpeted by a thick layer of green needles that covers everything except the furrows where the earth was sent flying. The savage, penetrating smell of resin has drawn the woodland ants. Massed in columns, they paint the western face of the hollow a rusty black and cover the wounded trees, the undulating skins of the snakes, and the broken birds' nests. There is something ominous in the annihilating march of their tiny feet, the groping of their pincers; something profoundly old and terrible erupting from a world of carbonous galleries, secret rites, and profanations. At daybreak, they burst out like a fierce, blind plague.

The two men, wrapped in their blankets, are awakened by the biting ants. Startled by the devouring horde that has landed on them, they can barely think before throwing off their blankets and slapping the ants off one another's clothes. Abandoning their leather pouches to the ants, they run helter-skelter down the gully, terrified, trampling small animals also fleeing, bouncing from rock to rock, gaping, open-mouthed.

As he jumps over a tree blocking his path, the Indian stumbles and rolls howling down the slope, finally coming to rest against another tree. He has landed on his wounded arm, and his face, barely raised above the pine needles, is gnarled with terror and flecked with ants. He tries to get up by using his left arm, but collapses, breathing hard. He only has enough strength to raise his hand. "*Negro! Negro!*" he shouts in anguish.

The slave jumps cleanly over the fallen trunk, takes a few strides, and kneels by his companion. He turns the *tameme* onto his back and drags him toward a rock. "Come on, kill me, *negro*. I can't stand it!" he wails, slapping his face with his hand. "Don't let them eat me alive," he sobs. The slave looks back up the ravine: their camp has disappeared under a boiling flow of insects. With a quick gesture, he draws the sword from his back, touching its point to the *tameme*'s jugular vein. "End it now," the Indian implores. "Listen, you dumb slave," he says, trying to smile, "four days toward sunrise and you see a river. The Mico mountains on the other side. Kill me, damn it!"

The slave looks straight at the *tameme*. Despite the fall and the tumbling, the dressing is still fastened to his stump. An angry swelling climbs along his mutilated arm, reaching the right side of his face. His cheek is a loose bladder, his eye a scabby, reddened wrinkle. With a hoarse, furious yell, the man tosses aside his sword, grabs the *tameme* by his left arm, and hoists him onto his back. Without looking backward, he starts running.

The one-eyed Indian observing the march of the ants

from the lookout tower can barely see the two men below in the forest. For a moment he thinks they may escape the columns of ants converging in the east, but soon, after calculating the distances with his round, birdlike eye, he crosses himself and leaves the parapet.

THE BROKEN FLUTE

for Carlos Fuentes

The old man stopped before the monastery's open door, lowered a big basket of white flowers from his head to set beside his unshod feet, and waited to be noticed by the friar who served as gatekeeper.

"What do you want?" the friar asked, looking askance at him, without an interruption in his operation of watering the plants in the flowerpots lined up along the wall of the wide entryway.

"I'm here to see Fray Bernardino," the old man said in a hoarse, low voice, not looking up from the basket.

"So, you've come to see Fray Bernardino," said the friar, leaving his watering can on one of the benches in the entryway. "You're the first. Yesterday two old Indians like you came, and there are three coming today. What's your name?" he asked, drying the water from his hands on his wide Franciscan habit.

"Juan Vallejo."

"Juan Vallejo," the Franciscan muttered, looking at the little piece of paper that he'd taken from his pocket. "Juan Vallejo . . . Here you are. All right, go on in. Clean your feet and wait here until Fray Bernardino sends for you," he added, pointing to the bench that was nearest the door.

The old man, watched closely by the Franciscan, cleaned the mud from his feet as best he could and walked into the entryway. Seating himself on the bench, he stayed as far away as possible from the watering can and placed the basket on his trousers' mended knees. As he did this, a protracted tinkling seemed to issue from within the basket.

"Judging by your wrinkles, you were born and raised in the time of idolatry, isn't that so?" said the friar as he entered the visitor's name in the register at his table. "The Christian faith in Mexico goes back fifty years, and you must be around seventy," he added, examining the old man's withered and undaunted face. "Are you a good Christian?"

The old man looked through the monastery's door, through which the morning's brilliant breeze was coming. "I was baptized quite a while ago," he answered drily.

"And how do you maintain the Christian life that our Lord gave you? Do you sell flowers?"

"I sell whatever I can," said Juan Vallejo. "Sometimes fruit and sometimes birds, or bulbs and pumpkins, or herbs for healing. Right now it's May, and time to sell izquixochitl flowers."

"Well, you do sell things, all right," said the Franciscan. "You know what?" he added, rising from his chair and turning toward the bench. "I'm going to buy all the flowers that you've got. They look fresh and they smell good. The flowers that I put out on the Virgin's altar Monday have started withering."

"I can't sell. They're already bought and paid for," said Juan Vallejo, clutching the basket as though afraid of losing it. "I can't sell them twice."

"We'll see about that, you old scoundrel," said the Franciscan, altering his tone. "What was that noise I heard when you moved the basket? Money? What have you got in there underneath the flowers?"

"I don't have anything," Juan Vallejo said, leaning over

to protect the basket. "Wet grass to keep them fresh."

"And what are you hiding under the grass, you reprobate? Something you stole?"

"There's nothing that's been stolen," protested Juan Vallejo.

"Let's have a look, you thieving Indian!" the Franciscan pressed, his wide neck thickening. "Let me see what you've been carrying in there!"

"It's nobody's business," said the old man, looking the friar in the eye. "It's just my things, old things that Indians have."

"Let me look, you heathen!" the Franciscan shouted, grabbing hold of the basket and pulling. As the two men struggled, the figure of a very old friar appeared quietly in the patio door. "What's going on, Fray Ambrosio?" he asked in a beautiful, soft voice.

Fray Ambrosio stopped tugging, moved away from the bench, and turned toward the old priest. "This man, Fray Bernardino," he said, panting a little, "has something hidden in the basket . . . I don't know, knives maybe."

When he heard the name Fray Bernardino, the old man raised up his head among the flowers: "I've come from Don Diego," he said, in a firm voice, as if mentioning that name would be enough to exempt him from any suspicion.

"Leave this man alone, Fray Ambrosio. What's in his basket has to do with me," Fray Bernardino said, and turning toward the old man, he added: "Follow me, Juan Vallejo. We have a lot to talk about and it's getting late. Did you bring all your things?"

The old man, without answering, lifted the basket onto his head with difficulty and followed Fray Bernardino into the monastery's interior.

*

For the past thirty years, Fray Bernardino had been work-ing tenaciously on his *General History of the Things of New Spain*. It's true that during those years he had not always had the support of his superiors. There had been times when they refused him the money to pay his scribes and informants, and at others they had ordered him to spend his time on matters nearer to the Franciscans' purposes in Mexico, whether preaching in the towns of the Texcoco region or teaching Latin in the order's schools. But one would have to conclude that what contributed most to delaying the work's completion was its monumental pro-portions and extraordinary complexity. Unlike the works of other historians of the Indies, Fray Bernardino's had two different sections: one that compiled in the Nahuatl language material supplied by hundreds of old Indians, people with good reputations who had lived in the times of Moctezuma and remembered the country's past cus-toms and beliefs, and another that he himself was writing in Castilian.

When Fray Bernardino invited Juan Vallejo into his office – a spacious room in the monastery of St. Francis the Greater filled with writing desks, lecterns, maps, and shelves holding reams of paper and rolled-up manu-scripts – he had just begun to revise the twelve books that made up the Nahuatl version of his *History*. For that day, Diego de Grado, the scribe who worked as his secretary, had arranged appointments for him with three old men. Their information was to nourish his final draft of the paragraphs dedicated to the god Tezcatlipoca, which Fray Bernadino had not been able to assemble to his satisfac-tion, although he didn't know why. What was really hap-pening was that the friar, essentially a man of the Renaissance, tended to associate the Mexica deities with the Greco-Roman pantheon. These parallels, although useful now and then, were not really suiting certain deities who resisted comparison. Tezcatlipoca, in whom the friar kept trying to see the attributes of Jupiter, was one of them.

The principal god of the Mexica cosmogony, Tezcatlipoca represented the arbitrary and inscrutable forces that controlled human fate. He was the most feared of the gods, as his acts were unpredictable and he rarely listened to those who asked favors of him; furthermore, one never knew if the scant moments of happiness that he handed out would carry one finally toward the most painful misfortunes. He dwelt in heaven, and from there he granted life. Nonetheless, when he came down to earth he would regularly unleash wars, famines, plagues, droughts, earthquakes, and all sorts of calamities without anyone's knowing why. His name, "mirror of smoke," alluded to the impenetrability of the sacred and the ubiquity of the illusory: the stroke of chance that tangled the thread of a life or simply cut it. Nothing went on that Tezcatlipoca didn't know about. No time or place was alien to him. For that reason they called him "The Lord of the Here and Now." That's why they said that all of life occurred in the palm of his hand.

Naturally, Tezcatlipoca had had his temple in the old city of Mexico – nobody used the name of Tenochtitlan any more. But in order for his invisible presence not to pass unnoticed for even a single day, a walking imitation impersonated him at all times in the streets and squares. This imitator, or human double for the god, was a young man chosen from among the handsomest slaves. His education, imparted in secret by haughty priests, was exhaustive and deeply transforming: when it was over, the young man had been made into an avatar of the divinity. Fray Bernardino's informants had told him that this young man, accompanied by eight pages, walked throughout the city very decked out, now dancing to the warbling of his flute, now smelling the flowers, now sucking smoke from his tobacco pipe, as was the custom among the gods. His face was painted black, the color of the sacred, and, in his waist-length hair, white feathers shone; he wore around his neck a garland of sweet-smelling izquixochitl flowers and a string of precious stones; he wore gold earrings and gold bracelets on his arms and ankles, and from his rich mantle there glinted little golden bells that made music when he walked. The melodies that he played on his flutes were nothing like any that had been heard before; he alone knew how to dance to them. He would greet sweetly everyone he met, and his words were so wise and delicate that nobody could comprehend their deepest meaning. Everyone knew that the young passer-by was the image of Tezcatlipoca, and they knelt before him and worshipped him whenever he came near.

The divine youth was to be Tezcatlipoca for one full year, beginning on the feast day of the god. This festival, whose date was movable and fell after Easter, was called Toxcatl and was one of the most demanding and intense of the Mexica calendar. Twenty days before Toxcatl came, the ritual surrounding the sacred youth changed radically: the stain on his body was washed off, his hair was cut and done up in the style of the most renowned warriors, and he was offered four young women named for goddesses to keep him company in bed. Five days before the festival came, the emperor retired to the depths of his palace and ceded his throne and court to the youth. Then they put on four solemn banquets and dances for him, one for each day, in different parts of the city. When the day of Toxcatl arrived, after all life's pleasures had been tasted, the youth took out the emperor's lavish boat and crossed the lake with all his retinue. On reaching a lonely point called Caoaltepec, he disembarked, while his women and his servants wailed. There, attended by his eight pages, he ascended the steps of a small temple. With each step, he broke one of the flutes that he had made music with. When he reached the last step and broke the last flute, the temple's priests swooped down on him and pulled him toward the sacrificial stone. There his heart was offered to the sun.

At that very moment, in the city, a new youth was being made Tezcatlipoca. As his double was sacrificed in the isolated temple of Caoaltepec, this young man went to the festive dance of Toxcatl, celebrated richly in the Great Temple's galleries, at the foot of the imposing *teocali* in the Plaza Mayor.

Diego de Grado belonged to the second generation of mestizos born in Mexico. Feeble and squinty-eyed from birth, he had tried to offset these deficiencies with the study of Latin and the four liberal arts of the quadrivium. Fray Bernardino, his tutor and employer, had a special regard for him, using him as a translator from Nahuatl, scribe, secretary, and stand-in at the Latin classes that he would dictate at the monastery. Of all the friar's collaborators, Diego de Grado – or Dieguillo, as Fray Bernardino called him – was the only one who had sincerely embraced the project of the *General History of the Things of New Spain*. Fray Bernardino managed to secure for him, an orphan, a lodging in one of the monastery's attics and to arrange for his board in the kitchen. As he was always busy, he had no friends nor did he pay much attention to what was happening around him. This bothered some of the friars who, feeling themselves ignored, believed wrongly that he was a proud man. Every now and then, Fray Bernardino put a few *reales* in his hand, which he would spend at the old-clothes dealer in the market to replace some piece of clothing that had been mended too often. He was an honest and religious man, and he prayed every night for his tutor's health. If someone had asked him what his chief desire was, he would have answered that it was to see all the books of the *History* completed and in print. Only a few days earlier, when the friar decided to revise many of his texts all over again, he had put together, at full speed, a work agenda. During the first week of that month of May he would look for informants to speak about Tezcatlipoca and the festival of Toxcatl.

With his habitual diligence, Dieguillo walked through the city's streets for three days looking for male informants over seventy – Fray Bernardino, as a matter of principle, did not employ women. This task was not at all easy, as the city of Mexico at that time was notable for its scarcity of old men. The extreme mortality of the massacres and privations of the conquest and reconstruction had contributed to this, of course. But apart from these calamities, the local population had been swept by successive epidemics. Given all this, Dieguillo could find only five old men worthy of his trust who would agree to help the friar in exchange for three *reales* per session.

Dieguillo found out about Juan Vallejo indirectly. One morning, as he stopped at the atrium of the cathedral to explore a beggar's random recollections, a disheveled woman who was selling *tamales* on that same corner had insisted that her father knew a lot more about the old idols. "When he gets full of *pulque*," she had added, "he starts talking about Tezcatlipoca until he falls asleep." The woman gave Dieguillo the house's address, telling him that the best time to find her father there was at nightfall.

That same evening Dieguillo set out for the house of Juan Vallejo, which was at the other end of the city in a miserable neighborhood called Santa Ines. With his quick step, it took him less than two hours to leave behind the Churches of the Holy Cross and St. Catherine and then reach the great monastery of St. James. To make his trip shorter, he decided to head diagonally across the Tlatelolco market's vast rectangle, even though it would fill up, at just that time of day, with some bad characters. As he scurried between two drunken Indians and a *zambo* who looked darkly at him, he thought that if Tezcatlipoca's double were to come walking through there they wouldn't even let him take ten steps. That crowd would stitch him up with knife cuts in a snap and quit him of all his gold and jewels. Finally, after splashing through the puddles on a worn-out path, he reached Juan Vallejo's hovel.

The women opened the door and it turned out that Juan Vallejo hadn't come home yet. "Please come in and sit down. I'll find the cooker and heat up a *tamal*."

Dieguillo cast a look at the caved-in chair and the grimy *petates* that served as beds on the floor, and he declined the invitation. "The heat took all the hunger from me. I'll just wait outside."

With night now coming, the woman drew his attention to an old drunk who, with a basket on his head, came weaving toward them on the path. "Well, here he is," she whined. "Dead drunk. The pittance that he makes he drinks right up as *pulque*. If I didn't make *tamales*, we'd have died a long time ago of pure want."

When the old man saw Dieguillo by the door, he tried to draw himself together. It happened that when he tried to pull up his falling trousers, he lost his balance and dropped the basket. When he reached to pick it up, he fell head first and landed face down in the mud. "You should have seen that coming!" the woman shouted angrily, lifting the old man to his feet by the armpits. "Aren't you ashamed to come home like this? What's Don Diego supposed to think? He's come to see you about a thing that's going to do us some good. Just stand up straight, and don't move!" she added as she wiped the mud from his face with her threadbare shawl.

To conceal his embarrassment, Dieguillo had begun to gather the white flowers that had flown out from the basket, putting them back inside. When he finished, he shook out his hands and said that he'd come another time. It was late already and the streets weren't safe at night.

"Wait, *señor*," the woman begged him, grabbing his cape and pulling. "You don't have to bother with another trip. Tomorrow I'll bring him with me to the cathedral. We'll be at the place where you found me. We really need those three *reales*."

Dieguillo, fearing for his cape, assented, said good night, and started walking back in the direction that he'd come from, asking St. Christopher to see him back to the monastery safe and sound. "At least there's a full moon," he muttered to raise his spirits. As he took a turn in the muddy path he heard, in the distance, the woman insulting the old man.

The next day, very early in the morning, Dieguillo brought up the question of Juan Vallejo with Fray Bernardino. The friar was taking little sips of hot chocolate – he almost lived on hot chocolate – and didn't say anything until he had finished. "More than ten years ago," he said, in his beautiful voice, "the name of Juan Vallejo was given to me by a trusted informant. His defects weren't hidden, and for that reason I didn't seek him out. Now that you've found him, I'll tell you this," and he raised his index finger toward the sky as though he were preaching: "Divine Providence doesn't generally knock twice. Go over to the cathedral and offer him six *reales*."

Dieguillo found the woman and the old man in the corner of the atrium. "Here he is," said the woman. "I scrubbed him up and put clean clothes on him." Then, poking the old man with her elbow, she said: "Come on, tell Don Diego something."

"Good day, *señor*," the old man said obediently, without even looking up.

To keep from stretching out the matter, Dieguillo went directly to the point. He told the old man that Fray Bernardino de Sahagún, of the monastery of St. Francis the Greater, was interested in him; he told him he was offering him six *reales* to answer his questions concerning the idol Tezcatlipoca; he said that he ought to be disposed to speak freely, that he had nothing to fear.

"Did I hear you right?" said the woman, clapping her hands. "Six *reales*! Now we won't get thrown out on the street, praise God!"

"Six *reales* is all right," the old man said in his quiet, hoarse voice.

"Only if the information merits it. If not, it's three or four," said Dieguillo.

"It will," the woman said. "You're going to hear a lot of mysteries and marvels from the old times."

Juan Vallejo, leaving his corner, took a few steps through the atrium. After he'd looked for a while at the people coming and going through the plaza, he turned toward Dieguillo: "How much will the friar give me for my treasures?"

"What treasures?" the woman shouted in alarm. "You

don't even have a place to drop dead."

"How much?" the old man repeated, ignoring the woman.

Taken by surprise, Dieguillo did not answer right away. "You'll get nothing if it's something that you stole," he warned.

"The treasures are mine," said the old man, calmly.

"*Ave María purísima!*" the woman whined. "He's drunk and crazy."

"They're things that I've kept hidden," the old man said, swelling in importance before the woman. "My things, things that have to do with Tezcatlipoca."

Dieguillo thought the old man was referring to the *papeles pintados* that served as writing for the Mexica people. Fray Bernardino kept a valuable collection of them, and he thought of illustrating the books of his *History* with them. There weren't many of these papers left, since at the conquest's end they'd been tossed to the flames as trappings of the devil. Every now and then one of Fray Bernardino's informants would quietly pull one from his garment and offer it to him. People were still being hanged for idolatry; trafficking in these was a dangerous business.

"What will the good friar give me?" the old man repeated, a hopeful glint in his watery eyes.

"Well, I don't know," Dieguillo said. "Maybe ten or twelve *reales*. "He'd have to see what you've got . . . That's Fray Bernardino's business, not mine."

Astonished by what she was hearing, the woman had gone silent. Unwrapping a *tamal*, she started nibbling on it.

"Then I'll bring it all to the monastery," the old man said. "Tomorrow?" he asked.

Dieguillo took his schedule from his pocket and looked

at it. "Not tomorrow. Fray Bernardino is busy all day. Maybe, let's see . . . the day after tomorrow, early, because he has two visitors coming in the afternoon."

"It's better that way," said Juan Vallejo. "Now maybe you could help me, *señor*."

"Help you do what?"

The old man went up to Dieguillo and whispered something in his ear. The woman, coming out of her stupor, shouted furiously: "To hell with you and your secrets and your treasure! You're not my father any more!" and throwing the rest of her *tamal* down, she grabbed her pan and walked into the church.

Dieguillo didn't know what to do. Leaving the old man in the corner, he started walking nervously through the atrium. The deal had taken an unforeseen turn, a turn quite foreign to his life as translator and scribe. Breathing last night's *pulque* in his face, Juan Vallejo asked if he would come to the forest of Chapultepec with him that night; his things were buried there at the foot of a tree. He could see the old man's trepidation. If someone saw him digging up *papeles pintados* he could be accused of idolatry. On the other hand, if he were to accompany Juan Vallejo, it all could be cleared up by mentioning Fray Bernardino. Still wavering, he turned to face the old man. He could hardly believe what he saw. With no regard for those who were coming in and leaving the church, Juan Vallejo stood there urinating proudly, as though he were beyond all human judgment, sending his abject spurt into the corner's empty hollow.

Dieguillo walked quickly down the atrium's steps and left the question of Juan Vallejo up to providence.

Fray Bernardino pushed the old man gently into his office and signaled him to put the basket on a table. Then, with a delicate gesture, he dismissed Dieguillo, who had handed him a clear copy of the notes scrawled out the day before. On seeing that his secretary looked surprised, he told him not to worry about his wanting to talk with Juan Vallejo by himself. "You'll always be my right hand, but I think that in this case it's better for our work if this man talks just to me."

As he left the room, Dieguillo couldn't help taking a quick look at the basket. But aside from the scented tumulus of izquixochitl flowers almost spilling from it, there did not seem to be anything else there. Feeling a little cheated, he left the room, and with nothing better to do, he remembered that he hadn't had breakfast and went on toward the kitchen.

Fray Bernardino, who by that time could handle himself pretty well in Nahuatl – he had also learned to read the glyphs on the *papeles pintados* – addressed himself to Juan Vallejo in that language. Following his custom, the first thing he asked him was what his name had been originally and what sign of the old calendar he had been born under. Experience had taught him that his informants, on being called by their Mexica names and reconnected to their old traditions, felt more secure and spoke more freely.

"Me they called Uitztli," answered Juan Vallejo without looking at the friar. "I was born in Tlatelolco . . . on day *ome tochtli*.

"That's not a good day," Fray Bernardino observed. "Day of the Four Hundred Hares, day of drunkards."

"Yes," the old man responded laconically, twisting in his chair. His blackened, worn-out hands began to tremble in his lap.

Fray Bernardino kept silent for a while. When it seemed to him that the Indian had become calmer, he asked: "What's in the basket that you want to show me?"

Juan Vallejo seemed not to listen to the friar's question. He stayed stiff and silent in the chair, looking downward.

"Perhaps you want to sell me something?" asked the friar. "Some *maguey* papers?"

Juan Vallejo kept his lips pressed together, looking at his sorry, splayed-out toes.

Fray Bernardino got up from his armchair and walked over to a small cupboard. He took out a silver cup and a flask of wine. "Would you like some?"

Juan Vallejo shook his head. Then he looked up and studied the friar's face. "I am" – he began, with a tremor in his voice – "I am Tezcatlipoca."

Fray Bernardino blinked, and like a wooden image of some kindly saint, he stood there with arm held out and wine cup in his hand.

"I'm the last Tezcatlipoca," said Juan Vallejo showing his bad teeth in a kind of grimace. "The one who couldn't die. The one who couldn't give his heart up to the sun. The one who walked the streets when Cortez took Tenochtitlan."

Fray Bernardino nodded. A slow smile of comprehension came over his face. "Now I see it," he said in Spanish. "Of course, there was no Toxcatl that year," and holding out the cup again, he added: "Drink, the wine will do you good."

Juan Vallejo drank the wine down in one gulp, and without even a word of thanks, got up, walked away from the friar, and went toward the basket. When he emptied it, a sweet ringing sound went floating through the room. There appeared above the flowers and the grass a golden diadem adorned with an obsidian mirror, various gold bracelets and anklets, strings of precious stones, jade pendants, several brief bone flutes, and a rich mantle sewn with golden bells.

"My God!" the friar exclaimed, lifting his hands to his biretta, breaking the bubble of decorum that covered his strongest feelings.

"I'll sell everything," said Juan Vallejo in Spanish. "It's all for sale," he repeated, in a ferment, taking the cloak and shaking it in the air until he made it ring unbearably. "How many *reales* will the good friar give? A lot. I want many, many *reales*. None of this is stolen. I may be a drunken Indian, a piece of shit, but I am not a thief. All this is mine . . . Look at the gold . . . Many *reales* . . ." And dropping the mantle to the floor, he knelt on it and buried his face in his hands.

"God's mercy on you," said Fray Bernardino. "No money in the world could pay you fairly for everything you've lived through. I cannot help you. Nobody can; only God."

The Indian stood up slowly, and taking the diadem, walked to the room's only window. When there, he raised it to the sun. A sudden ray eclipsed the friar's vision. Covering his eyes, he backed up toward the door; he crashed into a lectern and then fell with it to the floor and bumped his head against the corner of a bookcase. There, his senses dangling from a thin thread of consciousness, he felt the room dissolve around him: the wood cracked, papers flapped like birds. Still dizzy, Fray Bernardino heard a beguiling sound of flutes and little bells. He forced his eyes open, and through a mist of blood that fell into the room, he saw the god in all his glory, dancing nimbly on the piles of paper and the broken furniture.

After he had finished his breakfast, Dieguillo decided to make the round of the Plaza Mayor and see if he could find another old man to serve as an informant. As he passed by his tutor's office, he couldn't resist the temptation to find out what was happening inside. Retracing his steps, he pressed his ear to the door: the only thing he heard was his own breathing and his guilty heartbeat. Surprised by the long silence, he pushed on the door and peeked. At first he thought that there was no one in the room, but when he looked down, he saw Fray Bernardino on the floor, his forehead bloody.

When Dieguillo came back with Fray Romualdo, the ancient military surgeon in charge of the monastery's hospital, Fray Bernardino had managed to sit up in his chair, and he was looking around wildly. As Fray Romualdo washed the wound, Dieguillo placed the lectern back on its base and picked up the pages of the *History* that had rested on it.

"Thank God it's nothing serious," said Fray Romualdo. "The wound has stopped bleeding; it's so small it doesn't even need a stitch. I'll go to the kitchen for some soup; that's the best way for him to get back his strength."

"Not soup," said Fray Bernardino, with a weak smile. "Hot chocolate."

"Hot chocolate then," said Fray Romualdo, happy to see his old friend now the same as always. "I told you. It was more a fright than anything else. Now some rest. Tomorrow he'll be like new. Careful with those lecterns," he recommended from the door. "At our age we have to watch our step."

Once Fray Romualdo had left, Dieguillo took his tutor to the small contiguous room that he used as a bedroom. After stretching him out gently on the bed, he asked him with his usual delicacy whether he had been alone when the accident had happened.

"It's all the same," Fray Bernardino answered, and pulling the cover up he turned his body toward the wall.

The next day, when Dieguillo went to inquire about his

tutor's health, he found him walking calmly through the patio, as was his custom after breakfast. On his right temple there was a small swelling and a tiny scab of dried blood. At the very moment at which Dieguillo was going to remind the friar to pay more attention to his health, the bell at the entryway rang three times, the sign that something unusual was happening outside the monastery.

Fray Bernardino and Dieguillo were among the first to reach the entryway. There stood Fray Ambrosio, the gatekeeper, with the bell cord still in his hands. Without waiting for the other friars to arrive, Fray Ambrosio began telling what had happened: The old Indian who had come in yesterday morning with a basket of flowers, one Juan Vallejo, had gone into one of the Cathedral's empty confessionals. "He took off his rags in there and came out dressed like Moctezuma, his whole body glimmering with gold and jewels. Things he stole from God knows where," he said with a triumphant look that ran all over Fray Bernardino top to bottom. "Then he went out onto the atrium and began to dance and play the flute. Of course, the beggars swooped down on him, and they left him naked on the steps. When order was restored, you could see that the old idolater had a knife wound in his chest."

"What happened to the gold?" a friar asked.

"Confiscated by the viceroy's guards."

"And the dead man?" asked another.

"They've got him lying on a *petate* in the Plaza Mayor. Nobody has claimed him," Fray Ambrosio responded. "They don't know what to do with him and there's talk of dragging his body through the streets as a warning to idolaters."

Fray Bernardino asked no questions and said nothing. He left his birreta on a bench in the entry, and pulling his hood over his head, something that he rarely did, he left the monastery quickly.

He came back fatigued and out of sorts. When Fray Ambrosio came up to him with his birreta, he pretended not to see him and went through the entry with his arms crossed above his chest and his face hidden among the folds of his cowl. In his office, Dieguillo saw him open the cupboard and leave the pieces of a broken flute next to the silver cup.

"Would you like me to stay until I've finished with these papers?" the scribe asked gently.

Fray Bernardino assented with a grunt, and after tossing his hood back over his shoulders with a brusque gesture, told his disciple that the time had come to leave Tezcatlipoca in peace, that it was time now to leave him and take a look at some other texts that ought to be revised.

VERACRUZ

Letelier looked out the porthole, felt the slap of a wet splash, and breathed the bitter taste of a rainstorm carried in an unexpected breeze. Wrapping his chest up in his cape and pulling his hat down over his eyes, for he felt a little feverish, he climbed up to the *Vaillant*'s bridge. All the signs of stormy autumn were painted in the sky: low, darting clouds that unraveled like old bedsheets; behind them a fugitive sun that took on strange appearances, now a copper coin, now a yellow woolen tassel, and the waves were swelling on the ocean, curling at the top, their cadence quickening. He went back to his cabin and walked up to the compass stand. There he pondered for some minutes over a sailing chart and made what was to him the only sensible decision. Surely he could not go back now through the Windward Passage; that would run the risk of shattering his squadron on the coast of Cuba or Hispaniola. The best idea was to let the storm keep pushing them right into the Gulf of Mexico and then hop on the current that would send them out into the open sea through the Florida Strait. After all, that exit wasn't new to him: he'd taken it eight years before on sacking Santiago de Cuba. Yes, things being what they were, this was the best expedient. When could he reach Bordeaux? If everything went right, perhaps by mid-November, maybe by December. He sighed. What might happen in the worst case? He leaned his elbow on the compass stand. Coughing and gasping, he gave rein to his imagination. One precaution that he always took was to think of every possibility, never to be surprised.

Days later, still coughing every now and then, Letelier leaned over the thick paper of his chart. There he had marked, in black ink, the course that the *Vaillant* had followed during that week of storms, but of course it was an estimated course, a course in line with his desire to shorten his return trip. In any event, at the end of the line that he had traced there was no sign of the huge breakers he'd just looked at from the bridge. He went over those fatal days with pen and ruler in hand, consulting his ship's log, and he concluded that his squadron was now in the depths of the Gulf of Mexico. Yes, some place near the Gulf Coast, but where, exactly? Could those shoals he'd just left to leeward be the Triangles? If they were the Triangles, he'd have both Campeche and San Juan de Ulua within his reach. But were those reefs really the Triangles? Had he gone that far inside the Gulf? The Portuguese pilot whom he had captured in Cartagena swore that he had sailed with the Spanish fleet; perhaps he'd recognize them. But it annoyed him to have to resort to pilots in times like these. He generally only asked them about practical matters, usually unimportant ones. Pilots liked to presume, and that Portuguese was capable of spreading the idea that he and he alone had saved the squadron. And that, of course, could incite the usual malcontents to say they'd pay him in exchange for taking them back to France immediately, and there you'd have a mutiny, and God only knew his battered ship could never stand a mutiny, and neither could his spirits.

Letelier, after having celebrated his fortieth birthday with an attack of malaria, drunk on bitter wine, and flabbily collapsed on top of a Negress from Cartagena, had resolved to make this his last voyage. The decision was irrevocable: of the beautiful smile of his adolescence, scurvy had left him with but six blackish teeth, and his lungs worked the air like a pair of leaking bellows; the lush hair of his youth, one of his little vanities, had been devoured by lice and the lingering rashes of equatorial climes; from his face, once expressive, the sun and salt had made a wrinkled, featureless leather mask whose hardened cheeks would scarcely let him part his lips. It was true that his funds in Bordeaux were well invested, but had it been worthwhile in the end to sacrifice his health and his appearance to a strung-out squadron, a farm in Gascony, and eight or nine thousand gold coins? Many years before, when he'd been a ship's boy to the legendary Jean Florin, he surely would have said it would be; now, seeing himself an old man in the mirror, he was sure that it was not. The hour had definitely come for him to leave his calling, marry, have some children . . . and he stopped for a moment to think about just exactly what that meant. It was then that, for the first time in his life, he felt sorry for himself; he saw that twenty-four years at sea had robbed him of any notion of civil life, and that words like home, marriage, and family no longer had any real meaning to him, they were just empty concepts, eggshells dried out in the sun. Overcome by a furious grievance, he blasphemed the memory of viscount Jean d'Ango, who in an evil hour had gone up to the king with the idea of creating a band of corsairs. Definitively, all those enterprising youths, who might have been great navigators like Jean Cartier, had surrendered to the awful life of war at sea: boardings, sackings, burnings, ransom; a life of cannon volleys, blunderbussings, pistol shots, pike stabbings, hatchetings; a life of hangman's noose and headsman's blade, of robbery and rape; a pirate's life, as had been that of Jambe-de-bois Leclerc, like that of Sores, Balier, Bontemps, and of course his own. Was it already too late for him?

Could those greenish shoals be the Triangles? – he asked himself again. If they really were the Triangles, he'd have no choice but to put in at Campeche or San Juan de Ulua, although Campeche would be preferable; it did not sit upon the route of the Spanish fleet, and the port's defenses couldn't amount to much. Clearly, he was imagining the worst. Perhaps the storm had not punished the ships as much as he was assuming; maybe his foremast would withstand the voyage home, and if so the only thing he still had to do was get provisions at any town along the shore and leave that shitty coastline for all time. For the moment he'd order Mendeville to check the rigging; then he'd send him out in a boat to inspect damage to the rest of the squadron.

Antonio Delgadillo was worried. The fishermen who had arrived that afternoon had no news about the fleet. They spoke at length about the big northeaster that had pushed them into the Gulf, and about the four sloops that disappeared, but not one word about the fleet. Everything brought them back to telling tales of their misfortunes, drinking *pulque*, and asking for assistance as they rerigged and took provisioning for a return to Cuba.

The story of bad weather was not news to Captain Delgadillo, who was commander of the garrison at San Juan de Ulua. Eleven days before, on looking out the window toward Veracruz, he had seen, uneasily, the unaccustomed whiteness of the snows of Orizaba and, above all, the volcano's monumental pyramid seemed to have neared the town by two or three leagues. And that illusion, as everyone had known for a long time, was a sign that an inevitable storm was coming from the sea; if it happened in December or January, the storm would bring on drizzles, sea-swells, and a cold north wind; but the month of October had just started, and so now there was reason to suppose that it would bring enormous waves and downpours, with winds that could knock down the most shored-up houses in Veracruz. In spite of this, however, he hadn't thought at first about the fleet. He'd only had a mind to take a close look at his own island, after which he had ordered the iron workers and carpenters, with the aid of a few soldiers, to reinforce the cannons' carriages and the planking in the slave barracks. On the pier that faced Veracruz there was little to be done: the packet that went to and fro from town was safely moored, and even if its anchor gave way, wouldn't be in much danger. As a matter of fact, the island of San Juan de Ulua, port of Veracruz, was a reasonably secure place; the jetty that surrounded it would function as a breakwater, and from a military point of view its defenses were first-class; in the spacious rectangular esplanade a battery of bronze culverins pointed out toward the anchorage and the channel, and another battery defended the long wharf where the packet that went to Campeche and the lightest ships of the fleet tied up; to one side of the esplanade there stood the tower that served as residence of the fort's commander, and at the extreme opposite side were the solid buildings of the storehouse and the garrison's quarters, and the barracks where the slaves slept.

Since Delgadillo did not like to take unnecessary risks, he made another top to bottom inspection of the island, but the only irregularity he observed was that the rat population in the storehouse had grown, which he noted in the diary that he kept meticulously. And it wasn't exactly that Delgadillo was a punctilious officer, but rather that he wanted to be transferred to Mexico City, and so he would do anything he could to make his efforts praiseworthy. He was a bachelor with courtly predispositions, and he had the idea that only in the capital could he make a career for himself, and this, to him, meant the éclat of the viceroy's court, in clever phrases and silk clothing. At times, when the heat kept him awake, his imagination ran free, and, as children do, he'd make up variegated adventures which invariably ended with his being promoted to the rank of general with the title of count and with a noble fiancée. But being the chief of San Juan de Ulua gave no room for fulfilling any of those ardent dreams. There, in the depths of the Gulf of Mexico, no French corsair ever ventured, nor any English contrabandist either; there, among shoals and sandbars, nothing ever happened, and the only days with any life at all came when the fleet arrived or left.

In any case, one never could be absolutely certain whether some high personage was coming in the flagship. That was why Delgadillo, whenever he heard an alerting volley, would convoke upon the esplanade, under a blanket of drumrolls and trumpet calls, his well-drilled host of soldiers, artillerymen, and Negro slaves to rehearse for one more time the complicated ceremony of obeisance that he'd worked out through the long hours of his idleness. But in the five years and as many fleets that he'd seen come and go, there had landed nobody but ambitious second sons like him, as well as endless flocks of bewildered peasants and a lot of people dressed in cassock and biretta destined to fill up the monasteries.

When he found out that the new viceroy, Don Martín Enríquez de Almansa, son of the Marquis of Alcanices, would arrive with the next fleet, Delgadillo took to organizing a reception that would be remembered forever in

Mexico's annals and chronicles. Considering that the crossing over to neighboring Veracruz could generally be made without time lost, the reception had to be brief, and so he had to think of something that would magnify it through intensity. Overcome by dreamy nervousness, he walked up and down the wharf by night, in cap and nightshirt, now talking to himself, now directing smiles and gracious bows toward one or another pelican then standing on the parapet. There was talk among the troops of the Negroes' getting ready to rebel, and the latter looked disgruntled when he made them, every day, sing out and dance a sarabande as they carried on their backs the heaviest coffers and barrels in the warehouse and even the extra masts that some galleon might need for its return. At other times he'd make the archers tie colored ribbons to their arrows and then launch swift, concerted rainbows toward the sea. One morning, his eyes red and his voice unsettled, he awakened six artillerymen to have them mix their powder with cochineal that he kept beneath his cot, a gift from some rich *hacendado* who was going back to Spain to buy a famous castle. On that morning, the Totonec Indians, fishing for their lunch from the deep holes along the shoreline, left their nets to the beating waves and ran to tell their elders about the cannons of San Juan de Ulua that belched clouds of bloody smoke, a sure foretaste of death and ruin. That afternoon, their bedrolls on their shoulders, many were seen fleeing down the road to Jalapa.

When the weather worsened and the stormy days were beating on the coast, Delgadillo began to worry about the fleet. Perhaps the storm had overcome it as it threaded through the channel at Yucatan, and in that case there was no reason to expect much, since the waves that now were beating on the reef, painting overwhelming scenes of foamy spray, would certainly have smashed all the galleons on the shoals of Cozumel or Catoche: goodbye reception, goodbye celebrations, goodbye viceroy, goodby palaces of Mexico, and goodbye wealthy nubile maids. The crew of the Cuban sloop that came that day was of no use at all. They were a bunch of ignorant fishermen who did nothing but whine about their luck and hold their hats out through the streets of Veracruz.

Don Martín Enríquez de Almansa, the Marquis of Alcanices' son and Mexico's new viceroy, called for his valet to support his head, and in three retches spewed into a basin everything that was left in his stomach. Still choking, he dropped himself into the unmade bed while the servant wiped his beard off with a silk handkerchief. There was something deeply artificial in the man's solicitude: maybe it was that way he had of executing quick touches with the handkerchief, as though working with a powder puff, or perhaps it was his outraged gestures, too insistent, too pronounced, or that finicky way he had of pursing his lips, of using his fingertips to sprinkle rosewater on his master's face.

"That's enough now, Avelino. Let me rest," the viceroy ordered with finality. "Ask Don Luis if the storm has ended and when we'll get to Veracruz."

"As the lord viceroy commands."

"Ask him also if he knows of some remedy other than wine for seasickness. No, no. Don't tell him about my puking. Don't tell anyone; they might think I have a weak nature. Understand, you rascal?"

"*Sí, señor.*"

And Don Martín Enríquez de Almansa, stifling a groan, threw off the sheets and sat up with dignified pauses. As he dismissed his servant with a quick gesture, his clouded eyes took notice of the basin and its contents, which he regarded with incredulity. "Stop, you knave. Can't you see that somebody has dared leave his bile in my silver basin? Take that stinking garbage out of here."

Avelino took the basin, made a complicated bow, and went out to the passageway. When he saw that Don Luis was talking softly with his pilot, a mysterious little man, he decided that none of his master's messages were important and that perhaps he just might squeeze a few coins out of this if he could overhear that suspicious conversation; he emptied the basin over the lee rail, and after wiping it with a rag, threw himself down upon a coil of rope, pretending to sleep; when he sensed that the men were withdrawing toward the other side, and not wishing to call attention to himself, he opted to go to sleep for real, for the viceroy's nonsense had scarcely allowed him to shut an eye all week.

Don Luis fixed his glance on the distant breakers that had appeared to starboard. Without looking away, he said to the old man beside him: "We'll have to turn south."

These words, spoken in a neutral tone, could as easily have been a command as a consultation. It was something that Don Luis had learned in eleven years of ocean voyages with his pilot, Sebastián.

"It would be a better idea to turn west," the old man said soberly, incidentally, looking at an object surrounded by wires that he held in his brown, scaly fingers.

"Perhaps we're close to the Cayman Islands," said Don Luis, cautiously.

"More likely it's Veracruz, *señor*," the old man said, putting the object into his pocket. "These breakers are the Triangles and, God willing, the day after tomorrow we'll get a look at San Juan de Ulua."

"That's what I was thinking, except that I didn't want to

fool myself into thinking that we'd end this hard voyage so soon. Go and tell the good news to the viceroy, for it would be a shame to wake up his servant," Don Luis said, pointing to Avelino, now a balled-up skein on his ropey nest.

On finding himself alone, Don Luis marveled at how little had yet been learned about cosmography and piloting, and about the inexplicable imbued knowledge that certain men like Sebastián possessed. That must be a grace of God, like the ability of hemostatic healers or the way that some people could discover mines and subterranean waters by witching them with ash wands; he had studied the quadrivium, and Marco Polo and Toscanelli's books, the apocryphal voyages of the Arabs, the treatises of Ptolemy and Mercator, and the papers of Henry the Navigator, and he still had no clear idea of where the fleet was after a week-long storm; nonetheless, Sebastián could just take his little cage out of his pocket, wiggle it a few times, and judging from the tiny hops that the cricket inside would essay, he'd fix the ship's position with an exactitude greater than one they'd get with the most precise instruments.

Don Luis had met Sebastián in a lively tavern in Triana, very near the bridge, in which he would pass the hat after his troupe of famous crickets had finished choosing slips of paper indicating people's fortunes, danced a courante and a chaconne, acted out passages from the *Amadís*, and played out the four stages of the great battle of Pavia upon a sheet gauded with rivers, mountains, and hamlets. Don Luis, who embarked the following day on his first voyage with the fleet, and had gone to the tavern to dispel the stomach cramping that the order to sail had left him with, happily lay down a copper coin to get the cricket to pick out, brushing it with his feet, a little ball of paper with his fortune in three words imprinted on it. But when he opened and unrolled the paper that Sebastián handed over, he saw with surprise that there was nothing written on either side of it. He decided right away to let the matter rest and not ask for a refund of his coin, which was just small change. He asked for some cheese, sausage, and another draught of wine, then set himself to watch the band of crickets leaping before the walls of Pavia – Sebastián described this as the fiercest stage of the battle – when suddenly he felt a shiver and a freezing cramp in his stomach: the blank paper could mean death. Wringing his hands, he waited for the public's attention to settle on the stage, where a fiercely applauded Lope de Rueda was announcing a performance of *Cornudo y contento*, the latest of his productions. Then, while Sebastián picked up famous crickets from the corners and underneath the tables, he went up to him slowly, mute with fright, shaking the little piece of paper. Sebastián got out of this squeeze by saying over and over that the blank text meant that a very happy future was waiting to be written by the hand of providence; when dealing with a young and elegant *caballero* it was not at all unusual that the famous cricket should decide to respond so prudently, since many sons of important families wind up getting lost when they rub elbows with rogues and sluts, ruining forever the promising futures that they had rights to in being born *hidalgos*; he had seen more than one of them sell his cape and sword to set out on the road with no other catechism than that corrupt *Vida de Lazarillo* that had come from Burgos and Alcala along with the New Christians who were looking for passage to the Indies. Don Luis answered that he was very far from committing any of those foolish acts, that the cloak of a *pícaro* would never suit him, and that the roads that his uncles had opened for him, since he was an orphan, did not go on land but rather over the sea and with the fleet to the Indies, except that he didn't have it all together yet because, being ignorant of the art of sailing, the thing he feared the most was being lost at sea.

In fact, Don Luis lacked any calling as a sailor, but his two maternal uncles, who manipulated, behind the scenes, certain of the Board of Trade's more tangled threads, had pushed him out to sea with the idea of placing him there in the fleet to be a front for silver smuggling. But in the days of his meeting with Sebastián, his sins were yet to come; he was a strapping youth with sad eyebrows, who was very fond of proverbs and wise maxims, collecting them in a slow, flowery hand in an octavo volume that he had bound in calf. If Sebastián had asked him then how he would most like to spend his life, he would have said in the old patio in Seville, at his uncles' house, his feet stretched out and basking in the sun, amid the sober fragrances of medicinal herbs, reflecting on the inexhaustible moral instruction flowing from some Latin apologia. Later, because this must have happened to him in his maturity, he would discover the classic severity that the proverbs hid beneath their homely crust and be astonished that they weren't the objects of deep study at the University in Salamanca. But Sebastián didn't care a damn about how Don Luis might most like to spend his life, and the only thing he asked him was whether he wanted to take him on as a servant, because ever since he was a child he had wanted to see the Indies; further, he would swear by the five holy wounds that from then on he would never have to be afraid of being lost at sea, because the famous crickets could divine, with perfect accuracy, the place upon the earth's surface where they ever might be situated. After all, daily they confronted problems that were much more difficult to solve. As the days went on, and counting on the opinions of the other pilots and the old mariners' formidable sense of direction, Sebastián would ascend to the post of chief pilot, at the same time that Don Luis, moved by the invisible threads that his uncles pulled, would advance to the envied post of Captain General of the Indies Fleet.

Diego Maldonado, from the bridge of his caravel, saw the approach of the longboat from the big ship without flags that had popped up at dawn at half a cannon shot's distance. It must have sailed up with its lights out, because the men on watch swore they'd seen no glimmer at all during the night. At first, after his page had awakened him to advise him of the situation, he had thought that they were dealing with one of the ships of the fleet. But on stepping out on deck he was disabused: he knew quite well what ships sailed to Veracruz that year, and the ship before his eyes was certainly not one of them.

Maldonado had joined the fleet at the Island of Gomera. For more than a month he had loaded wines in the Canarian archipelago destined for Mexico, charging this to the account maintained with good credit by the Genoese in Seville for whom he worked. The Mexican merchants' orders on this occasion had specified – the accountant had told him this before sailing – that they be wines of the best quality, preferably malvesie, for there were to be many celebrations at the arrival of the new viceroy, Don Martín Enríquez de Almansa, son of the Marquis of Alcanices. So that, following his intuition, he had visited the most famous *bodegas* in La Palma, Tenerife, Grand Canary, and loaded the most noble casks that could be bought. He had never brought such precious wines to the Indies, and all through the voyage he had the satisfaction of receiving, on his modest ship, the masters and pilots of the fleet, including the Captain General, Don Luis de Luján, who was transporting the viceroy on the galleon *San Lorenzo*. Flattered by those happy visits, where they tasted the dry sweetness of those unequaled draughts born of vines brought from the legendary Laconia, Maldonado would have wished the voyage to be endless.

When the storm unleashed itself and the ships scattered throughout the waters south of Cuba, Maldonado sank into a deep gloom. Only a miracle could put him once again anywhere near the flagship, and his project of asking Don Luis to intercede for him and get him named to something important in the fleet had suddenly gone sour.

On the morning when the winds died, Maldonado did not know if his caravel was inside or outside the Gulf. He flipped a coin, to stop thinking about it, and at midday he blessed his luck: there, on the southwest horizon, he could glimpse the breakers of the Triangles. Taking advantage of the calm, he repaired the bowsprit, reset all of the sails, and having recovered his good nature, gave out a keg of good wine to the men. He raised anchor a little before nightfall, and it was then that, far away to the leeward, he thought he could just make out a ship. He shouted up to the lookout, but was soon assured that what he'd seen was a flight of ducks. All right, then, here he was facing a flight of damned ducks, a huge ship with poop and castle as tall as his mainmast and no fewer than forty guns, a good number of them aiming at him point blank.

Without leaving the bridge, Maldonado sent his page to fetch his silk doublet and his hat with the green feathers. Then, turning toward his ship's master, he ordered him to bring a medium-sized cask of malvesie on deck and some silver goblets. He had reason to think that those men in helmets and cuirasses now approaching by boat were Frenchmen. Just that very autumn, when he was selling wines in Portobelo, news had come to the town concerning the crimes that Sores, Bontemps, and Letelier had committed all along the coast. So that Maldonado, thinking to die like an honorable man, knowing that on that morning his life wasn't worth a *maravedí*, got ready to play host to the pirates, but with the same enthusiasm, the same courtesy, he'd shown days earlier when receiving the commander of the fleet. Shaking off his grimace with a smile, he slid quickly into his ceremonial doublet, donned his floppy hat, giving it a Gallic tilt, and trimmed his lovely chestnut moustache in the unsteady mirror held up by his page.

Letelier and Mendeville climbed the ladder lowered at the prow and stood on the Spanish caravel's deck. Before they could even open their mouths, they almost tripped over a young and bedizened merchant who bowed reverently and then presented himself as Don Diego Maldonado, graciously offering them drink in silver goblets. After palating a quick sip, Mendeville cleared his throat and read out the paragraphs of the letter of marque that gave Letelier's squadron the right to take as a prize any island, port, city, town, or other territories in the West Indies, such as any ships that flew the Spanish flag which happened to be navigating through the North Sea or the South Sea, as well as the inhabitants or crews of said territories or ships, as well as their possessions in coin and specie, including Indians and slaves.

His smile never failing, Maldonado answered in his best French that all of that seemed very fine to him, the documents were in order, and that his person and his goods as well as his ship were at their free disposal. "Let's drink to our happy meeting here," he proposed, filling the goblets himself.

Carrying out his vow to get out of privateering altogether, Letelier had decided beforehand that he would spare the Spanish caravel. He only wished to know exactly where he now was in the Gulf and most of all if there was anywhere that he might anchor and repair his ships. "Excellent wine," he murmured, trying out a smile beneath the hardened wrinkles of his face.

"Malvesie from Tenerife, the best that one can drink," said Maldonado proudly. "What can I offer the *caballeros*? What would please them most right now?" he asked, taking in the caravel entirely with a broad and elegant wave of his arm.

Struck by a sudden coughing fit, Letelier signaled Mendeville to answer the question. "We'd like to put in somewhere to repair our rigging and to take on stores. How far is Campeche?" said Mendeville sourly. It was still hard for him to follow Letelier in sparing this attractive caravel.

"There's a solution for that," Maldonado assured him, without the slightest idea what it might be. "Let's drink another round," he proposed, in order to gain time. "But better yet, let's retire to my cabin, for the *caballeros* could suffocate beneath this awful sun. We'll feel much better there."

Letelier, a bit embarrassed that Mendeville might see him treating the Spaniard almost as an equal, told his men to return to the *Vaillant*. "And if you don't see me at noon on the bridge signaling to have the boat sent over, then board this stinking caravel and put its whole crew to the knife," he added, seeing the uneasy look that Mendeville sent his way.

After the seventh cup of wine, Letelier having fallen

into a thick drowsiness, Maldonado started feeling a warmth both sweet and dry that bathed him head to toe, clearing up his thoughts and showing him the benefits that he might get from this auspicious happenstance. Fate had put into his hands a future that was better far than that of having a small-time position in the fleet: a commercial future of the highest class, yes sir, first class. If his king's advisers had succeeded in convincing him to ban all trade between France and the Canaries, so much the worse for them, because now they'd have to answer to the Almighty for their scheming; if it was true that France's huge commercial trade was in the hands of Jews and Huguenots, that was not his business, it was a matter for the king or the pope; he had no relation to politics, nor with questions of religion; he was a little wine merchant on a 6 percent commission who risked his life on every crossing while his Genoese bosses swam around in gold doubloons without having to lift a finger; furthermore, and this was worse, they didn't even have to talk in Spanish. But finally his time had come. France, quite unlike Germany and England, was a land of drinkers of good wine, of gourmets. What Frenchman in his right mind could resist the malvesie of the Canaries? None, none. His fortune was now made. As soon as he could win Letelier's favor – and this now seemed a sure thing – he would flood France with malvesie; he'd drown her in good sack. Everything was coming together to his advantage. He'd start with Tenerife; he'd show the local smugglers how much easier and more lucrative it was to deal with France than with the Indies; at the other end he'd talk Letelier into putting all his ships, his wealth, and his name into the new enterprise, to escort first the smugglers' brigantines, and then to supervise unloading, storage, and distributing of the wines through all of France.

Of course, he'd be behind the operation, for he had enough experience in the buying and selling of wines, and he'd keep an eye out to make sure that the business kept rolling, in exchange for a 30 percent commission. His fortune was made; nothing, nobody could get in the way. And realizing that it was almost noon, he took Letelier by the shoulders and began to shake him. "It's not Campeche that you should be going to," he said as soon as the pirate opened his eyes. "Rather it's the isle of San Juan de Ulua." And gesturing expansively, on the wings of an effusive vehemence that let him fly above all treason and dishonor, Maldonado described to Letelier his ingenious project and how he would be able to close out his career with the greatest maritime victory the world could ever dream about: the taking of *all* San Juan de Ulua, repairing and provisioning *all* of his ships, capturing *all* of the galleons of the fleet and *all* of the new viceroy's court, and making off with *all* the silver and *all* the stockpiled merchandise of Veracruz.

Once Maldonado had stopped speaking, he fixed his glance on the corsair's watery eyes, on his hands, motionless on the chair's arms, on his legs that were resting on the table. The silence became unbearable to him, and when he was about to state his arguments all over again, Letelier assented with a sigh drawn out of his impassive mask.

Antonio Delgadillo, who was mending by candlelight, and with infinite care, a tear shaped like a seven that a nail had ripped in his best hose, heard the warning shot, jumped, and ran barefoot, in his underwear, out upon the fortress's terrace. "What have you seen, you dolt?" he asked the commander of the guard. The man just pointed toward the sea: there, almost entering the channel, still visible in the twilight, sat a group of big ships in full procedure of furling sail and dropping anchor.

It might be the fleet.

It should be the fleet.

It had to be the fleet.

It was the fleet.

Delgadillo dressed himself hurriedly, jumped over to the packet, and told her master to get going toward Veracruz to report the good news as soon as possible.

Bustamante, the mayor, was disporting himself in bed with his two nieces when Delgadillo knocked resolutely on his door: but it's eleven at night, Captain Delgadillo; it's not the time, *caballero*; go to sleep and leave me alone, *señor*; I'm not opening, I tell you, *hombre*, stop beating on the door and go to hell, you *mierda*; you should have told me right away the fleet had come, *hombre*; you should have begun with that, *señor*; I'm opening this minute, *caballero*; come on in, forgive the delay, Captain Delgadillo; take a seat and I'll be ready in a minute.

In 1568 Veracruz did not resemble in any way the city that it is today, for reasons that include its not even being in the same place. At that time, it was a precarious clump of shacks and crummy warehouses, a skimpy plaza of soft earth and a half-built church, all this surrounded by pale dunes and sparse coastal scrub. There the heat and the humidity were a lot like biblical plagues, and the heated wind that blew in from the surf filled the miserable streets with mountains of sand, huge, avid green flies, and a persistent stink of rotten seaweed and dead crabs. In the summer months nearly the entire population migrated to Jalapa, to Puebla, even to Mexico City, because the scourge of disease was so great that nobody was recalled as having lived through three successive landings of the fleet. As it happened, they resided underneath the incessant flying of a black cloud of buzzards, whose rapacity was a modest aid to sanitation. As September rounded, though, the climate started to become less intolerable – mosquitoes thinned out, big green flies had disappeared, puddles in the plaza dried, the dog-day heat relaxed its grip – and Veracruz stopped being a sleepy, miserable hamlet of Totonec Indians and turned into a big anthill crowded with merchants, functionaries, exhibitors, friars, vagabonds, and passengers to Havana or Seville; the mule trains wound their way down from cities and towns on the plateau, from the high valleys where the indigo and cacao were grown; they came down loaded up with silver, cochineal, spices, and jade stones. In those days the cost of a straw mattress for a night went up to a whole ducat, and a person could not sup on red meat or white for less than eight *reales*. In a little more than two weeks, Veracruz swelled up with those dusty and exhausted bands of travelers who, devoured by flies and lice, had flocked from every part of the viceroyalty to sail off with the fleet. Then, when roofs and awnings became insufficient and the plaza turned into a seething camp of stalls, when patients could no longer fit into the hut that served as a hospital, nor was there room for all the sinners in the church, a multitude of dissolutes, with unknown origins and destinations, opened up pathways through the dunes around the village, and the streets surrendered to an arrant mob of hawkers, charlatans, actors, musicians, grim-faced thugs, faith healers, card sharps, fortune-telling Indian women, cinnamon-colored mulatto girls, and slinky Negresses to obliterate first loves and recent passions.

The fleet's arrival instantly reordered that provisional world, kept it together in a single thought, a single watchword that could recognize no differences of race or class:

emptying the pockets of the new arrivals, and the sooner the better. And so, overcome by this idea, magnified on this occasion by the arrival of a new viceroy, the mayor Bustamante pulled Delgadillo across to the other side of the plaza, and leaping over card hands and foul-smelling bedrolls, knocked on the treasurer Marzana's door. It was not until almost dawn that Delgadillo's packet, dressed up now with a shiny canopy of silk brocade, made off for San Juan de Ulua, with the cream of Veracruz crammed on her deck.

At dawn Letelier gave the order to his battered squadron to raise anchor, get the sails unfurled and the cannons ready. At the same time he ran up the Spanish flags that Maldonado had given him. In spite of a strong morning breeze, their ships had difficulty in maneuvering; if any one of them was not missing a mast, it would be minus a boom or bowsprit, and they all were short of rigging. Following as best they could the *Vaillant*'s wide wake, the squadron's ships fell into line to take the channel which would lead them to the anchorage at San Juan de Ulua. As he approached the island, Letelier felt a growing confidence in Maldonado's project; out in front of him, facing his prow, streamers and banners unfurled above the fort, and on the dock a crowd was waving handkerchiefs, capes, mantles of the most varied colorations as a sign of welcome; now he heard the distant riffle of the drums, fifes, trumpets mixed in with the noise of shouting; now there was no going back, and things would turn out as they would. On coming into the first battery's line of fire, nonetheless, he took a dry swallow and assured himself again that this would be his last action as a privateer. An instant later, all the cannons of the fort went off in perfect unison, and his figurehead cut through the lovely crimson cloud that had so frightened the Totonecs some two weeks earlier. As she started the slow task of anchoring, the *Vaillant* took in a volley of feathers, flowers, ribbons, and butterflies that lit upon her planking as on a garden path.

Mendeville tossed away over the side a gardenia that had fallen on his ear and was about to salute Delgadillo's imaginative cannonades with a broadside of grapeshot. In fact he was furious, and he didn't hide it; for the first time Letelier had not revealed his entire plan to him, and he foresaw that there was something fishy in this business concerning San Juan de Ulua; his instinct was telling him that Maldonado, with his courtly ways and his casks of malvesie, had not just gained Letelier's confidence, which was obvious, but had also brought them together in some promising enterprise that would leave him out. Well, fine, he'd settle accounts with Maldonado later; the main thing now was to carry out Letelier's orders to the letter, because if everything went well it was quite possible that things would go back to being the way they'd been before.

After launching a gob of spit over the rail, Mendeville climbed up to the bridge and made sure that every man was at his post; he looked out toward the *Nouvelle France* and saw that Bonadieu was taking off his hat and waving it in the air; to his left, Pitou repeated the gesture, indicating that the *Neptune* too was ready; behind them, *La Gascogne*, *Le Tonnerre*, and the *Dauphin*, which had anchored in the channel, had already filled their long-boats with men bearing shields, crossbows, and harquebuses, and these were coming up speedily, impelled by oar and wind. Beyond the channel, at a distance of three culverin-shots, one could just make out the pinnaces *Sophie* and *Melissande* and Maldonado's caravel, now under Cussac's command, which were designated to be on the watch for any Spanish galleon that might turn up on the horizon. Each ship was in place; every weapon was filed sharp; all the fuses had been lit; each man was waiting for the signal. He looked over at the dock and saw that Maldonado and Letelier, all dressed up in white silk garments, had just disembarked. Ringed with a guard composed of the squadron's best harquebusiers, they walked now, one behind the other, into the shouts of "*Viva* the good lord Viceroy! *Viva* Don Martín Enríquez de Almansa! *Viva la flota y viva España*!" The crowd, just come from Veracruz in everything that floated, could hardly be contained by the ring of halberdiers that had been posted there by Delgadillo; making the pier's planks creak, it lurched toward the gaudy figures, asking for money and for favors with arms outstretched and open palms. Moving ahead a few paces, Maldonado placed himself beside Letelier, reached into the leather sack he carried at his side, and began showering left and right the silver pieces that Letelier had picked up in Cartagena. With disorder now spread all along the dock, Letelier took out his purse and tossed it over the parapet that separated the two batteries. The effect was instantaneous: all of the artillerymen abandoned their posts and spilled out on the esplanade to look for gold pieces and pearls. It was the signal, and Mendeville, a fervent Huguenot with a religious hatred for the Spaniards, allowed himself the pleasure of lighting the fuse of a falconet loaded with grapeshot, whose firing brought down the great red and yellow flag that had waved above the tower. Then he ordered that the Spanish flags be lowered from his masts to allow the hoisting of the fleur-de-lis. While the reception committee and the petitioners jumped into their boats and shoved out over the water, the cannons of the

Vaillant, the *Neptune*, and the *Nouvelle France* swept the esplanade of Spaniards.

Over to the east, right on the horizon's edge, the *San Lorenzo*'s lookout had discerned what he believed to be two or three fishing boats and, farther out, a snub-nosed little brown blur that could turn out to be a cape or island. Don Luis, who was striding on the bridge to take the morning air, sent someone out to fetch Sebastián, and when the latter came, he asked him, pointing toward the prow: "Do you think it's strange that we should be arriving at San Juan de Ulua?"

"I wouldn't call it strange, *señor*," replied Sebastián, shaking the cricket's little cage. "This famous cricket tells me that the land in sight now is indeed San Juan de Ulua."

"That's what I say!" Don Luis said. "I'd think it strange were it not so," he added, and visoring his eyes with his right hand, he looked ahead once more. The fact was that, although he'd seen San Juan de Ulua seven times before, the isle had never two times looked the same. He sighed deeply and began to search his memory for some bit of received wisdom that might explain his having been so often mistaken, whereupon a proverb came to him so apt it left him in a cold sweat. When he had recovered, he told Sebastián sententiously: "Appearances can be deceiving." Right away, he went to tell the viceroy personally that almost all of the ships of the fleet had reunited overnight and that the voyage, thanks be to God, was almost at its end.

The first to recognize the galleons of the fleet were the men of the *Melissande*. The pinnace, sailing before a breeze, followed by the *Sophie* and Maldonado's caravel, paused for a few minutes at the side of the *Dauphin*, the last of the ships that had been anchored in the channel. When the news, running from ship to ship, reached Mendeville and passed on from him to Letelier, the batteries had already been taken. Now, at the petty officers' command, there began the task of turning the culverins around and training them upon the fortress tower, where, stuck on a broomstick and waving from a porthole, there was an old torn Spanish flag.

The fleet's arrival halfway through the operation was no surprise to Letelier. Certainly he would rather that this happen a few hours later but, in any event, it was something he had foreseen, and now it was just a matter of speeding up the capture and securing of the island. The last of the halberdiers on the dock, bunched up on the stone stairway leading to the esplanade, could not decide if they should use their arms or lay them down, but when they saw that they were targeted by a dozen smoking harquebuses they threw down their halberds and kneeled in surrender. Clearing a path through their laments, Letelier climbed the steps in four strides and reached the esplanade with one dashing leap. He realized quickly that he could hardly breathe and that his heart had hit upon the rhythm of a bailing pump in a shipwreck. He tried to take a step in the direction of the artillerymen to order them to forget about the tower and put their guns back in their original positions, but the least movement of his limbs upset him so much that he decided to wait until he got his breath back. Feeling betrayed by his lungs, he tried to give orders by shouting: he only managed a couple of snorts and smothered whistles that he himself could barely hear. Stuck there, alone, immobile, dressed in white, with his mouth agape and his hand to his chest, he looked like a tragic sculpted marble figure that someone had left behind. Captain Delgadillo, from one of the tower's embrasures, took careful aim, lit the fuse on his blunderbuss, then saw the corsair fall into the arms of his men, who had spilled out over the stairs.

Mendeville, observing the progress of the attack from the *Vaillant*'s bridge, saw Letelier's fall. The shot was to the head, and it was clear that nothing could be done. For the moment he would mourn the loss of the man who'd been his teacher, his commander and adventuring companion, and he felt himself about to cry. But he pulled himself together quickly: now suddenly the whole responsibility was his. "Fire at the tower!" he ordered, and he signalled to Bonadieu and Pitou and also to the land batteries to follow suit. The fort, defended gallantly by Delgadillo to the last man, was reduced to a huge pile of rubble in a little over twenty minutes.

Maldonado, on receiving Letelier's broken head in his hands, could see that all was lost; he knew that the Frenchmen hated him, that his being alive at all was a matter of the corsair's having done him a favor; likewise he knew that he could expect no better than the noose from his own side. Wiping the blood from his hands onto his silk doublet, he cast a final look at Letelier's body and ran to the other end of the esplanade, where the packet that went back and forth to Veracruz was anchored. Halfway there, the whistling cannonballs forced him to the ground, and lying there, shaken by the explosions, he waited for the bombardment of the tower to come to an end. His mind, though, kept working: it occurred to him that his flight would be safer if the slaves helped him; he'd go into their barracks; he'd tell them they were free, and he'd arm them with whatever he could find in the warehouse; afterwards, he would board the packet, head over to Campeche, take the town, and then build a fort there; then he'd come up with a plan. He ran head-down in the direction of the Negroes' barracks. He found an open door, but inside there wasn't anything but empty sleeping mats and here and there a tattered blanket. On reaching the pier, he saw that the packet, loaded with Negroes, was pulling out while trading harquebus shots with five or six Frenchmen who were standing behind a parapet. "Stop right there!" one of them shouted to him, aiming a harquebus straight at his face. With no other recourse, Maldonado jumped into the sea, thinking that he could swim easily to the mainland. But as he lifted his head from the water he saw that it was hopeless: between him and the sands of Veracruz was interposed the *Vaillant*'s longboat, just poking around the isle's extreme south end. After he was pulled from the sea, they shoved him toward a bench where there sat, tied hand and foot, the mayor Bustamante and the treasurer Marzana.

For more details about what happened in San Juan de Ulua that October 9, see especially the files numbered 15.251.EM and 48.357.LT of the *Archivo de Indias*, in Seville; see also the viceroy Enríquez de Almansa's correspondence in the National Library in Madrid, as well as Mendeville's diary, published in 1888 by the French Academy of History. There are several important secondary sources, among them a fervent biography of Letelier written by Sismondi, and also *Los corsarios de la casa de Valois*, which the Spanish Academy of History gave a prize to while the book's author presided over said institution. Although their approaches might be thought contradictory – in the first Letelier is portrayed as a kind of Ulysses, and in the second he is called the Attila of the Indies – they are both well-documented works. Curiously, neither of them mentions any legal proceedings against Maldonado. Now, on the level of conjecture, one might imagine that the latter had figured out how to avoid leaving behind any evidence of his treason, perhaps by cutting some unknown deal with the viceroy Enríquez de Almansa. All sources concur as well in their mention of a curious event: when the clash between French squadron and Spanish ships seemed imminent, the pilot of the fleet saved everything with a negotiating session which, with the cooperation of all concerned, and underneath a white flag, was held on the galleon *San Lorenzo*. These sources say that after the pilot's proposal to settle the conflict honorably was accepted, he wrote down, on pages torn out of his logbook, the thirty-six possible outcomes that could issue from the situation. Folding the sheets and placing them in a circle on the table, he took a cricket from his doublet, and immediately it hopped onto one of the tickets. To everybody's consternation, the paper was blank on both sides. After an all-night discussion, it was agreed that the blank paper signified peace. With matters standing thus, Mendeville repaired his ship's damages, placed an agreed-upon floral wreath at the grave of Delgadillo – promoted posthumously to general – and, keeping Letelier's remains in a lead vessel, left San Juan de Ulua in the viceroy's hands.

Each side claimed victory, and by the time they started toasting Mendeville in Bordeaux, the music and the dancing had not ended in the turbulent and always unsung Veracruz.

ST. MARTIN'S CAPE

Perhaps Don Pedro de Valdés, having leaned until this moment on his newest galleon's taffrail, will decide to go below into his cabin's cozy shadows. Perhaps he'll do this to keep the midday sun off some tender project that he's hatching in his head, or perhaps it's just to order up a lunch that could be composed of stewed eels, ox tongue, fresh greens, and white bread, all purchased that morning on the docks. Perhaps, before he goes down to lunch, he'll search the horizon for San Lucar's port, receding steadily, or perhaps he'll fix his eye on the small, two-masted *zabra* sailing half a cannon shot away and slowly drifting off its course. Perhaps he'll smile as he imprints the vessel's windswept April outline on his retina, its billowing white triangles, its bulging sails amidships that look like a dragonfly's wings above the long, low, elegant hull. He'll think, perhaps, that he'd done the right thing in designing the boat himself, taking time every other day to cross the rowdy plazas of Seville to reach the Shipyard, sprinkling coins into the carpenters' and caulkers' caps. He surely will recall the anterooms and rituals of politeness that he went through when he got the Board of Trade to open up its warehouse to him, yielding wood that had been cut in the West Indian forests for his masts and hull ribs; the leisurely discussions with master Joseph, who only when encouraged by gold would forge, four separate times, in

German fashion, copper for the bowchasers and cannons; the pleasure, bittersweet, of sailing, perhaps for the last time, along Asturias's beloved coast in search of the right men and then, in passing, to pick up, in hidden harbors watched by the smugglers, Saracen scimitars, neat English muskets, accurate compasses and astrolabes, and above all those whispering canvas sailcloths, light as gulls, that France's most renowned privateers used to fly away on. And all those trips and dealings, that whole year of coming and going, during which he took along Fernando, reveling in his happy nature, had made him young in body and soul again as if he'd drunk from Florida's wondrous fountain. With Fernando's yellow feather's first appearance on the *zabra*'s deck, a surge of pride will lift his breastplate, smoothe his brow, and put a humid sparkle in his eye. For an instant he will see his own wrinkled forehead and his beard's old silver reflecting on Fernando's face; his trembling fingers will reach out to touch that vision, surely a foreshadowing, he'll think, a revelation meant to show him that the destinies of son and father had been linked beneath the seal of this royal enterprise. Still leaning on the rail, the *zabra* galloping to starboard, he'll beg Christ to extend his favor with the grand Duke of Lerma, who had plucked him from a long, unhappy service in the Andalusian fleet to make him Cuba's governor and captain general.

"Times have changed, Don Pedro," Lerma would have said a scant one year earlier, and he'd toss a rabbit pie in the direction of a big, black, frightening dog that he'd tied there to a column.

"Forgive our ignorance, Don Francisco, we don't know politics or government. From a galleon's bridge, things hardly seem to change at all: always the same job of sailing, the same sun, the same stars out every year on the same days."

"Don Pedro, don't be clever," the duke would say. "Look here," he'd say, pointing to the dog. "Know what I call him?"

"I think I heard you call him 'Turk.'"

"Do you know why?"

"No. I don't, Don Francisco."

"I call him 'Turk' because he's ugly and he's black; because he's hungry all the time; because he's always snarling even though his former master tried to beat it out of him; because I'm fearful that some day he'll break his chain, attack my table, and sink his fangs into my throat."

"And yet you keep him next to you?"

"You hardly know what I must do, Don Pedro."

"I don't know what you mean, *señor*."

"Since God has made me serve His Majesty by helping him to administer his realms, I have to stay alert. But try some of this Bohemian wine, and make yourself at home. How is it?"

"It's excellent."

"Well, drink up, my friend. I was telling you about my duties. Yes, in fact you can't imagine how worried it makes me to realize that a word from me on any subject gets weighed and generally followed by His Majesty. *Ergo*, as we used to say in Salamanca at the university, I have to keep my focus on the world as sharp as I can make it. One quick remark, one bit of bad advice, one nod in this or that direction . . . Drink up! Drink up! Don't take all this so seriously. You like that capon? Well, eat it up before Turk can snatch it. I'll have to throw mine to him pretty soon. You get me?"

"Get you?"

"I guess you old seafarers, with all that howling wind

and water in your ears, need things put to you straight. I share my supper with Turk . . . But tell me, though, how does that painting strike you?" Lerma then would ask, turning toward a canvas of St. Martin that was hanging on a panel to his right. "You know El Greco was a painter that the old king, who rests in glory now, did not like much."

"I don't know anything about painters or their paintings, Don Francisco. There's been nothing to my life but sailing and fighting for Spain."

The duke would ponder. "That's true, you've fought enough," he'd say, "although you haven't had much luck."

"My honor is intact, however."

"That is a fine response, Don Pedro. But we're not concerned about your honor now. I'm speaking of your prospects. Don't you have a son?"

"Fernando, señor. This year he'll leave the university to learn to be a sailor. As a matter of fact, if you think you could, perhaps . . ."

"I'll get around to your son," the duke would interrupt. "I want to talk about El Greco's treatment of St. Martin. Do you like it?"

"I told you, sir. I'm not a connoisseur, and I can't say if it has good colors or proportions. But I might observe that the painting shows St. Martin's generosity. I think the painter, showing us the saint as he shares his cape with a poor man, tries to set a standard of compassion. The rich and powerful should learn from it. I find it useful and instructive."

"That's how I see it too, Don Pedro. I'm sorry that the old king, mirror that he was to all the Christian world, chose thornier paths than that of generosity on his way to heaven," Lerma would say, sighing. "Finish your wine," he would add then, when he had drunk down his own and casually thrown half his capon to the dog. "Let's retire to the next room, because I suspect that Turk can understand Castilian as well as a *morisco*. Come on, let's leave the monster to the custard, fruit, and chocolate. Let's say goodbye now to St. Martin."

By working some mechanism beneath the table, Lerma would move the panel with St. Martin to a place behind the curtains. The spacious room that this disclosed, filled with lights and rare aromas, soothingly ventilated by the movement of big palm fronds, seemed to be the duke's private library. Thousands of books revealed their spines on shelves of ebony, mahogany, cedar, olivaceous quebracho; rolled-up maps and bundled parchments tied with ribbons spilled out over stools and tables on the rug's fabulous plumage; from the ceiling there hung down, as in a rain of wonders, bracelets by the dozen, jade and gold amulets, bells, obsidian mirrors, necklaces, rings, brooches, little idols with protruding gems for eyes and navels; portraits of coppery-faced men and women, variously adorned, lined up along the walls beside displays of all their handicrafts; through a worked-silver blind there slid the sound of reed flutes and tambourines.

"Sit down, Don Pedro," the duke would say as he dropped down amid a half dozen cushions. "This is my secret parlor; I read here and reflect upon the Indies. Everything you see around you came from the New World. The water clock over on that table has a drop from every river, that hourglass a grain of sand from every beach, that rug a feather from every kind of bird, those books, whose titles seem so interesting to you, are bound with hides from many forests. Weavings, dyes, spices, perfumes, drugs, seeds, woods, objects, races, metals, precious stones, musicians . . . I need only dictate a letter to my secretary to get each locality to send me what they've got. It's true that they don't always respond, and that frequently an order under His Majesty's seal is not obeyed, and sometimes the bundles and the boxes, and His Majesty's one-fifth, get lost, stolen, or shipwrecked. What do you expect, the probity of local administration leaves a lot to be desired. But something always comes, thank God," Lerma would have said, describing a wide quadrant with his arm. "Ah, Don Pedro, what wouldn't get here if things were running well; how many riches would the king distribute then among his faithful subjects? But the Indies' towns and seas are lacking in good men, and there are too many pirates. Spain gets weaker every day, and more endangered. Do you know who our worst enemies are?

"Elizabeth Tudor? . . . Maurice of Nassau?"

"You're wrong. Elizabeth's last fit was beheading Essex. As a queen she's a cadaver, as a woman she's doddering. Hawkins, Drake, Cavendish, Frobisher, and all the others who used to carry her royal mantle on their masts have been burning in Hell for some time now. Also, she will have a hard time putting down the Irish Catholics. No, Elizabeth won't launch any real attack against the new king. If she lives past her allotted time she'll have to abdicate in favor of James Stuart, and he has no deep animosity toward Spain, I can assure you. As you see, England is not our worst enemy. I can understand how you, who commanded one of the luckless squadrons in the Armada, ill-named the Invincible, that the old king sent out against the English, should be of that opinion. But, my friend, we are in the first year of a new century. Times have changed. I'll say to you in confidence that the Christian unity of the West, the reconciliation of the Catholics and the Protestants around the idea of Christ, Erasmus's dream which no one ever understood . . ."

"Don Francisco!"

"Don't worry, we're not standing before a tribunal of the Holy Office. Let me finish my sentence . . . But perhaps you think that wars are cheap? Ah, Don Pedro, Europe has been bled; it has been ruined by religious wars. I'm not condemning the old king's politics, God keep me always from presuming that. If I'd been in his advisers' shoes, I would not have hinted any other course to him than that of fighting against infidels and Lutherans. They brought everything down on us, and there was nothing left to do but close ranks, clutch the crucifix, and burn heretics at the stake. The roads of Flanders, Italy, France, and Germany, the rivers of the Indies and the seas of all the world are running on above the helmets and the swords of our dead soldiers. And they fought, Don Pedro, ten times more than for their nation, a hundred times more than for their king, they fought and suffered and then died for their idea of God. You know that very well. So if politics sometimes advised adoration of the stubborn image of a Spanish God . . . Now don't start to gesticulate or say things that you may regret, because your being here is nothing but good fortune for you. I'm as good a Catholic as you are and, forgive my boasting, I know politics far better than you do. In any case, the stake and the rack were necessary, as were our sons' deaths. But other winds are blowing now, Don Pedro. And they are winds of poverty," Lerma would say gravely, rising to his feet. "The poets and playwrights are calling me a leech who sucks Spain's treasures. But what treasures are they talking of, my good man, when to cover the crown's most pressing debts I've had to agree to move the capital to Valladolid just to get that city's burghers to contribute their *escudos*? What treasures, if it has been necessary to mint copper merely to hear something make a noise inside the royal coffers? Spain doesn't have a *maravedí*, and what's worse it has no credit, *señor* Don Pedro de Valdés; Europe is bankrupt, *señor*. The wars have borne everything away, they have devoured everything with their fangs of iron and fire. All that's left is copper coins."

Don Pedro would observe that the Lord of Denia, first Duke of Lerma since a few months earlier, had aged little. His voice, although a bit sharper, continued clear; his figure, his shoulders, and his limbs, were fine, and his step was quick; his hair, cut one inch from his scalp in the Italian style, seemed not to have gone gray, and his face, in spite of the tragic expressions he was using to support his arguments, was almost what it had been twenty years before. "If you're not averse to telling me, Don Francisco, what does Spain do with the riches that arrive from the Indies?"

"What does it do? You tell me. Where does wheat for the country's bread come from?"

"From Castile, from almost all the center and the north of the peninsula."

"Where else?"

"From Sicily. The Baltic as well."

"And that's bad news, because it means that Spain can't produce the wheat it eats and used to export," the duke would say, stopping before a globe. "If that happens with the wheat, and with cod, and now and then with wool, what won't we buy abroad? If this keeps up, I wouldn't be surprised if before long we were eating Greek olives and drinking the Frenchmen's wine. Let me tell you a state secret, Don Pedro," the duke would say, as he turned around to face him, with his finger to his lips. "Genoa, Hamburg, and other cities run by moneylenders and traders supply five-sixths of the manufactured goods that we consume, and they control nine-tenths of the total commerce with the Indies."

"Impossible!"

"To do this, they use the names of Spanish merchants, duly entered in the register, to whom they will consign a premium in kind. If this matter interests you, you can read about it in those files," Lerma would say, with a vague gesture. "Ah, Don Pedro, the conquests, the wars, the plagues, and God only knows what else have left us without men or forests or sheep; the moneylenders and the smugglers and the pirates have left us without trade. For a hundred years we've spilled the New World's gold and silver everywhere. And now, with the last ducats and doubloons, we adorn our knightly figure with brocades and taffetas from here and there. Do you know that houses are not built now with true-cut stones, and that we've spent, in Seville alone, ten million ducats to buy Negroes instead of selling them in Veracruz or Portobelo, Cartagena or Havana?"

"You really distress me, Don Francisco. A day that started happily has clouded over."

"No more wars in Europe, *señor* Don Pedro!" the duke would then exclaim, kicking down a pile of cushions. "Extend the peace with France, make peace with England, negotiate a peace with Holland. That's my politics. I don't care if the men in togas call me inept and those with swords make jokes about my lack of spirit. You think that Maurice of Nassau is one of our worst enemies, and I ask you: What can Holland do without the help of England? Nothing, *señor*, nothing. Without the English, Maurice would have to give up all his ships and towns in a matter of months. In any case, let him keep his slice of Flanders in exchange for a peace that's backed up by the English crown and a trade concession. Do you understand yet who is our real enemy, the enemy of all of Europe?"

"The Turks?"

"You've hit the bull's-eye, Don Pedro."

"Congratulate me, *señor*. I see it clearly now."

"I'll seek to unite Spain with all the European powers. Whatever the Holy Father thinks of it, we'll go elbow to elbow with the English, with the Huguenots, and with the German Lutherans. Everyone against the Turk!" he would exclaim, putting his hand on the globe. "I'll reopen the epoch of the Great Crusades. The booty that awaits us will match the riches of a thousand Croesuses. But, let's be careful," Lerma would say, lowering his voice and looking all around as if someone were spying on him, "first we'll have to clean up the citadel. How many *moriscos* do you think there are in Aragon alone? Not more nor less than two hundred thousand. Well, I'll have them expelled for being restive and ignoring their taxes, and if they resist, I'll have them executed. When everything that smells of camel has left Europe, and that includes the entire Mediterranean, we'll see our way to another politics. At least the Christian kings will have bagged a good prize and I, old friend, will have fulfilled my vow, and," the duke would smile, "then nothing will oblige me to share my dinner with Turk, for I gave the damned dog that name to keep my mission in life before me."

"Tell me what I can do, Don Francisco. As God is my witness, I have never feared the Turk. You must remember that when young I was a galley captain in the Mediterranean."

Lerma, in silence, would approach the three-legged silver table and would pour, from a finely ornamented flask, a wine that was aromatic and full-bodied. "You're a man with experience, Don Pedro," he would say, staring into the cup. "For more than thirty years you've beat against all kinds of enemies, and you must be familiar with the seven heads that Ovid attributed to intrigue. In those documents you see there by the water clock, there is an account of your career beginning on the day you left the royal galleys to go to Florida with your relative Menéndez de Avilés, may God reward him for his deeds. I've had you summoned here because after having read them over and having searched my memory I have gathered that you are a man of high endeavor."

Don Pedro would have noticed a change of inflection in the duke's voice. He would watch carefully the duke's steps, now calmer, through the chamber; on reaching the partition the duke would pull twice on a black silk braid, and the Indians' music then would stop. "There was a time," Lerma would say, returning, "when my own star scarcely shone, and I desired to be your closest friend," he would add as he stretched out on the cushions once again. "Certainly you did not avoid me, but that strict courtesy with which you generally cover up your generous, frank nature kept me from coming to you with my projects. Today, Don Pedro, I am His Majesty's right arm and my star shines in broad daylight, and in spite of the cool courtesy with which you treated me in the past I've kept you in my mind."

"Thank you for this demonstration of your friendship and benevolence, Don Francisco. But I'd be lying if I didn't tell you that you too were present in my heart, and if I never opened it to you then it was because I thought of you just as you thought of me. Tell me what I ought to do, because I only want to be of service to His Majesty and to you."

Lerma would look for a long time toward the tray that held the flask of wine and the cup. When he must have seemed most absorbed, he would raise his head: "You'll go to the Indies, Don Pedro," he'd quietly affirm. "But before I put your name before the king, there's something I have to know about you."

"Ask, *señor*, just ask; I'm ready to satisfy you. Although I thought the Turks were your main worry."

"The young will march on them, my friend. Such an ardent enemy calls for the greenhorn's pluck, for his natural urge toward stunts and honors."

"In that case, take my son Fernando, *señor*. He yearns more than anyone to put the laurel of victory at His Majesty's feet."

"Calm down, calm down, my dear Don Pedro. We'll get around to your son," Lerma would say with an air of annoyance. "A while ago I told you that we might achieve a peace with the princes of Europe. That peace is feasible because Spain will offer them some religious toleration and, more than anything, a chance to dump Byzantium's gold, enhanced by a century and a half of interest, into their empty coffers. But this peace will hardly reach the Indies if at all," the duke would sigh. "By now I guess you know what's in the Vervins Treaty's secret clause."

"I've heard rumors."

"And haven't you lately come across some pirate out of La Rochelle?" the duke would have asked sardonically. "Well be advised, His Majesty Henry IV of Navarre has thought it well to embrace His Majesty Philip II of Austria, but only to the north and east of the Azores, which you well know from your unfortunate campaign. Below that line and out to sea, pirating and illegal trade continue. And the worst of it is that I'm afraid that some such clause might mar any treaty that Spain should come to. Do you know what the French call the Azores line?"

"No, Don Francisco."

"I swear you don't know anything," Lerma would say languidly. "They call it *the bound of friendship*, since war proceeds outside."

"God damn them! You know I've never trusted any Frenchmen."

"And so it seems that peace will not lower its latitude, *señor*. It won't go down because the Indies constitute a mythological reward, a prize for demigods. To renounce a bite of the Indies is to give up Eldorado, Jauja, the City of the Caesars, Cibola, the Font of Youth, in short . . . to give up dreaming. Many Jasons and their argonauts you'll see throughout those seas, *señor*. So let's leave the holy wars to the boys and let's look among the old captains for those who, like Ulysses, can rely on craft and judgment to win peace for the New World. If Spain should lose a war with the Turks, she will always come back, but the loss of the Indies would make the empire disappear for good."

"Ah, Don Francisco, don't go on like this. Such a disaster won't occur. Do you think our Lord would take away with one hand what He's so freely given with the other?"

"Adam and Eve lost paradise, dear friend. But don't you worry, it's not going to be God who grabs the Indies' riches from us, but our own ineptitude. You know as well as I that there are whole towns of smugglers on the islands and coasts of the Indies who are depriving Spain of hides, sugar, indigo, tobacco, precious woods, and even pearls and silver. Isn't that true? Now I ask you: how many soldiers have we got in the Windward Islands?"

"None."

"And in the Leeward Islands?"

"There aren't any that I know of, Don Francisco."

"You're right. Where the islands that have no gold are concerned, we think of them as nonexistent, or rather, we call them the *useless islands* and erase them from the maps we carry in our heads. But they are there, Don Pedro," Lerma would say, pointing to the globe. They're there, and our rivals can at any moment occupy and colonize them."

"I'm not unaware of that, *señor*, and I think, as you do, that it's a shame. Give me enough ships, give me a license to recruit the men and food and stores from ports in the Indies, and I'll bring you all the intruding ships in tow."

"And how many sails do you need, *señor*, fifteen, thirty, fifty? Do you want me to pull the galleons we've lost in twenty years up from the bottom of the sea?" And looking fixedly at Don Pedro, he would add softly: "Do you want me to give you back that ship you handed over to Drake amid the Armada's sad reverses?"

"Ah, Don Francisco, you know that I was in the Channel all alone, waiting for help that never came. My battered ship was helpless before the English squadron. If I had engaged, four hundred Spaniards would have died to no avail. I beg you to give up that point which, along with my honor, has been cleared up entirely."

"I haven't wanted to offend you," the duke would say, "but you're imagining a naval war that's impossible to wage because we lack the ships. You will serve His Majesty on land, and your main mission will be, on the one hand, to fortify the cities and raise local militias, and on the other, to hang everyone who trades with the foreign ships, and first to hang those who are buying slaves."

"I fear that you've not been fully informed, Don Francisco. In the Indies, especially in the islands, nearly everyone, from monk to mayor, participates in commerce with the smugglers."

"I'll give you special powers. As soon as the guiltier ones are hanged, you'll have the rest of them clamoring for more cannons to fire on the ships that violate our waters. And also, if you need more men, take slaves from their masters, put pikes and machetes in their hands, and promise them their freedom if they fight well against intruders. Tell their masters that a compensation from the crown is coming, and if it doesn't come you can lay the blame on me. You're a resourceful man," the duke would say, getting up. "Excuse me, Don Pedro," he would add, lifting his hand to his forehead. "A little while ago I wanted to ask you something, and now I can't remember what it was. Of course, with so much in my head . . . I guess I'll just have another cup of wine," the duke would say, pouring one for himself. "I don't offer one to you, because it has some Mexican powders that you're not used to."

"I've eaten well and drunk at your table, Don Francisco. I couldn't put another drop into my stomach now; the years and troubles have made me a bit delicate."

"Strange wine," Lerma would say on drinking it. "Thick and fragrant as a syrup, but it has the virtue of clearing up the head."

"May it serve you well, Don Francisco."

"It's a good thing that I thought of you. It's been good to see you here," the duke would say, rising to his feet. "I'll take you before His Majesty tomorrow, and I'll have you launched on your new mission right away," he would add, in a tone that meant the interview was over.

"But Don Francisco, you still haven't told me my destination."

"Destination? Oh, yes, that's right. I told you, the kingdom's complicated affairs are making me more distracted all the time. It's a bad sign, a bad sign, Don Pedro. We're getting old, my friend," the duke would sigh, sitting down again. "Well let's see: His Majesty's intention is to replace the viceroy in Mexico, but that position would cost more than you could afford, because the one who gets it ought to pay at least a million to the king. He also intends to replace the governor of Cuba, that Maldonado Barnuevo, who hasn't known how to make his authority felt and keeps begging us for money to make sugar in Havana. On the other hand, I've just heard from Santo Domingo that Don Diego Osorio has died . . . Ah, *señor*, I tell you the memory is a curious thing. Now I remember what I meant to ask you."

"Tell me, Don Francisco, tell me."

"Why did it happen, since Drake was then the worst personal enemy that Spain had, that you were given so many privileges as his prisoner?"

"Privileges? . . . None, Don Francisco. What are you trying to insinuate? I told you already. That episode has been explained. The three hard years of my imprisonment in England . . ."

"Which you spent drinking, hunting, and gambling with Drake and his cronies."

"A libel!"

"My informants are trustworthy. Absolutely."

"Trust me, *señor*, you have been ill informed. Someone who wants to bring me down has been deceiving you."

"Watch what you say, Don Pedro," the duke would say, with a frown. "I have evidence that you turned your galleon over to Drake in exchange for a share of the plunder."

"Evidence, *señor*? What evidence do you have? I was cleared of all guilt by the commander of the Armada, the Duke of Medina Sidonia himself, *señor*!"

"Well, let it be, Don Pedro, it's your business whether you want to recognize your sins or not. You've been playing dumb for the past two hours, as if you didn't know a thing, and all the while you've got money in Amsterdam that could easily buy a viceroyalty and a magnificent palace as well. So that's enough posturing and double talk; it doesn't suit you anyway at your stage in life."

"Ah, Don Francisco, you're passing over details that would argue in favor of my honor."

"Details, Don Pedro? I could give you all the details that you want. Here they are," Lerma would say, turning his head disdainfully toward the papers by the water clock. "But after you've read them you still will have delivered to the enemy one of Spain's most powerful galleons and, along with it, a half million ducats, a hundred barrels of powder, fifty cannon, four hundred soldiers and sailors, and a dozen coffers full of jewels and gifts to buy the Irish with. If the old king had known this, he'd have had you beheaded on the spot. How do you expect the new king to react?"

"Oh, *señor*, have mercy! I don't ask this for my own sake, but for my son Fernando who, being innocent, would be dishonored. What would you gain by denouncing me? Do you want money? I'll give you all I have. Do you want my head this minute? Here it is; behead me and throw my body to your dog, but spare my son."

"Calm down, Don Pedro. Stand up and straighten your collar. Would you like a little wine? Whatever you want. I think it's time to get away from this unpleasant subject."

"And then . . .?"

"I have a proposition for you, and it has nothing at all to do with your well-deserved punishment."

"Give me an order, Don Francisco. Tell me what to do; my life is in your hands."

"Do you know the business of buying and selling slaves?" the duke would ask as he looked at the documents piled on the table. "Don't bother to answer; you'll say you don't know a thing about it."

"I know a little, Don Francisco. The business is in the hands of the Portuguese, which means it's in our hands."

"You astonish me. Well, you ought to know that a few years before the old king died, when the ruin of Spain was almost palpable and the country's credit had hit bottom, he resolved to issue a license to Pedro Gomes de Reynal allowing him to sell forty thousand Negroes in the Indies over nine years. In exchange for this privilege, the crown received nine hundred thousand ducats. All right, now I'll tell you that I am in business with another Portuguese, a certain Rodrigues Contino, who is interested in getting a similar license from His Majesty. A short while ago I got a letter from a mainland governor, I think it was from Cumana; he was requesting Negroes with the desperation of a starving man who begs for bread; he complained that his subjects had abandoned their corrals and plowed lands to run off to Peru, and they were doing this because there was a lack of Negroes there to do the work." Lerma would get up from among his cushions, and once again he would approach the globe. "I've made a study of the business of slave trafficking, believe me. I could tell you about it from the times the Portuguese landed in Guinea until the beginning of the contraband in Negroes, some forty years later. Apart from the English and French, another naval power is now sticking its nose into the business. I don't know if you've heard that a Dutch squadron was captured in Angola. In any case, the demand for slaves is growing; of course the competition is growing too; it's only natural, the business is great, you know. A Negro's price on the West African coast is a barrel of sour wine, or sixty bad knives, or four pairs of woolen stockings, or twenty pounds of glass beads, or a big iron bar. And a slave sells on the mainland for more than two hundred ducats."

"It really is a big business."

"Yes, Don Pedro, it really is a big business. In the mines of the Indies, you can put the native, because nobody knows better than he how to work them patiently, as they did under the pagan kings; but for other types of work you want the Negroes: nobody surpasses them in leading mule trains, in pearl diving, building fortresses and roads, in rounding up cattle, in cutting sugar cane, in cutting stone and working in the fields, and even in cooking and being servants. A Negro is worth four Indians, much more, in fact, if you take into account that the latter, being by nature weak and sickly, die of fevers, colds, and the shits by the tens of thousands, and already there are hardly any left on the bigger islands. That lesson has been learned by now all over the New World, and the demand for Negroes is going to keep on growing."

"What can I do for you, then?"

"I'll have you named governor and captain general of Cuba, an island that you've visited already. As I said, you'll stop the illegal trading there, which for the most part is in Negroes. This will discourage the foreign ships, and before long they'll stop coming to Cuba. If you're able and diligent, you'll be able to conclude this first stage in two years. Make use of every necessary means, as I told you; use the gallows without thinking twice, wipe out and burn the towns if that is needed, but make sure that you stop the contraband in Negroes. I'll send a magistrate for you to dispatch as your lieutenant to Baracoa, to Bayamo, Puerto Principe, Santiago, Trinidad. Write down those names, especially Bayamo, because they're nests of smugglers. You'll stay in Havana, so that when the justices in Santiago complain about your methods your lieutenant will pay for the broken dishes."

"Could you give me a galleon and two or three light ships to fight off the enemy? I know Cuba's waters, and I have always had success there fighting pirates."

"I'll give you the *San Pelayo*, a new galleon, and you can build a *zabra* or two, but no more. Take your son with you, so you can see him be distinguished in some way that the king will notice."

"You are magnanimous, Don Francisco. My son and I are your eternal servants."

"Stop the bowing and hand kissing, Don Pedro, because if you make a mess of this you'll pay me with the money that you've got in Holland. By the way, when you get to Havana, be sure to live and behave like a prince. Don't be afraid of the sin of pride; it will make everybody hate you, but also fear you and respect you. I'll give you the power to confiscate, in His Majesty's name, all the Negroes that you need to defend the island; as I told you, set one or two of them free so that everyone tries harder to do his duty. Also, confiscate any Negroes whose owners can't prove that they were legally bought; these slaves, of whom there are very many, you will resell, even to their former owners, for three times what they're worth. If there aren't any more, they will buy them. Don't ever think of keeping part of this money for yourself, because in the long run you'll be accused of being a thief, and you won't be of any use to me then. Send everything on to me, together with the king's one-fifth, and I'll find a way of rewarding you through other channels. One more thing, you must never dare to send a letter to me; always write them to the king, because I'll be the first to read them."

"Don't worry about me, Don Francisco. I will carry out your wishes. What shall I do when the two-year term you've set has run?"

Don Pedro would see Lerma walking toward the partition. Now he would note a certain stiffness in the duke's movements, as if a steel breastplate had been hidden underneath his rich silk jerkin. Lerma would pull the black braid several times, and a clamor of cowbell and drums would mark out a strong African rhythm. "When the two-year term is up, Don Pedro," Lerma would say above the fervent beating of the drums, "all the people there will come to you to ask for slaves."

"I don't understand you, Don Francisco."

"Everyone will ask you for some slaves!" the duke would shout as he came nearer, and then he would add: "You will send these requests to the king, and right away ships loaded with Negroes will cast anchor in the ports that you want them to."

"Ships loaded with Negroes? I swear I don't know what you mean. You just told me to put an end to the slave traffic."

"But these ships you'll leave alone, Don Pedro," the duke would interrupt, "because they'll be the Portuguese ships of Rodrigues Contino, my business associate. The Negroes will sell at four hundred ducats apiece, and there will be a commission for you. Furthermore, when the business in Cuba is over I'll have you appointed in whatever other place, where you'll do the same thing. As you can see," Lerma would say, smiling, "I divide my cape in two just like good St. Martin."

Perhaps Don Pedro de Valdés, having leaned until this moment on his galleon's taffrail, will decide to go below into his cabin's cozy shadows. Perhaps he'll do this to prevent the midday sun from glaring down on the bilious fever that's beset him, or perhaps it's just to try a bite or two of an inviting lunch that could consist of turtle soup, broiled porgy, pork ribs, greens, fresh guavas and bananas, all bought at daybreak on Havana's docks. Perhaps, before he goes back, he will look in the distance for the gloomy Morro castle, or the little Punta fortress; then, squinting in the resplendence, he will extend his view toward the dressed-up brigantines and longboats roofed with palm leaves that have come outside the port to bid the fleet farewell. Perhaps, in walking to his cabin, he'll smile weakly to the ship's master, who will see in his embittered face the failure of his six years of governing. He'll think, perhaps, as he walks below decks with his head down, that at the end of those interminable months he's going home defeated by that rabble from the land where they smoked the Indians' tobacco, engendered mulattos, and danced the *caringa* until dawn; those impudent, rebellious creoles who would bet everything they owned on a cock fight, who breakfasted on three glasses of rum, and who burned houses to amuse themselves; who because they lived in the Indies and a long way from Spain would ignore tithes and excommunications, who lived scandalously all the time, and who hid under their cots indecent books and Lutheran Bibles translated into Spanish by Flemish Jews; that stew of whites, browns, and blacks, all of them with souls of runaway slaves, who took up a machete as readily as a guitar; that shameless pack who wiped their asses with royal licenses, governors' pronouncements, and lieutenants' summonses. Perhaps now, about to go into his cabin, he'll be sorry that he brought his son Fernando, maimed now forever by a pirate's bullet in the Windward Passage. He'll regret, more than anything, his having let Lerma scare him, when it would have been better to have faced the consequences of his past actions than to take on that commission. In any case, whatever would result from it, for now he hardly cared for his life at all. He had made it quite clear in his report that it was not possible to eradicate the contraband in Cuba; there the buying and selling of slaves was a privilege that belonged to everyone except Spain, and the skiffs and anchorages swarmed with slave traders and buyers, auctions and fiestas; and if he sentenced twenty guilty ones to hang, two hundred went up to the mountains to work banditry; and if a pirate was caught, another came and stole whatever there was, the very nails, from Santiago, Puerto Principe, or Trinidad, for it was one thing to look at the Indies from back there and another to live them here, and he would make this point with the weight of the proofs that he carried in his trunks, and he would sustain it in front of the king without taking one step backward, although Lerma might denounce him or withdraw his favor along with his wretched bit of cape.

WINDWARD PASSAGE

The old black man is out there hammering on the bell again . . . three . . . four . . . five . . . six times. He stops, and now he'll rest for three Our Fathers; then he'll go on ringing. Yesterday, after you arrived on muleback to inspect the church, the old man sat outside waiting on a rock, with the mallet between his legs. The bell hung like a bronze fruit on a ceiba tree, and you asked if he could ring it loud enough to reach the cattle ranches. It's an old mill bell, and it doesn't have a clapper, and God knows how it ended up in this weird smugglers' town where the air smells not of sugar but of cowshit, rotten carcasses, and hides curing in the sun. The old man seems odd, too. He's toothless and he's chewing a tobacco wad between his gums. Deaf as a post. When you asked him what his name was, he got up and started banging on the bell. They told you he would be your slave, but a slave is not the same thing here as it is across the island. What the mayor meant was that he'd be your servant while you stayed here preaching in the town. They haven't even got real slaves here, or if they do, they deal with them like honorary family members.

You decide to peek through the hole in the dusty curtain that separates the sacristy from the church's public space. In spite of the old man's hammering, there's no one out there yet, not even the mayor's children, who will help you with the mass. The dusty curtain makes you sneeze. You'll have to tell the old man to take it down and shake it out outside; also he should sweep the floorboards and get the spider webs out from the corners. You sit down and wait. Midday is approaching and the people ought to be here soon. You take a look at the red silk chasuble that the archbishop gave you, hanging proudly from its perch. It has already acquired the nature of a sumptuous disguise, as if removed from some Venetian carnival, lacking but a mask, though that would be unnecessary – don't you always wear one? In any case, the Italian chasuble looks so out of place that you decide that you won't even wear it. You'll serve the mass with just a robe on, which suits this shit church perfectly. Besides, it's starting to get hot.

There the old man goes again, hammering six times exactly, as though he's lacking energy for more, or perhaps he does, perhaps it is the custom here: six rings, three paternosters, six more rings and on and on until the people come. How many do you think are coming? Don't get your hopes up. You have a doubtful place here. On the one hand, they're glad you're here for weddings, baptisms, and such, and on the other hand they all suspect you. It's as though they knew your mission here. It was a mistake to come by boat, especially in the archbishop's brigantine. If you'd come across the mountains on a donkey, your coming would have seemed less official. They're all polite, but they avoid you. They've limited their hospitality to offering the old man and one mule. And nothing else; they haven't even given you a sacristan. Yesterday you had to work alone with vinegar and ash to clean the tarnished silver chalice and the monstrance, then put *copal* resin in the censer, holy water in the font, cut up *casabe* cakes to make five dozen hosts, and shake dust fiercely from the altar and the crucifix, no less, the dust that had been building up since the last priest died six months ago. But still they take good care of their Madonna portrait, a sickly one from Portugal (Baby Jesus' head looks like a smiling olive): fresh flowers, candles, offerings pinned to her frame, silver coins left in the donation box. The woman keeping you, the dead priest's sister, calls her by the name of "Virgin of Good Hope," another name to fill out the roster of dubious patrons rendered homage in the New World. Over here, unlike in Europe, every village has its Virgin, just as it has its local Christianity. The cult of the Virgin, Rome's biggest winner since the time of the Crusades, the best defense from Calvinist asceticism as well as Luther's practicality. But you have to recognize that, apart from Michelangelo, the Madonnas have had a better run of luck than all the Pietàs. You might expect this; the Pietà is filial love from just one side, the side of death, and the Madonna, on the other hand, is the symbol of a life including every kind of love; the Madonna is the beginning, origin, and center. And suddenly, still peering through the curtain's hole, the memory of your father's hated figure strikes you, your father with his pompous mien and in his uniform as captain of a Flanders squadron, your father with his heavy hand down on your adolescent head: Get on your knees now, son, your mother's dead. The Lord has called her to reward her for the things she's done, and her soul is flying up to heaven, although it must be said that there were times when she had need of me to guide her conduct; her passionate Sevillan nature led her to excuse the weaknesses that I saw in others. In your case, she was a tolerant Madonna who forgave you everything. You were always her sweet prince, conceived after many years of anxious waiting; she never saw that these times aren't meant for our rejoicing at the mystery of birth, but rather for the extirpation of the heretics who conspire against the Holy Church of Rome. My son, the Virgin doesn't need more infants in her arms; now is the time to die for Christ, and Christ needs soldiers. As soon as you are old enough, we'll enlist you in my squadron. Meanwhile, you'll learn to ride and use the lance . . . But many things were yet to happen before your father took you, sick and disinherited, on the broad rump of his horse to push you not into his barracks but into the St. Omer Jesuit seminary, an old monastery needing nothing but a drawbridge to resemble all those ruinous castles on the Schelde, from before the reign of the counts of Flanders. Around it: bad roads, impenetrable forest, fog. Within it: porous stonework, etched green by the ooze, interminable winters filled with phlegm, coughing, mustard plasters, sad rosaries and litanies, holy water frozen in the font, and in the basilica a thick iridescent halo made by humid air above the candles, the Mass a ghostly ceremony of faded chasubles and ashen pomp, a thing for catacombs, and then, in the refectory, a singsong reading of some martyr's life, usually a Roman child who had been thrown into the circus, on the table barley soup with a turnip in it, steaming in a chipped bowl into which a lay brother may have dropped a piece of herring, and oh that hard and bitter bread, those cabbages that smelled of doctrine, and the shadowed, whispering corners where the Jesuits always lurked. It wouldn't hurt you to forget all that.

The mayor's children enter dressed as acolytes. They are twins, mulattos like their father. Their robes don't reach their ankles; they must be twelve years old, the age when masturbation starts. You pull back the curtain a little and tell them to go out and let you know when they see the public coming up the hill. You see in their faces an amalgam of respect and fear. They haven't even dared talk to you; they nod, and then go tiptoeing out with arms crossed, the big hypocrites, as if you didn't know the vile things that they do with calves and sows at night, things that unfortunately they won't shut up about when they find you inside the confession box. You know damn well what they'll be thinking then; they'll think as you once thought, that their sins are abominable enough to leave a confessor scandalized. At least that's what you thought at the seminary when you knelt to give confession. How could you whisper through the grate of the confessional to that thin Irishman, trembling with ascetic fervor, that your father had surprised you with your prick inside a sow he'd bought for Christmas dinner? A sow, no less, your father wailed, an animal that demons frequently make use of, succubi especially, at witches' sabbaths. Do you realize, you degenerate, that it's quite possible that you've had carnal knowledge of a succubus? Have you an idea, you nauseating rogue, of your enormous sin? On your knees! Kneel down and repent this act with all your might! Go on, Frasquita, go get my sword, bring it here so I can snap the spine of this young dog, I'm going to beat the demons out of him! But the flat blade on your father's ancient sword, given to him by the Duke of Parma, would not fall directly on your shoulders; one swing knocked off Frasquita's cook's bonnet and the other clipped harmlessly the full skirts of your young Aragonese stepmother, Doña Pilar; both women had protected you with their bodies, hugging, throwing themselves over you, leaving your father with the sole recourse of going out back to attack the sow, and then you got up from the floor and fear would now be tinged with laughter as the yard became a merry-go-round with your father, too enraged to strike home with his blows, hopping after the affrighted sow from one end of the yard to the other, etching pinwheels with his sword, piercing, cutting in the air, until finally a bloody ear flew through the air, a chunk of snout hit Doña Pilar's neck, and a stream of blood and guts on the yellow grass marked out the animal's noisy death throes, which had their macabre end beside the trough where Frasquita threw the table scraps; then everything was silent, your nervous laughter and the women's shouting ceased, and your father, huffing and puffing from his protracted chase throughout the yard, tore up some grass and started slowly cleaning off his blade with it, his face distorted in blind fury, lips and cheeks gone white as he continued wiping off the steel, and suddenly he raised his head, looked right at you, and murmured somberly: If only you were not my son. You'll never be a soldier now; you'll be a priest, so you can reflect on your repugnant sins. Next week you're going to the seminary.

But that whole scene of your father and the sow, which you decided, after much hand wringing, not to recount to the Irish Jesuit, and which causes you to smile now in this miserable church, turned out to be a mere preamble to a real *Walpurgisnacht*, except that the witches here, rather than meet their devils in the Harz mountains, had chosen that year to fly on their broomsticks toward St. Omer to come down on upon your father's roof and then to whisper in your ear, while you asked God's pardon for your terrible sin, that after all to spend yourself inside a sow was not so awful, and couldn't be as bad, for instance, as to take another person's life, or steal their property, or to eat meat on Lent, and anyway the person most to blame here was the gardener, who had trapped the sow in a corner of the yard and offered you explicit demonstration, and then you'd wanted to find out what it felt like, and it was amazing, and there was no succubus inside the poor beast, because if one had tried to inhabit someone in the household it would have picked Frasquita, who lets the gardener squeeze her behind, or even Doña Pilar, who when she's suckling little Juanito opens up her shirt entirely and takes out her two breasts, and then your father hates you, he's always hated you, because your mother loved you more than she loved him, and now he hates you more because he has little Juanito, and all he says is that Juanito has his very nose, his very mole beside the navel, and it's you whose ears he pulls on and slaps for no reason after anything you do, because as far as he's concerned you don't do anything well, and if he speaks a word to you it's always the same thing, that the Holy Church in Rome says this or that, and that the Holy Father says or doesn't say, that Jesus did or didn't do, and that the Lord God and Most High and the Creator and the Holy Spirit and the Most Holy Trinity and so forth, and everything gets him talking in this way, as if he were an evangelist rather than a captain, although you might as well get used to it, because next week you're going to the seminary and they're going to say the same things there, and what a good thing it would have been to be a cavalryman, to pass the time in taverns, drinking wine up to your ears, playing cards and screwing farm girls, milkmaids, kitchen maids, laundry maids, and whores who follow behind the troop when it goes off to the campaigns, and you'd do it and you'd do it and you'd do it until you felt like stopping, felt like getting married, for if you weren't to go to the seminary you'd be able to have a sweetheart and then marry her, and you'd give it to your wife your whole life long, yes sir, how good that would be, the life you'll never have. And the best you could do now was root up something in the kitchen, because your father would have gone to sleep and Frasquita will give you something to eat, maybe a chicken wing, a piece of cheese, a sausage, something anyway; but that something without a definite taste was materializing to the beat of your coming down the staircase, sniffing like a bird dog at the nobly welcoming smell of meat turning on the spit, and with your mouth watering you skipped over the final steps because you knew that Frasquita, whom your father sent to the butcher with the sow's remains, had forgotten some good piece of roast and left it in the wheelbarrow to take out and enjoy alone, and this wasn't the first time you'd surprised her, but this time your gastronomic complicity took an unexpected turn, for when the lascivious sow's ribs had all been chewed and picked, you raised your greasy fingers to Frasquita's bodice, and she let them stay there while she occupied herself in sucking marrow from the bones, and then suddenly, with a quick shake of hands and shoulders, Frasquita pulled her bodice up over her head and kept on sucking bones like anything, gluttonously, lip-smackingly, one of her big breasts sticking halfway out of her smelly chemise, and she kept her sucking up while you applied yourself to nibbling and nursing, and when she'd finished she started grunting like the sow, and a rank, sweet vapor rose between her legs, and she took you by the hand and led you to a corner, and groaning softly she undid your fly and looked at you, took hold of you, palpated, kneaded you and fondled you and greased your prick with warm lard that had been dribbling from the spit; then she tucked up her skirts, got down on all fours and nuzzled like the sow, and she was steaming down below, and there you were, and suddenly she started rocking back and forth as your father and Doña Pilar walked into the kitchen. Naturally in the next two hours you suffered all the tortures of the Inquisition, and your father came near to castrating you with the carving knife, but luckily just then they notified him from the barracks that they had captured two Dutch spies and were waiting for him to come so they could hang them the next day.

Now come to think of it, despite the royal caning that you got there in the kitchen, you came out rather well that night, and not only that one, but now, as you stand waiting for your new parishioners, whom you're going to threaten with excommunication if they don't follow the commands you've brought, you realize that it was that long gone day at St. Omer that had marked your life forever, made you into what you are, a hypocritical and nonbelieving priest, an opportunist looking only to get by at the expense of other people's faith. Just maybe, if your experience had been nothing else but to try the porcine flesh of a sow and that of a poor dumb servant, being unable to repress your own most primitive desires, your life would have turned out more sincere, less hopeless, but it wasn't to be like that; it happened that on that very day there was unveiled to you the mystery of the flesh throughout its range: bestial, vulgar, and sublime. With your father now gone in a commotion of arms and horses, Doña Pilar came unexpected to your door, in a nightgown with a candle in her hand, and she turned the lock and without saying anything blew out the candle and began to kiss and toy with all the welts your father had left on your body, head to toe. Filled with pity for yourself, you started crying as she lay down by your side and tucked you in between her breasts. And then, in the same warm, soft tone of voice your mother had used to speak to you, you heard her say that you were fifteen now and it was time to learn to do things right. And a little while later, as you sat looking through the window at the slowly moving lights on the pinnaces as the current carried them downriver, trying not to look at the sheets filled with moonlight and abandonment that your stepmother's body had just left, you swore that never would you tell a confessor what had happened between you and her on that enchanted night. And you've kept that vow, for better or for worse, unto this day.

But here you've got the mayor's children to advise you. You realize that for some time you've been listening to their voices without hearing them, like listening to the rain. They ask your license to go into the sacristy, and when you give it they stumble walking through the curtain. Now they're looking at you helplessly. They're nervous. They must have forgotten how to do the Sunday rite. After seven months without a Mass, no boy could be expected to remember the Latin like a parrot. Why must the Mass be said in Latin anyway, a tongue that only educated people comprehend? Wouldn't it be more natural to perform it using words the people understand and speak? And now the boldest of the twins is stammering a request for flint and tinder to light up the censer. As you point to the worn-out chest of drawers, the other twin takes down the chasuble and holds it forward carefully by the shoulder seams as if he were going to hang it on a rack. You see his eyes ablaze with wonder; he's never seen so fine a garment. And why not flaunt your vanity again? You stretch out your arms to let him fit you with it, then turn to let them both admire you. Their faces, openmouthed, are the best mirrors you could have. You're going to shine like a ruby necklace on a pile of cowshit, like an emperor's crown upon the altar of this miserable church, which is not much more than four adobe walls and a palm-leaf roof, the pulpit a rough slab platform looking mostly like a scaffold. It's a good thing you're not staying long. Two months or three at most, until the soldiers come and burn the town down. The archbishop told you that. But now it's time for you to get out there. If you put it off too long you'll lose half your audience. Quickly you pull out your handkerchief to mop the sweat on your nose and forehead, then you open up your chasuble's folds and part the curtain to face gloriously all the sheep of your new flock. And there they are: blacks, whites, mulattos, mestizos, and *zambos*, all colors tossed together like vegetables and meat in a stew, an *ajiaco*, as they say here in these islands. You can't even tell the difference right away between masters, slaves, and servants. There are whites out there who wait on Negroes, carrying their benches and stools and pillows and straw pallets to kneel down on, and all this is so natural, as if the color of their skin bore no authority whatever; you see blacks and *zambos* waiting on mestizos, and mestizos serving whites and blacks, and of course you'd seen some of these mixed castes and colors back in Puerto Plata, but even there, when you come down to it, no white would have waited on a person who was anything but white himself. But Puerto Plata was much closer to Santo Domingo than this godforsaken place, Puerto Plata almost bordered on the captain general and the Inquisition, and that's why it is no more; it almost bordered on the land of treasurers, inspectors, magistrates, constables, captains, mayors, planters, merchants, lenders, slave traders, notaries, and bishops and archbishops, priors and precentors, the crème de la crème of the very shit itself, the New World shit, colonial shit, the worst shit of all because it has no self-awareness, doesn't smell itself.

A whiff of *copal* brings you back to the present. As

Puerto Plata fades away with its flames and nooses, your face takes on its everyday mask. One of the twins tugs on your chasuble. Let's get on with it.

Carefully you climb the shaky pulpit stairs. You go up without looking at your feet, as if your piety would make you levitate. At last you reach the platform, and you spread out your arms to tell the people what you always tell them when you get to a new church; you say that before the mass begins they should all say three rosaries, or else thirty Hail Marys and three Our Fathers, which will give you time enough and more to get a good look at every face in the congregation. Suddenly, and somewhat inexplicably, as the rosaries fade into enthusiastic implorations of the Virgin, you think you'd like to know their names and family histories. There was a time, years earlier, in which you also would have wanted to find out their sins, let's say the secret life of that fair, low-necklined woman, with tits not for disdaining, who looks rapturously on that lustrous and red-kerchiefed black, or perhaps the intimate life of that red-haired dwarf, dressed in silk, whom everyone greets warmly and is followed by a little harem of three sweating mulatto girls, their charms occulted by finery smuggled in by a Rotterdam merchant, yes who *is* that dwarf sultan, that proud jester, and no matter who he is, will he tell you all his sins in the confessional one day? Let's hope not. Let's hope he keeps them to himself as you do with yours. You can't stomach any more sins. You've had your fill of crimes, betrayals, adulteries, incests, thefts, abortions, buggeries, unnatural couplings, heresies, impieties, and sacrileges; you've heard so many that you simply cannot swallow any more, you just can't stand it, and now you can't see anyone without labeling him a rogue or cuckold or whoremonger.

Why can't you just accept that red-haired dwarf as just

a red-haired dwarf, and those three mulatto girls as just
his maids, or slaves, or cousins, friends, half-sisters even?
But that's not the worst of it, the worst is that you can't
admit that you're no better than they are, you're just the
same. And when you think about it, you're worse than
they are, because you look on Christ as an example
impossible of imitation and you've always doubted the
church's legitimacy, and yet you live for and from it. You
haven't even had the courage to hang up your robe and
become another public sinner, one of so many. Certainly
you've had a chance to do it, you've had plenty of them,
starting at St. Omer seminary when you jumped the walls
to stay one night with the gypsies who had camped out by
the woods. And now, as you remember it, you find yourself a young man again, trying to distract yourself during
the Hail Marys and Our Fathers by imagining what you'd
write in the book you know you'll never write now. And
you'd write exactly what your memory holds, and now
you see what once you saw from your cell's window slit
in a back tower of the monastery. And you're looking at a
garden crammed with cabbages, turnips, radishes, and
onions stretching toward a bare wall. Behind the garden
there's a gray road, muddy, with a surface of sinuous furrows left by wagon wheels. And that sad road you're
looking at now bends rightward toward the solid ground
of a low hillock, and beyond that it disappears in a forest
of elm and linden trees. The treetops are all bare, and the
fallen leaves, compacted by the autumn showers, are
mixed in with the mud. And then you start to hear a far-
off sound of tambourines and strings buzzing like a
bumblebee, and it's the gypsies from Spain. Now you see
them in the road. The children and the women are on foot,
beside three big wagons pulled by double mule teams.
The children are splashing in the puddles, and clayey

water has left their bare legs with a crust that looks like riding boots. The women sing and dance as they walk along; they too are barefoot, but their multiple skirts hide everything above the ankle. The men are crammed together in the driver's seats; some hold the reins and some are making music. It's a lovely thing to watch the women dance. On seeing the forest, they have run ahead, still dancing, dark hands raised above red, green, and yellow bodices, toying with their fringed mantillas, playing on the castanets. When they reach the forest's edge, the wagons leave the road for an encampment, and old men wrapped in black mantles come out, and small children, and thin dogs that lift their legs beside the tree trunks; the men bring out dry firewood, cast-iron pots and bundles of all sizes; the women and the children, baskets in their arms, walk into the forest; they must be looking for blackberries and mushrooms. A black-haired girl, however, keeps on dancing, singing. Knowing that you're observing her, she has stayed there in the road, and she lets her hair down, claps her hands with feeling; now she undulates her figure, stretches, arches it, laughs gaily staring at you. And now, as in a dream, you see yourself stuck to the window slit, devouring that beckoning flame that's setting fire to the afternoon, that's burning monastery doors down, making ashes of the sacred ornaments, the supplications, the grave organ introits. And that night, when you ran off unsuspected, when you smelt, below the sheepskins, gypsy girl-musk as you slid inside her, you discovered roundly that you weren't born to give the sacraments; your tonsure and your robe, vows and rosary would serve you only as disguises, migrant shepherd's masks, clown clothes belonging to a grinning windbag gypsy on the paths of God. And that night, like on your night of incest, like many others in your thirty-year pilgrimage through the churches of the Old World and the New, you have kept from everyone; those nights are your secret life. Yes, it's true, you could have changed from one life to another at any time; you could have said I am just what I am. But you were afraid of being excommunicated and branded as a heretic, afraid of being treated like a renegade priest, like vermin. You've always been a coward, and your cowardice has made you a loyal tool of bishops and archbishops, priors and inquisitors. Even worse, it is quite possible that they will make you Inquisitor of the Holy Office here on this shit island; the post is vacant now. If you refuse it you will be suspected. Someone else will treat you to an inquisition. Of course you will accept whatever the archbishop offers. You've achieved the condition of a draw animal, with no balls, an ox who ruminates about his bullish past while he meekly pulls the plow. And you had better get ready to say whatever you're going to tell these people, for the prayers are over now. It's time to put on your Savonarola mask.

As you must, you speak the Latin name of the three-personed God. But following the group's "Amen," as you look on the straying sheep, you see yourself among them. If there's a shepherd in the church, it surely isn't you. And now a fraternal feeling rises to your heart, one that you can't remember having had before. Fraternal is not right, exactly, fraternal comes from *frates*, a word that usually bends in your teeth like a false coin. The right word is complicity. Yes, He already said it about stoning the adulteress. Then, if the lesson is that we're all guilty, why are you going to stone these people, whose only sin is selling cowhides to the Dutch? To start with, you're not going to say the mass in Latin, but in Spanish; then, we'll see.

You enter the sacristy dripping with sweat. You take off

the chasuble and throw it in a corner. It doesn't seem like a disguise now; it's a bloody hide ripped from a cow's back. You look for the holy water urn and pour a little in the sink. You wash your face. You drop into a chair, exhausted. You unbutton your robe. You close your eyes. You'd give your life for a cigar, but you left them back in town, inside a drawer. If you weren't so tired, you'd get on the mule right now and go back to the dead priest's place, to Father López's house. There you'd drink some pineapple juice, smoke a cigar, and stretch out for a nap in the hammock beneath the carob tree in the backyard, a kerchief on your face to keep the flies off. Yes, you'd do that in just a little while. And when you think about it, the house is not that bad: Father López's little room, the bed under its mosquito netting, the feather pillow, a bit of veal on the table, and on the night stand nothing less than the lives of St. Francis and the ingenious hidalgo of La Mancha. The hammock takes you back to one you once had in Havana, same height, same curvature, your body sunk voluptuously in the cotton net. It seems that López weighed the same as you and had your figure. What could he have died of? His sister, who must be about fifty, told you that he was her younger brother. So López must have died at your age, forty-seven more or less. You wonder what he'd think of what you're doing. The archbishop told you López had protected contrabandists, but that isn't saying much: on Hispaniola's north and western shores, where cattle are, the clergy is supported by the contraband. That's nothing new, and furthermore it must be like that: the Dutchmen pay two times what hides bring in the capital, and they sell their merchandise for six times less. The contraband in hides is the natural economy here, just as it is sugar, legally exported, on the island's other side. That's why slavery here is different;

it's not the same thing to cut cane for sugar mills as it is to ride twirling ropes through the open fields. But none of this interests you. What you're worried about is your personal situation. When you get down to it, López never had his choices set against each other as yours are. On the one hand are the orders from the archbishop and the governor, which you must carry out, and on the other is that curious comradeship you're feeling toward these people. It was enough that you gave the Mass in the vernacular, which is sure to carry consequences, to have you seen as taking a political stance. You, no less, who have never had political opinions. Now you've done it. They almost carried you in triumph from the church. And now, of course, you think that there's a vigilant eye observing you, and your behavior hasn't passed unnoticed. Maybe the governor has spies, who knows? You're squirming in your seat. Now the old fear is coming back, the fear that they can read your thoughts, that your secret life is visible. The feeling of being watched is so intolerable that you open your eyes: two identical heads are jutting from the curtains; it's the mayor's boys. They've kept quiet because they thought you were sleeping. Still seated in the chair, you wave them in. They're not frightened of you now; they're smiling foolishly, like the Madonna's olivaceous child. You ask them what their names are. They're called Julio and Esteban, and they have a message from their father, a dinner invitation for tonight, at sunset, and they'll come for you. This matter smells of a conspiracy. Naturally, you refuse. The boys begin to back away; they look serious and cheated. You close your eyes again. You feel endlessly fatigued. You feel like shit. You're going to sleep.

You wake up bathed in sweat, you're hungry and thirsty, mostly the latter. You walk to the urn of holy water and take a long drink from it. Despite the heat, the water is cool. It tastes unbelievably good. The old man brought it the day before from the town fountain, and you blessed it in his presence. As you were doing so, he took off his hat and fell to his knees, pressing his hands together the way that praying children do. You couldn't help giving his head a little sprinkle, too, and blessing him. The old man thanked you. He didn't say a thing, but he looked you in the eye and moved his head. Maybe he was saying that you could count on him. Where do you think he was born, in Africa or over here? If you heard him talk, you'd know. And now you realize that he's never said a word to you. You don't even know his name. He must be a deaf-mute. You take another drink.

The mule is rather old, but it obeys you and moves fairly well, even downhill. It's a good mule. Strange that yesterday you didn't notice. Nor did you notice that you could reach the church along two different roads, one running toward the west, in the direction of the town and the ocean, and the other heading inland, toward the ranchlands. As a matter of fact, you don't know a damn thing about the layout of this region. This morning, when you unpacked the chasuble, you saw the map the archbishop had given you. You'll have to examine it in more detail. They say that from the northern mountains you can see the coast of Cuba. That could well be; the Windward Passage is just fifteen leagues across, you were told. You stretch your neck, shade your eyes, and look to the horizon. It's no use, you've got the sun in front of you and you see nothing but the flashing sea. Your eyes hurt, and you look down. Now the mule seems to have four ears. You blink, and now your eyes are better. You think that the Madonna cult must be quite popular, since this path looks worn by heavy traffic. The land is red and loose. It must

drain well. The best land for raising cattle. The clay in the
soil allows for puddles, and the hooves can even rot
sometimes. Where did you read this, in Italy, in Spain?
The town's rooftops are now coming near, the smell of
carrion and drying hides gets strong. You guess that a person gets used to this, but never to the flies. You've never
seen so many flies.

The road has widened out into the town's main street.
The people stop to look at you; they show their faces in
the doors and windows. Now you're a celebrity; your latest mask: revolutionary priest. Whoever would have
thought? López's sister stands there waiting for you
underneath her house's canvas awning. You can't remember what her name is, Antonia, Ramona, something like
that. Beside her, sitting on the ground, his back against the
wall, you see the old man; he's weaving a straw hat. On
seeing you, he stops as quickly as he can and comes forth
to take the mule. Tomorrow you'll give up the robe and
ride straddling the mule, which in Santo Domingo you
could never do.

As soon as you go in, a disagreeable surprise awaits
you: an entire delegation, headed by the mayor, is in there
waiting for you. One of its members is the red-haired
dwarf, whom they introduce to you as the richest rancher
in the place. You'd have to see it to believe it. They've
reserved for you the house's only armchair, where López
must have read one of his two books and where now
Antonia or Ramona does her sewing; the other seats are
leather footstools. The mayor fires the first shot; he tells
you straight out that he wants to know the governor's
intentions. Everyone looks fixedly at you. With your sermon you have opened up Pandora's box, and now they're
going to hound you with their questions. They've started
with the easy ones, but you know that more are coming,

which if you answer them will compromise you hopelessly. This time you'll begin at the beginning, with the governor's order, something you unfortunately failed to mention in your sermon. You answer that, obeying the royal writ that calls for an immediate end to contraband, the inhabitants of the north and the west coasts will have two months to round up all their cattle, load their belongings into wagons, and set out for the new towns now being built near Santo Domingo; when this time is up, the soldiers will appear and burn whatever they find; anyone who disobeys this order will be excommunicated by the archbishop, and in accordance with their guilt, will then be jailed or hanged without regard to sex or civil status . . . And so you fired the first cannonade. Your words, official; tone, magniloquent. And to remove all doubt, you add a thing you weren't even going to mention in the sermon: you were there when Puerto Plata was destroyed and those who disobeyed were hanged. And that's it. They aren't going to pull you from behind those words; you will repeat them until they're tired of listening. Of course they are all silent now. After you'd preached in church that you were on their side and wished to help them however you could, they had hoped for something else from you. It hurts you to have disappointed them, but what the hell were you going to do? You let out a sigh and take a look at the mayor; he has begun to work his anger off by pacing through the room. You look at the dwarf; he licks his lips with his little pink tongue, and you think he's going to speak. Seated on the footstool, he resembles a Dutch doll. But his words are far from doll-like, supposing such could speak. Without even getting agitated, he declares that when the goddamned soldiers come he's going to stampede forty thousand head, and then he adds that the shit and guts those bastards leave behind there in his pastures will help the grass grow thicker. As if that were nothing much, the mayor, when he sits back down, not even looking at you, says there's no priest who's excommunicating *him*, that the pope alone could do it. You can see it's going to be a long and torturous evening.

You've been hearing the birds sing and the flies buzz for some time. You open your eyes: through your handkerchief's thin cloth the bright daylight filters through. You think: finally it's Monday. Your head aches so much it feels as though you could give birth through it. Must be the cigars; when you retired to the hammock, you left behind four cigar butts on the plate that Doña Ramona set next to your chair. As soon as you lit up the first one, they all started smoking. You'd never smoked so much, nor had you seen such smoking. Even the dwarf, with admirable tenacity, reduced a ten-inch *tagarnina* to a pile of ashes. You notice that your kerchief smells of smoke; it must be your breath. You pull it off and blink. You get up; beyond the shadow of the carob tree, there's Doña Ramona watering the plants. She hasn't seen you waking up, it seems, and you turn to rest your aching head inside the hammock, covering your face again. Right now you don't want to think. You want only to want nothing, worry about nothing. Here you're all right, inside López's old hammock. You start humming in your head a madrigal of Palestrina's, and from there you go to Monteverdi's latest, which you heard last year in Italy accompanying the archbishop. And suddenly, from among *Orfeo*'s notes, Doña Ramona's words slip through, for she must have seen you stirring: the twins, a message from the mayor, he wants to know if the Thursday meeting can be in the church, a lot of people want to come. Without taking off the handkerchief, you assent. What else could you do?

You crossed the Rubicon last night. Or rather you crossed the Windward Passage, the most notorious strait in the New World, the only thing that's here to cross. At any rate, you're inside the conspiracy now. You're one of them now, no, you're one of us, one of the communal country folk in Lope de Vega's *Fuente Ovejuna*, a democratic work at that. And the best part is that you yourself took on the role of banished priest. You started with the governor's command, and before midnight you'd already stripped him of his operation. It must be that your brains went soft from listening to all those sins. Or perhaps you're getting old and sentimental. But no, my friend, you're not the shameless cynic that you've always thought yourself to be. Leave that to the archbishop. Your skin is not as hardened as you sometimes think. You knew that as soon as you arrived. You're just a cowardly priest who thinks in terms of me and mine, strictly in first person. It's just that the business in Puerto Plata was too much; it was the coup de grâce that killed off your last mask: the mask of the hangman's helper. You'll never forget what that woman said to you when they were about to string her up. Only you and the hangman heard her words: "Stick that crucifix up your ass, you're just as much a fake as all the rest. Why don't you go to hell and let me die in peace?"

You're sitting down to lunch. Doña Ramona has served you a heaping plate of *ajiaco*. You think the meeting went quite well. It lasted until dawn, and they took the Madonna out for the march. The old man had fun ringing the bell. Then he gave you a straw hat. Nobody's moving to Santo Domingo. They're dealing with two choices: defend the area to the last, or cross the Windward Passage with as many bulls as they can. From what they've told you, almost all of them have relatives in Cuba. One way or another, you're always going to be with them, and you're going to give the mass in Spanish. The *ajiaco* tastes damn good.

SUMMER ISLAND

for Caz, islander

The duel will take place on an island in the Caribbean, one of those minute territories that were late to be colonized because they lacked both pearls and precious metals. This island's previous history is not relevant here, nor are its flora and its fauna. Right now it is enough to know that Christopher Columbus put it on the map and that four languages were spoken there at the moment when the duel was arranged. This linguistic pluralism ought not to arouse any mistaken ideas about the size of the local population, which did not surpass six hundred people at the time.

We need to know the island's interesting mountain system for our archeological work. It must be stated that there is a volcanic ridge running through the middle of the island and that its rugged slopes, with caves and waterfalls, divide east and west. The highest elevation, an old spent volcano, stands at exactly 3,792 feet and has a lake in its crater. So no one ought to be surprised that the aforementioned duel – or any other kind of meeting between warring factions – should occur precisely on this lake's rocky shores: he who controls them rules the island.

The early years of Harry Poole and Alain Pentier are not recorded. We know only that they went by in parallel fashion in the cities of Dieppe and London. This has hardly anything to do with the duel's origins, although someone is sure to bring up the age-old, bitter enmity between the Normans and the Anglo-Saxons. However that may be, in our investigation of this forgotten matter we're going to look at every curious hypothesis, including this one.

It is possible to know with astonishing exactitude the actual date when the lives of these two who were to duel converged in a common destiny. It was March 29, 1615. What was the extraordinary decision Poole and Pentier took that day? There wasn't any. The dueling scheme had been elaborated by a power machine over which the two men hadn't the least control. This power or hidden force, this dictate of the gods or else of history, is what Ovid and Virgil knew as *fatum*; Poole and Pentier called it *destiny*.

To the king of England, James, however, what was going to happen on that morning of March 29 was hardly written in heaven by a transcendent hand. On the contrary: it was his own hand that should have signed or not the decree concerning imports of tobacco that had lain upon his desk for several weeks. We ought to recognize, in truth, his moral quandary. In the first place, James hated taking any profit coming from tobacco, a product he sincerely loathed because he thought its use to be injurious to health and good customs. In the second place, he had already taken a public position alongside those who condemned the practice of smoking. After all, his *A Counterblast to Tobacco* had been welcomed in England's most prudent households, and it had been rumored that the Latin motto printed on Bushell's defiant pamphlet *"Fumus patriae igne alieno luculentior"* – translated by the author as "Better be chokt with English hemp than poisoned with Indian tobacco" – had been written in Whitehall by the diligent royal pen. But of course, arguing the other way were James's depleted treasury, his growing debts, and the unpopularity that would accompany his loading up his subjects with new taxes. In these circumstances, James finally stopped wavering; he decided to sign the decree giving him control over the tobacco trade, under the pretext of limiting its importation. He knew that there was now more and more smoking in London's inns and taverns, that the price of tobacco would rise like smoke, and that if he required a 50 percent commission of the merchants he could earn more than twenty thousand pounds in a year. With a sigh of resignation, James stamped the paper with his signature. His thoughts flew presently in the direction of George Villiers, the beautiful young man with whom he'd fallen hopelessly in love. Of course when he signed the decree James was very far from thinking that he'd created the conditions that would allow Poole and Pentier, years later, carrying their arms of choice, to come together on a Caribbean island's rugged peaks. Nor did Poole and Pentier ever guess that it was the king's moral inconsistency that gave rise to the discords separating their two bands. This kind of karmic explanation can start one thinking.

In any event, we may imagine that in the spring of 1623 Poole was robbing whatever he could on London's streets, while Pentier helped his father sell old clothing in Dieppe. Possibly – here I invoke the curious symmetry of lives destined to cross – Poole one Sunday morning would regard the flowing Thames as the surest route to adventure, while Pentier would look at the arrivals and departures of the Atlantic's famous corsairs with the same longing in his heart.

But the time has come to introduce two new characters, or rather, if you like, a new array of forces whose historic role was to extend the consequences of King James's lack of principle. Their names, unlike those of Poole and Pentier, can be found in library catalogues and encyclopedias. They are: Sir Richard Crumber and Pierre Bélain, *sieur* d'Esnambuc.

What can we say about these men that their biographers have not? Certainly not many things, although it should be noted that the whole point of their respective relationships to Poole and Pentier has been consciously unrecognized until today. For example, if d'Esnambuc raised anchor in Dieppe on April 26, 1625, it was because Pentier had found and picked up, on the wharf, a Turkish talisman that the former had lost (a gold babouche, the size of a cricket). Without this object, which he carried always around his neck, d'Esnambuc would never have sailed on a Wednesday, a day he considered dire because an infallible gypsy had told him so. Correspondingly, if Pentier had not found the little babouche, d'Esnambuc would not have taken him aboard as a reward for his good deed. But, naturally, Pentier *had* to have found the talisman because James had signed the tobacco decree. (In the future, to keep from stretching this postmortem out, I'll try to cut down on these didactic cases.)

What is certain is that Pentier departed aboard a ship that was destined for big endeavors. Notice that I could have said: "What is certain is that Pentier departed aboard a ship commanded by d'Esnambuc, a man marked for great things." But those would have been a historian's, not a sailor's words. All of the world's sailors – beginning with Noah – have always and will always know that on the ocean only ships have destinies. This is so much the case that if d'Esnambuc had left Dieppe in a bigger ship, it is quite probable that he would not have gone down in history as the colonizer of Martinique and Guadeloupe, those green gems set in the Caribbean Sea. Luckily for him, he was suffering through a hard time and could barely raise enough money to buy a brigantine with three cannons and enlist a crew of thirty-nine unsteady hands, including Pentier. As you might expect, d'Esnambuc was defeated in his first engagement with a Spanish ship.

Where was it that this naval combat happened? At the entrance to the Windward Passage, a point exactly equidistant from Jamaica, Cuba, and Hispaniola. There d'Esnambuc's ship was intercepted by an enormous galleon, which with one volley cut her crew by 25 percent. In an all-or-nothing gamble, the brigantine aimed its prow toward the deadly Cayman shoal. Kept from pursuing through those shallow waters, the galleon swung around to shoot its final volley. But the iron cannonballs fell short, just managing to smash the little boat the brigantine was towing. Under these conditions, with all hope placed in a prophetic northeast breeze that had just begun to blow, the brigantine had stumbled on the very course that was to carry d'Esnambuc to glory.

Now let's pick up Richard Crumber when he wasn't yet Sir Richard Crumber; let's take him when he was still one of King James's guards. He was a young, good-looking man then, whose duty, according to an old courtier, "Was but to tell tales, devoure the beaverage, keep a great fire, and carry up dishes, wherein their fingers would bee sometimes before they came to the King's table." That was not all bad if one had no further ambition in life. Only it so happened that Rebecca, Richard Crumber's wife, did have them: she wanted her husband to be rich, which was impossible at King James's destitute court.

One night, with the moon waxing auspiciously, as he was serving supper at the royal table, Crumber heard from James's lips that Roger North, the brother of Lord

North, was about to sail off to the Spanish Main. His mission was to discover Eldorado. Fascinated by this conversation, Crumber never tore himself from James's right side, from which he made quite sure that the king's chalice brimmed with malvesie – a wine James was particularly fond of. After having put down six or seven cups, James took Crumber's steady arm to leave the dining room, followed by Prince Charles and by George Villiers (who by then had been made Earl of Buckingham). When he reached the door, the king turned facing Crumber, and after some kindly patting on the shoulder, named him on the spot the captain of the guard.

When he had finished his night duties, Crumber went to his cramped quarters in the east wing of Whitehall. There he asked Rebecca what to do. Should he take advantage of his new court rank, or should he go away with North on the expedition to Peru? With hardly any reflection, she replied: "My dear, as a captain you won't be able any longer to walk through the streets of London in a mended cape, and you'll have to buy a pair of expensive leather boots, a hat with a white feather in it, a red silk cummerbund, two shirts with cuffs of Holland lace, a brocade baldric for your sword to hang on, a silver-handled pistol, and some kid gloves. I advise you to sail off toward Peru with North." Crumber argued that just two years before Raleigh had lost his head for not discovering Eldorado. Rebecca answered: "My dear, they cut Raleigh's head off because he was an intriguer, but you are a loyal and inoffensive subject. I advise you to follow North to Peru." Crumber answered that if he were to stay at court perhaps the king would pay the back wages that he owed him. "My dear," replied Rebecca, "the king is now quite spent and will die soon. Then the new king will replace the guard, and we will lose the room and board we have today in Whitehall. I advise you to leave for Peru with North."

As we all know, North's first trip to Guyana was a total disaster. As far as having money is concerned, Crumber came back poorer than he had left. But money is not everything in life: a pair of pretty feet, intuition, baldness, and many other things cannot be got with money. And so Crumber came back from the Wyakopo River with empty pockets but a memory filled with valuable experiences. For example, on arriving at Guyana, he encountered several bands of adventurers, most of them Irish, who were growing tobacco to be smuggled into the kingdom. Six years earlier, the low price of tobacco would never have made up for the risks of such an operation, but after the merchandise had fallen into King James's hands, the prices just kept going up. Along the Wyakopo nobody believed in Eldorado anymore: they talked only of varieties of tobacco plants, of freightages, of companies, and how to get around the royal monopoly. It was taken for granted that the Guyanese plant was better that the Amazonian one, and that either one of these was better than the Virginian, which had an ugly yellow flower. The best plant of all seemed to be the one that grew on the Summer Islands, but who dared defy the Spanish galleons that patrolled these waters? "At any rate, all Europe has become a chimney," he'd been told, in faulty English, by one of the Hollanders who had encamped upriver, "and I wouldn't be surprised if women and children soon began to smoke. Eldorado isn't made of gold; it's made of leaf." But a few days later sixty Spanish harquebusiers emerged from the sleeping vegetation growing by the shores of the Wyakopo, wiping out the Dutch encampment. A Spanish captain judged the few survivors, sentencing them to eat three pounds of cured tobacco each. It was then that North decided to pack up his men for a return to England.

Of the twenty-five Normans who reached the island, only d'Esnambuc arrived with his mental faculties intact; heat, hunger, thirst, despair, and scurvy had turned the brigantine's whole crew into a squalid bunch of madmen. Pushed by the winds of destiny, the ship had run aground into a stubborn sandbank near where a little river met the sea. There placidly it stayed, like an old barrel, swaying amid the languid waves and squawking gulls. When midday came and with it the low tide; the hull stopped teetering, and d'Esnambuc took notice that it wasn't going to sail again. Overcoming the oppressive funk he'd fallen into a few days before, he made his way up to the poop; from there he saw his men as they shambled silently along an empty beach of granite sand, whose low dunes shone like heaps of shattered glass. "Perhaps they think they're dead," he thought. After making sure that the powder in his horn was dry, he loaded one of his pistols and fired it in the air. When they heard the report, Pentier and his companions turned their forlorn glances toward the brigantine. Then they fell to their knees and began to weep and laugh despondently.

When dusk came, as they all still played like children in the stream's fresh water, six gentlemen, correctly dressed, appeared. One of them, a tall man with a feather in his hat, stepped forward two paces before shouting out "Ici la France!"

Who was this Frenchman?

How had he got to that island?

What did he intend?

There are two versions of this. Some historians, among them J. W. Jackson, who wrote *The Richard Crumber Story*, say the man with the feather in his hat was a certain Monsieur de Rombe, whose ship had been wrecked on a horseshoe-shaped coral reef up the coast. But if we look at Pierre Margry's *Bélain d'Esnambuc et les Normands aux Antilles*, we find that this man was none other than the famous captain Levasseur, the very one who years later was to found the fearsome Brotherhood of the Coast on the island of Tortuga. Naturally, since my investigation is not immune to the allure of famous names, I warmly support the claim that this man was Levasseur.

However that may be, d'Esnambuc and his men cleaved unto the people of the predetermined Levasseur (Monsieur de Rombe to some), to form a small colony of Normans guarded by a stockade, a lookout post, a flag, and three cannons from the brigantine. Once he had got over all of the long voyage's privations, d'Esnambuc learned from Levasseur that the island harbored a contingent of tobacco-growing Englishmen. This they had been doing since two years before. The plantation had been sited on the island's northwest corner, beyond the mountains, and it had New Road for a name. In a voice laced with disgust, Levasseur told him how the Englishmen refused to board an envoy of his on one of their ships, arguing that there was no telling if when he returned they wouldn't be at war with France. Something like that had happened with some Dutchmen who were mining a big vein of salt at a site they called Araya, a small peninsula of the mainland, and whose hookers put in at the island every three or four months to stock up on wood and water for the journey home. "In any case," Levasseur added, "we decided to grow tobacco anyway, which we trade to the Hollanders for wine, clothing, powder, and lead balls for our firearms. We feel no hunger here; there are fruits and vegetables, and no shortage either of fish, crabs, conches, quail, and ducks. The Caribs, also, bring us a kind of bread they call *casabe*."

"Caribs?" asked the startled d'Esnambuc. "You have the Caribs here?"

"About three hundred," answered Levasseur. "They're mostly transients, heading for the bigger islands, Martinique or Guadeloupe."

"But they're cannibals!"

"No more," said Levasseur reassuringly. "It's said their grandfathers ate the Arawaks, but there are none left of those on any of the islands around here," he added, and when he saw that d'Esnambuc's unease had not abated, he said: "They'd never eat white men's flesh; they think we're poisonous. It seems that years ago the ones on Dominica ate a Spanish priest, and a few of them went mad. The news of this has spread all through these islands. And so the fact is, *cher ami*, that we are quite safe from being eaten," said Levasseur.

D'Esnambuc learned that the Caribs lived in a village of palm-leaf huts in the middle of the island, where they grew tubers of various kinds. Levasseur told him that they smoked a lot of tobacco and were given to free love. For no apparent reason, they liked getting up and heading for the other islands. They would travel in canoes they hollowed out from tree trunks, rowing jubilantly and shouting. For hunting they used blowgun darts and arrows, tips smeared with deadly substances. The big lizards and the rodents that they killed were smoked on a hardwood grill they called a *boucan*. Meat they cured that way would last for many days without going bad, and though some men of his were repelled by it, he had tried it and found that it tasted quite good. The women went with their breasts uncovered; they were ungovernable and spoke a language different from the men's. The village chief was a good friend of his, and had him to thank for having discovered hats and trousers. D'Esnambuc also learned that this man, whose name was Temereme, had formed a bad opinion of the English because they wouldn't mingle with his people. "I wouldn't be surprised if they got together some night and attacked their plantation," said the future lord of Tortuga.

D'Esnambuc's natural talent for diplomacy came out right away. Arguing that the French and English had a common enemy in the Spaniards, he lay out to Levasseur the benefits of their signing an alliance with the people of New Road. "Moreover, when you think about it, we could offer to divide the island." Levasseur answered that he thought the English were too haughty to line up behind a deal like that one. "They're organized by law beneath a company in London, and we're nothing but a band of wrecked privateers with no trading house to back us up." D'Esnambuc conceded this to Levasseur, but only for the moment. "If you get your men to join with mine, we'll put the brigantine together in a month or less. Then it's off to Paris with your tobacco crop, and we'll get the money for a company. You'll see. I've some connections there."

When the time came to depart, Levasseur decided not to go. A daughter of Temereme, a broad-shouldered girl named Barbe, had taken over the Norman and his Roman profile, invading his hut with her store of domestic utensils (stone, conch, and bone), and a big basket of *casabe*. Levasseur had never told him the real reason that he'd had for staying on the island – he'd said it was for his health – but d'Esnambuc conjectured that his countryman had chosen not to interrupt a passionate romance. But he was wrong. Levasseur, whose real name was Gaspard de Baudry, was wanted in all the cities of France for killing unlawfully – in a duel without witnesses or seconds – the only son of the renowned Marquis of Carabas. To evade what was sure to be his judges' prejudice – which the two thousand livres at his disposal weren't sufficient to suborn – Gaspard shaved his moustache and goatee, donned a blond wig of his sister's, and left Rouen at a gallop down the long and tedious road to Caen. Days later, in a crummy tavern in Cherbourg, he found what he was looking for: a new identity. It was there that he bought the name of Levasseur from a privateer who was sick from consumption, along with the man's letters of marque, his folder full of maps and notebooks, and an old Portuguese caravel with a crew of seventeen. Between his gulps of wine and bites of barbecue, this worn-out corsair, now without a name, told the new Levasseur of his enterprising plans for the island of Tortuga.

Needless to say, Gaspard would never have met this privateer if he hadn't killed the Marquis of Carabas's son in some alley in Rouen. Just think, if his sword had deviated just a half-inch right or left of his adversary's femoral artery, the latter would have gone on limping happily through one or the other of the two palaces that his father kept in town. But the steel blade, guided by the hands of fate, entered exactly where it had to in order to make Gaspard de Baudry – *dit* Levasseur, *dit* Monsieur de Rombe – run at a gallop down the route that would lead him into the history books.

Rebecca listened to everything that Crumber could remember about his blistering and endless days beside the Wyakopo. Looking up from her sewing, she fixed her husband in the eye and said: "My dear, the things you've told me could be worth a lot of money. Thank God you listened to me and went to follow North off to Peru. What was that mountainous island called, where you took on water?"

"I can't remember," Crumber answered. "All the Summer Islands have their names in Spanish and are hard to keep track of."

Rebecca left her sewing on the table and got up to stoke the dying fire in the hearth. When she went back to her sewing, she told Crumber: "My dear, take the money from the mattress where I keep it, and get North's pilot to sell you the chart he used on the voyage. Then use the rest to buy a dozen oysters, two big sausages, a rabbit pie, and a bottle of Spanish wine. We'll celebrate your coming back, even though tomorrow we may dine on cabbage soup and turnips."

Adjusting his hat before the sorry mirror in the vestibule, Crumber heard his wife's last admonition: "My dear, tell that man to draw a circle in red ink around the island where you took on water."

Two hours later, Crumber returned with a purple nose, complaining of the cold. He unrolled the chart before Rebecca's eyes and said: "There's the island. Don't you think it's too small?" Rebecca looked at him pityingly. "My dear, it's the map that's small."

After a happy supper, Rebecca made her husband try on his royal guards' uniform. Crumber found that the Wyakopo expedition had robbed him of four inches of flesh, but Rebecca assured him that the only clothing that couldn't be altered was that which was too tight. As she worked with needle and thread, she asked Crumber to find the inkwell, the pen, and three sheets of paper. Then she dictated point by point everything that needed to be done the next day.

Clenching in his frozen hand the papers that he carried in his pocket, Crumber arrived at six in the morning on the doorstep of Jack Merryweather, London's biggest tobacco merchant. He told the servant in a nightgown who opened the door for him that he had brought some papers for his master worth five thousand pounds. The servant thought immediately that Crumber was one of the many who beset his master to get him to invest in harebrained projects, but when he noticed the royal guards uniform he thought that no one from King James's court would get up at daybreak in midwinter for a thing of no importance. After settling Crumber in an armchair, he took the papers and went upstairs. Twenty minutes later, wrapped in a thick wool dressing gown, Merryweather came down. When Crumber saw that the merchant was receiving him with a sincere smile, he was then completely sure that they weren't going to throw him out.

Repaired feverishly in under a month, d'Esnambuc's brigantine was readied for an ocean crossing, although when it berthed at Rouen's docks it came apart like a paper boat. Nevertheless, some of Levasseur's tobacco could be saved, and with the money from its sale, d'Esnambuc was able to distribute twenty livres among his men, buy some clothing made out of good fabric, and take a post-horse down the busy course that ran along the Seine.

Paris was not a new city to d'Esnambuc, and after taking his lodging at a hostelry on la rue des Lombards, he rubbed the Turkish amulet that he wore on his neck and went to see his cousin on his mother's side, who ran a business around the corner that sold imported products. Before entering the establishment, d'Esnambuc stopped to watch the unloading of a big cart. Two robust youths were arranging in a line, beside the door, great bundles of hides, barrels of molasses, tobacco bales, and a dozen boxes of sugar and indigo. When d'Esnambuc began a mental calculation of how much all this was worth, his cousin Ducharme stepped out into the street, followed by three underlings. At the time, the cousin didn't notice him. A group of rubbernecks had bunched up near the cart, looking with admiring eyes at the exotic merchandise that spilled out on the street as if from Ceres's horn of plenty. Before being recognized, d'Esnambuc registered that his cousin Ducharme had changed considerably since the last time he'd been in Paris, seven or eight years before. There was a pocket of fat hanging from his jaw, and his belly rounded out the white mantle that he had on above his clothes. But it was not just a physical change: there was an aura of prosperity to his plump figure, to the nervous way he pointed with his finger at the barrel or the crate to be loaded in his storeroom. D'Esnambuc was cheered, of course, when his cousin recognized him and ran up to squeeze him to his padded breast. "You're the same as ever," said d'Esnambuc, letting himself be taken by the arm and led into his cousin's office on the upper floor of the establishment.

D'Esnambuc didn't beat around the bush. After ascertaining that the goods he'd seen unloaded on the dock were not the fruits of piracy, but rather of commerce, he took a cured tobacco leaf from his jerkin and lay out his plan to Ducharme.

"It seems like an excellent business," Ducharme said, smelling the fragrant leaf. "This is tobacco from the islands of Peru, with a pink flower. The best kind of all. But what I like best is that you've stopped being a privateer, a profession that has come down in the world and is no longer meant for wellborn people such as you. I have it on good authority that Cardinal Richelieu, the king's right hand, thinks that the kingdom's future lies with the overseas companies. Once more I congratulate you for this wise decision, made now in the best years of your life. Try a bit of these pineapple and guava preserves while I write a note to Madame Cavelet, who is my best client and who knows the cardinal well."

Events progressed at such a rate that d'Esnambuc came to suspect there was a conspiracy to be amused at his expense. Madame Cavelet, a widow with the bearing of a musketeer, came to meet him in person to hear him describe the island. She unrolled the chart he gave her and asked him to point out the island he had described. She also wanted to know the exact number of Caribs and Frenchmen living there – d'Esnambuc hadn't said anything about the Englishmen – and if the Dutch had shown an interest in colonizing it. Finally she took the tobacco leaf, smelled it, and passed it over her tongue; then she crumbled it in her powerful fingers, and, inserting two pinches of the powder into her nostril, she sneezed colossally and sprinkled the map with a yellowish juice. "This is good tobacco," she said, after she had blown her nose into a napkin. "I'll tell the cardinal."

The next morning, as d'Esnambuc was washing his face at the hostelry, a maid knocked at the door to let him know that a Madame Cavelet was asking for him. D'Esnambuc dressed as quickly as he could, brushed his boots, rubbed his little golden babouche, and bounded downstairs. The widow was waiting for him beside a man who wore the uniform of the cardinal's guards. With a gracious bow, d'Esnambuc invited them to breakfast, pointing to one of the few free tables. But Madame Cavelet didn't answer; she pushed him toward a chair and handed him a folder that the guard had been carrying beneath his arm. Then she sat down across the table and ordered a jar of wine, six egg yolks, and some writing materials.

That very afternoon, d'Esnambuc bade farewell to his

cousin and rented a coach. In his right boot he was carrying letters of credit for forty-five thousand livres payable in le Havre. Richelieu had suggested that the company be called *La Compagnie des Iles de l'Amérique*, a visionary title which, sooner rather than later, was to back all the enterprises overseas that d'Esnambuc would conjure up.

Of the five men whom d'Esnambuc had left on the island, it was only Pentier who had interested Levasseur. There was something about him – perhaps his pale face and bulging eyes – that reminded him of the son of the Marquis of Carabas. (This vague resemblance, naturally, had been drawn out years before by destiny's hand.) Since the new tobacco crop was in the ground, there was hardly anything to do on the little Norman plantation. Now many of the men, to while away the time, began walking naked down the beach in the hope of being ravished by the Carib women. Levasseur and Pentier, their friendship growing tighter, played cards or went out hunting quail along with Barbe, the athletic Carib maid. At first it had been only Levasseur who fired. Out of every two shots, he could hit the target once. At that point Barbe, amused by all the noise and smoke, would run to fetch the prize. One morning, seeing that Pentier was getting bored, Levasseur offered him his brace of pistols. "Try not to miss," he said. "We aren't going to have much powder until the Dutchmen get here."

"I've never used a firearm," said Pentier, unsure of himself.

"Don't worry," Levasseur said, inwardly regretting what he'd done. "When the quail take off, shoot at the whole flock and maybe you'll hit one."

Scarcely had Levasseur said this when a quail stuck out its head from a bush. Barbe pointed with her arm, and

Pentier fired almost without having aimed. When Barbe returned, laughing, from the bush, she had in her hand a bird whose head was blown right off.

From that time on, Pentier would occupy himself with hunting. With a good musket he could hit a *casabe* cake at three hundred paces. Everyone marveled at his incredible dexterity with firearms, and for two months there were always plenty of ducks and quail at the Norman colony. When the Hollanders arrived, the tobacco plants were still too young, but Levasseur cut a deal with Temereme, whereby the latter gave him cured tobacco in exchange for three hats and a gold-filigreed copy of *Gerusalemme Liberata*. As was always the case, the arrival of the Dutch and the sale of tobacco was celebrated with huge libations, fricassee of duck, roasted fish, violin music, and shouts of "Down with Spain!" Pentier competed successfully with the Dutch ship's best sharpshooters, and on a dare from one of the ship's gunners, knocked down a distant palm tree with his first cannon shot.

Filled with wonder at his friend's useful military gifts, Levasseur told him about his project as they sat eating the farewell banquet's leftovers: "North of Hispaniola there's an island called Tortuga that it turns out is deserted, or rather, it's filled up with wild pigs and cattle that the Spaniards set loose there to reproduce. My plan is to land on that isle and take it over."

"You'll run the tobacco plantation, and I'll be in charge of hunting," interrupted Pentier, his mouth full.

"Not entirely," Levasseur responded. "We aren't going to run a tobacco plantation, but rather one of bacon, lard, and roast beef *à la boucan*, all of which we're going to sell at whatever prices we set. Think for a moment of how many people come down to this sea to do their business: pirates, privateers, slave traders, merchants . . . And they all come here hungry following an ocean crossing. Remember that I'm not talking just of French ships; we're going to deal with the English, the Dutch, and all who travel to the New World despite Spain and her blockade," concluded Levasseur, picking up a roasted duck thigh.

"That sounds like an excellent idea," Pentier responded. "But I don't see how we're going to leave this island. You're going to have to argue this with d'Esnambuc, if he ever should return."

"We'll see about that," said Levasseur, evasively. "But what I just told you was just the first part of my plan. Listen here: once we have the money, we'll buy ships and take on crews in Brittany and Normandy. Using Tortuga as our base, we'll then attack the silver galleons, and then we will attack Santo Domingo, Havana, Cartagena, and Portobelo. What do you think?"

"Impossible," said Pentier. "We're not at war with Spain."

Levasseur took a long drink of wine. "*Cher ami*," he said, after he had used the back of his hand to wipe his moustache, "the island of Tortuga won't be French; it will be ours." Then he stood up and stepped outside the shadow of the tree that kept them from the midday sun. He opened his arms toward the sea like a prophet and said, in a fervent, quaking voice: "Tortuga will belong to everyone and no one, a republic of men without countries, like us: *boucaniers*. Yes, that's it, *boucaniers*. That's what we'll call ourselves . . . Our flag is going to be black."

That same night, when the wine-drunk Levasseur and Pentier were wagering at cards their future spoils as buccaneers, Barbe walked in and interrupted them, pointing to the sea and enunciating slowly the word *huracan*. After a short while, they saw her leave the fort with a basket on her head.

The dawn came late and cloudy, and soon the wind changed from east to southwest and the surface of the sea began to curl. With almost no transition, a thick rainstorm came in from the horizon and put out the morning fires at the Norman fort. A leather-faced man who had sailed twelve years with the authentic Levasseur said that in those seas the autumn storms were terrible, and the fort, being near the beach, could easily be borne away by the surf. "We should climb into the mountains and find refuge in a cave."

The arguments that would persuade Jack Merryweather to invest in Crumber's – actually Rebecca's – project could hardly have been weightier:

1. *Any English settlement on the rivers of Peru is bound to be wiped out by the garrisons at the Spanish outposts.*
2. *The only settlements that could survive would be those which, protected by the natural barrier of the sea, were to be built upon the Summer Islands.*
3. *Although it's true that such settlements can be attacked by galleons, any naval expedition is quite costly and requires indefatigable preparation: thus it is improbable that an encampment will ever be attacked more often than once.*
4. *In the hypothetical event that there should be a Spanish invasion, the colonists will disperse into the mountains, frustrating any organized attack.*
5. *In the aforementioned hypothetical event, it might be assumed that the Spaniards will destroy the tobacco plantation before leaving the island. In that event, our people will descend from the mountains to build a new plantation in another place.*

Following Rebecca's instructions to the letter, Crumber pulled out the navigating chart from within his jerkin, and showing Merryweather the little red circle noticeable on the right side of the sheet, said to him: "Of all the Summer Islands, this is the best one for tobacco: it has four bays and several rivers, high mountains and dense forests, a healthy climate and much fertile land. What's more," and here he lied, "it's the only one on which no Caribs live."

"It seems like a good proposition," said Merryweather, as he examined the chart to check its authenticity. "Clearly there will always be a danger of invasion by the Spaniards."

Crumber, repeating what his wife had thought, reduced the rich merchant's doubts in no time: "What could thirty dull peasants and an unimportant man like me be worth to the Spaniards that they'd spend their time and effort on us? Wouldn't they get much more benefit from having their galleons protect the ports of Peru and its commercial traffic?"

One month later one of Merryweather's ships sailed off heading for Virginia. In it were the Crumbers and twelve more or less close relatives. Their departure must have been stealthy, since, apart from the notes taken by Rebecca in her *Journal of a Lady*, no other information about this voyage exists. (I have searched fruitlessly for their names in John Camden Hotten's *Lists of Emigrants to America 1600–1700*.) Thanks to Rebecca's detailed and slightly repetitious account, we know that the Crumbers rented a ship in Virginia, which left the couple on the island, together with their relatives, eighteen servants, one hundred and five sacks of cornflower, three pregnant sows, a team of oxen with their plow, twenty-two copies of the King James Bible, a barrel of gunpowder, and seven muskets. The settlement was founded on the 14th of August in 1624, with the name of New Road. Far from showing hostility, the Caribs happily made room for the newcomers. According to Rebecca's diary: "The duke of the pagans, an indecent man named Tanamama or something similar, supplied us yesterday with tobacco seeds and *casabe* bread in exchange for a pair of old boots, a hat, a glass eye, and six nails."

With autumn having come, shortly after Levasseur's boat had shipwrecked on the reef, Rebecca wrote simply: "Now we have some twenty Frenchmen on the south side of the island. Let's pray God that they are not Roman Catholics."

When the ship sent by Jack Merryweather came for the tobacco, it brought news of King James's death. At what surely was his wife's insistence, Crumber left for England thereupon, to seek official protection and spread the word that his tobacco plantation had been prospering. Once in London, thanks to Merryweather's influence, he obtained an interview with King Charles and Buckingham (now a duke), who remembered perfectly the night King James had made him captain of the guard. To flaunt his new authority in front of Buckingham, King Charles, on the representation of Merryweather and under the Great Seal of England, issued a letters patent appointing Crumber (now Sir Richard): "Governor of All the Summer Islands in Main Ocean toward the Continent of America which are inhabited only by Savages and Heathen people and are not nor at the time of the Discovery were in the possession of any Christian Prince, State or Potentate."

With a praiseworthy stoicism, Crumber turned down a banquet in his honor offered by the Merchant Adventurers and a private supper with Lady Jane Wallingforde, the most beautiful widow in King Charles's court. He knew that a ship was soon to sail from Bristol heading toward Virginia, and now holding the money given him by a pool of merchants headed by Merryweather, he followed Rebecca's instructions and left London as quickly as he could.

After the hurricane had crossed the island, the Carib community felt a kind of telluric anger; in spite of the precautions they had taken, their fields and huts had disappeared, and the wild fruits and berries had fallen from the trees unripened; many of their canoes had been dragged to the sea, and the ducks and quail had flown to other islands. In this critical situation, Temereme found that his authority had lessened considerably: his magic, or medicine, whatever you might call it, had proved insufficient to allay the downpours and gusts of wind that had occasioned so much ruin. "The cause of all this," Temereme assured his explosive subjects, "is the look the hairy white people gave us when they were pretending to be our friends. That piece of witchcraft was the evil eye, the eye of Mabuya that destroys everything it looks at." In a public ritual, drunk from fermented guava juice and continual inhalations of tobacco smoke, Temereme would put the spare eye of some Englishman of New Road upon a rock and would reduce it to dust with his angry flint hatchet. After dancing for many hours to the frantic rhythm of the great hollow-tree drum, Temereme would call together a council of all the village elders. When this was over, they would all emerge from the sacred cave with their bodies painted for war against the white men on the island, no matter what flag they were under.

All of this, of course, is purely speculative. But what other reason could the Caribs have had for breaking with the Europeans? In any case, one has to recognize that Temereme gave signs of being a consummate strategist. Rather than sending his warriors against the provisional encampment that the people of New Road had raised after the hurricane, he decided to ask for military aid from the Caribs of the nearby islands. In the days that followed, Temereme's political future was ostentatiously manipulated by fate, or if you like, by the implications of the decree that King James had signed ten years before. Nevertheless, the first Carib to serve this purpose was not Temereme but rather his daughter Barbe: without even saying goodby to her family, the woman left the tribe to return to the arms of Levasseur. It is not easy to guess how Barbe managed to save the Norman from Temereme's conspiracy. The analogies between the Romance and the Amazonian languages are fortuitous, and it was probably the mute language of pantomime that did the trick. The fact of the matter is that Levasseur, before the imminent danger of the Carib attack, set aside his differences with the English and marched toward New Road to organize a collective European defense. Before he left, he discontinued his work of rebuilding the fort, and remembering the feat of valor at Thermopylae, distributed the powder to his men and told them to defend the mountain passes.

The events that followed can be examined in a wealth of detail in the volumes of the Hakluyt Society. Here we shall offer but a brief synopsis: the massive attack that the Caribs unleashed was repulsed in the island's heights; for each dead white, sixty painted corpses – including that of Temereme – fell torn apart by the cannons' grapeshot, the pistol, and the musket ball, the heavy cutlass edge, and the dagger blade.

When the days of war had ended and the Christian dead were buried in the places where they fell – the Caribs were thrown upon a bonfire – the European alliance dissolved to hardly anyone's regret.

*

Available information on Poole is extremely scant. About his life in England, we know with certainty only that he was born in London, *circa* 1605, and that he frequented the Globe theatre. (Among the few lines that Rebecca devoted to him in her diary, we find the following: "Once the duel had been arranged, it was agreed that our champion would be Harry Poole, whom Sir Richard Crumber had met at the entrance to the Globe theatre.")

What was Poole doing there?

It's possible that some romantic researcher might think that Poole earned his living as a Globe actor. In search of a sublime cause, this kind of person might lean toward thinking that Poole, as a child, would have acted the part of Miranda in *The Tempest*. That would go toward explaining an early fascination with the Summer Islands, and given this premise, nobody ought to be surprised that he'd enroll years later in Crumber's expedition. Nonetheless, the truth seems to be otherwise. According to Rebecca, the duel took place at night, and curiously, the rivals carried very different arms: Pentier, two pistols; Poole, a dagger. What conclusion can we draw from this? In the first place, that just as Pentier was a gifted pistol shot, Poole was a master in the art of wielding a dagger. And in the second place, that daggers belong in the orbit of the urban underworld. And so Poole worked in London as a thief.

What could have been the link between a decent man like Crumber and a knave like Poole? The very one there is between a flower and a honeybee. Stationed cunningly at the entry to the Globe, which was always crowded at showtime, Poole would attempt to rob Crumber: he would whisper to him that he'd better not turn around, that what he felt in his back was the point of his dagger. Except that Crumber, thanks to the many hours he had spent training for combat at Whitehall, was not an ordinary Londoner. In short, I would hazard the following sequence:

Poole goes to jail.

He is convicted and sentenced to serve time in Virginia.

He is among the servants that Crumber hires in Virginia.

He goes to the island without Crumber's having recognized him.

He grows tobacco at New Road.

He fights effectively against the Caribs.

He is recognized by Crumber.

He is chosen to fight against Pentier.

Of course, when the English and French parties arranged the duel, each would insist that the arms used should be those best suited to their respective representatives: Pentier, daylight and the pistol; Poole, the dagger and the dark. In the end, d'Esnambuc would concede to Crumber that the duel would take place at night but that Pentier would carry two pistols. But I have just mentioned the names of Crumber (whom we left in the outskirts of London) and d'Esnambuc (whom we saw leaving for le Havre). What happened next?

Here history's symmetries are so precise as to seem influenced by mathematics. Just look: Crumber and d'Esnambuc, each on his own, departed for the island and arrived there on the same dates; in both cases the total number of ships and men was the same (two ships and 253 persons per expedition); it is true that the English ships anchored at what is now Port Road and the Frenchmen at what now is Port Boucan, but if you were to draw a line between these points it would coincide exactly with the orientation of the compass's needle.

In any case, Crumber and d'Esnambuc waited about a

year before they met in person. One day of hurricane and three of war had been enough to devastate the tobacco fields, the stockades, the lookout towers, and the log cabins. In her diary, Rebecca writes at length about the long and sweltering days of reconstruction. With naive satisfaction, she writes how good her first cup of fresh milk in months had tasted to her, of her first efforts at cooking crabs and corn on the cob, of the sheets she sewed for the infirmary, and surprisingly, with no preparation, of how her little Bartholomew Crumber had the honor of being the first child born in Port Road.

Curiously, the Norman chronicles do not offer any domestic details. Obviously written by a man, they tell us nothing about home life in Port Boucan. The few references that they make to woman are in the worst taste, crude, in fact: for example, "From the fifty whores that we took aboard in le Havre, there came forth forty-seven legal marriages."

Once both colonies had been established firmly, the frigid tolerance that united Englishmen and Frenchmen was broken when Levasseur, with d'Esnambuc's help, tried to appropriate the services of the twenty-four Caribs who had stayed on the island. His argument was that, given his unquestionable right of ownership over Barbe, who was now the queen of the Caribs, the rest of the tribe ought to be under his authority. Advised by Rebecca, Crumber argued that the Carib village lay nearer to Port Road than to Port Boucan, to which d'Esnambuc responded – on paper sealed with the company's coat of arms – that if Barbe was a subject of the king of France, her subjects thus had also to be subjects of the king of France. The sealed papers came and went from one side of the island to the other for two weeks. In his last letter, d'Esnambuc claimed not only the Caribs for the flag of

France, he also was demanding that the island's territory be divided into two equal parts; in his last reply, Crumber said: "The first flag planted on this island was ours, and so we do not know the signature of Cardinal Richelieu and we take his bloody company as an illegal one," and he enclosed a copy of King Charles's letters patent with the clarification that the original bore the Great Seal of England. That same day Rebecca wrote in her diary: "Our souls are exalted. A war of religion seems inevitable. I pray God help us in our colonizing venture."

Was it really God who helped Rebecca, or was it simply her good judgment that gave her the idea of the duel? I don't favor either of these theories by itself: the incident had been projected toward the future at the instant in which King James signed the tobacco decree. Bear in mind that the idea of the duel as well as its conditions were accepted immediately and without any quibble by both opposing parties: if the Englishman won, the French would retire from the island; if he lost, the island would be divided in two and shared, as would the number of Caribs.

Given this situation, Pentier left the stockade at Port Boucan at five in the afternoon, the hour agreed on by the Anglo-French commission that would supervise the duel. Before leaving for the volcano's crater, he was embraced and kissed all around. Nobody doubted his competence: he had practiced shooting at night, and it was rumored that someone had seen him shoot down two bats on the beach, guided only by their squeals. As he was being hugged by d'Esnambuc, the latter acknowledged in public that if Pentier had not found his Turkish amulet, he never would have raised anchor on a Wednesday, he never would have met the Spanish galleon, and thus never would have come to the island.

Right after this, Levasseur asked d'Esnambuc to authorize a dance with a collective supper at ten in the evening, the approximate hour at which it was supposed that the duelists would find each other around the crater. "There is no reason to delay the celebration of our sure triumph," Levasseur proposed. D'Esnambuc vacillated a little, but finally he consented.

At Port Road, Poole was sent off much more chastely: nobody hugged or kissed him, and the only words that Crumber uttered in public were: "England expects that you will do your duty."

The only version of the duel that exists up until now is the one that Pentier put in his letter. I'm not going to reproduce it here in its entirety because it has been quoted in many books and publications. Nonetheless, I find that I have the difficult obligation of saying that Pentier's testimony is totally false: Poole did not die in the duel. On what do I base this judgment? Let's take it one step at a time. Let's start with the letter. As we know, this was nailed to a tree trunk with Poole's dagger. It wasn't just any tree, but a rubber tree, whose enormous spread could protect the runny ink of the time from the dew and rain. We can infer two things from this: the first one is that Pentier made sure that his letter could be read, even should it not be found right away (the original is now kept, reasonably well preserved, in the *Bibliothèque* in Paris); the second one is that it wasn't written on the mountain but rather in Port Boucan. How could we believe that the commission that supervised all the preparations for the duel would permit Pentier to carry the tools of writing with him, that is, table, paper, pen, and inkwell? Further, we can rest assured that Pentier was not carrying the letter with him as he started up the mountain; when his clothes were inspected by the commission, the note would have been discovered. So there can be no doubt that Pentier wrote his letter one or two days before the duel, hiding it in one of the caves near Port Boucan. All this, naturally, leads us to think about the existence of a premeditated plan: a conspiracy.

Who were the conspirators? More of them than one might think: Pentier, Poole, d'Esnambuc, Crumber and Rebecca, Levasseur and his men, Barbe and her twenty-four Caribs. How do we know this? Certainly not from d'Esnambuc's letters to Richelieu. In those, d'Esnambuc was very careful to say that Levasseur, on the night of the celebration, had left the island in a company launch, heading for Tortuga. What's more, Levasseur's name does not appear on any of the company's official documents. (In his correspondence, d'Esnambuc always called his predecessor on the isle Monsieur de Rombe.) If some historian should connect Levasseur with Port Boucan, this is because he was to recount, many years later, the story of his life to Esquemeling, the chronicler of Tortuga's buccaneers. Why did d'Esnambuc bend to Levasseur's wishes and send him off in the direction he desired? Because Levasseur's nature would never conform to the strict colonial requirements Richelieu demanded; Levasseur was an independent man, a free spirit whose staying on the island would turn out to be a problem. Of course, it was not only Levasseur who set out in the launch, his associates went with him: the eight survivors of his old crew, Pentier, and Barbe with her twenty-four Caribs. But d'Esnambuc had no room for them in his plans either. Pentier had ceased to be the young dreamer whom d'Esnambuc had taken charge of one Wednesday in Dieppe; he drank now, he gambled at cards, and he liked to show off with firearms – lately he had begun amusing himself with shooting out the pipes in smokers' mouths. As for Barbe and her unpredictable Caribs, I think everyone will agree that it was better for d'Esnambuc to have them keep their distance. So the best thing that d'Esnambuc did was to help them all to exit Port Boucan, although he did it secretly. How did d'Esnambuc explain the absence of Levasseur and his men? Easily: he'd say that they had gone to live with the Caribs in the middle of the island – after all, Levasseur's relations with Barbe were flagrant, and it was well known that he made a pretense of authority over her Indians. Nor was it hard for him to justify the loss of the launch that *La Concorde* – the company's biggest ship – had been towing. In Richelieu's registers, only the names of ships appeared, not those of their auxiliary launches; in the matter of Port Boucan, it was enough to say that the current had carried the boat off and the presumed responsible parties had been given twenty lashes each. Only Pentier's disappearance still needed explaining, but that was no problem either: Pentier had made it quite clear in his letter that, after he had killed Poole with a pistol shot, the Caribs had surrounded him to block his retreat. The last paragraph of his letter, perhaps dictated by Rebecca, says "In this terrible hour, Poole's shattered head, pallid in the moonlight, regards me closely as I write. I can do no less than to recount his last words: 'Tell my poor mother that I died praying and content at having done my duty.'" With his victory over Poole now proven, Pentier concludes: "What will become of me? The Caribs now are narrowing their circle, with me at its center. I see them not, but I hear their frightful shouts come ever nearer. I shall pin this paper to a tree and try to break the circle. I have one bullet left. Goodbye."

Of all these words, the only true one was his goodbye:

removing the letter from his pocket, Pentier nailed it to the rubber tree and then went off with Poole to meet Levasseur and his men at the place they had arranged, surely the cove from which the Caribs launched their expeditions. Details of their trip to Tortuga are not known, but remember that Esquemeling's book does not just mention Levasseur; in addition to the well-known names of Roc Brasiliano and l'Olonais, there are named a certain Captain Pole and a Captain Dieppe as well. This leads us to assume that everyone reached Tortuga safely, Caribs included – Esquemeling notes that among the buccaneers there were "Cannibals from the Summer Islands."

Now let's consider the British interests. Did it suit them to have Poole stay on there at Port Road? Of course not. Seeing him disembowel the Caribs right and left, just like a butcher, must have made Rebecca blanch. Nothing could have been more natural than that, when Crumber came back from England, Rebecca would have told him about that cutthroat, and nothing could be more natural than that Crumber, when he got a good look at Poole, would recognize in him his assailant at the Globe. Then, as Crumber concentrated on the duelling project, the best candidate to represent English interests could be none other than Poole. And if it should happen that Poole were to kill Pentier, wouldn't he then change into the hero of the British colonial venture? Well, it was possible; but the fact was that Poole was destined to become a sacrificial goat and he would meet a Christian end at the volcano's top. This, of course, was as far as the history books were to be concerned; in actual fact, both Rebecca and Crumber knew that Poole and Pentier had taken advantage of the circumstances of the duel in order to run off to Tortuga with Levasseur and company. Do I mean to suggest by this that the duel was just a farce, a trick, a fake that never really happened? Not at all; the duel happened, but it happened for the benefit of history. And since history happily perpetuates assassinations, battles, executions, and similar brutalities, Pentier's letter fit it like a glove.

Now the only thing that we have left to do is to enumerate the reasons that had moved Rebecca to propose the duel to Levasseur. Let's pick up Rebecca at the moment when she knows for certain that she's pregnant – the nausea, the urge to eat wild flowers, the periods missed. At that time Port Road was still known as New Road, and its thirty inhabitants worked furiously to rebuild what the hurricane had smashed. It wasn't known for certain on what date Crumber was coming back to the island; it could as easily have been the next summer as the one after that, and Rebecca, in charge of the colony, knew she must not weaken, she must impose her will upon the malcontents, the intriguers, and the faint of heart who cursed the day that they had left England. Let's imagine Rebecca there, tired, her hands blistered from rebuilding the stockade; let's imagine her stifled by the sun, sweaty, sad because she found that morning that hunger had made her gums swell and had loosened her teeth.

"*Bonjour, madame,*" Levasseur would have said to her, gallantly, recognizing her in spite of her dishevelment. "I want to talk," he would have added, in his brusque English, learned at the docks and taverns on the Channel ports.

"What can I do for you," Rebecca would have asked, mopping her sweaty face with her apron. "You can see how busy I am."

"I come as a friend," Levasseur would say, tipping his hat and bowing his head. "I have come to warn you of a danger."

Persuaded of the Norman's good intentions, Rebecca

– 164 –

would invite him to step into the English territory. There, beside the stockade gate, she'd have heard him out and she, in turn, would tell him what was on her mind: the Caribs will attack us, when? in three or four days, but you are the Caribs' friend, the Caribs have no friends, how many Caribs are there on the island?, it doesn't matter because many more will come, we must flee inland to the mountains, that's just what I was going to tell you, we should fight together, you have read my mind.

As often happens, after the victory the alliance began to crumble. In this case it would have been because of some religious point having to do with the burial of the dead. Nevertheless, Rebecca would soon understand that although the Frenchmen were Normans and Roman Catholics, it was convenient to have them as allies, and not only because of the Caribs but also because of the Spaniards. Furthermore, the island was big enough for the two settlements. She was ready to sacrifice her religious hatred for the cause of the common good, but clearly, she was an exceptional woman who did not let herself be blinded by emotion and knew what she wanted. The problem was not with her, nor was it with Crumber either, poor Crumber was always open to her guidance; the problem was Crumber's family, who were all fanatics, and the ignorant people who had come there from Virginia. What was to be done? She would test out Levasseur as soon as the dead were buried: I come to say goodbye, madame, we are returning to our fort now, what fort? Port Boucan we call it, some fancy name for a ship-wrecked sailors' hut, Captain d'Esnambuc will soon be coming back with many ships, hundreds of colonists and a company, Captain Crumber will bring that back too, I wish you all the best, madame, there will be hundreds of the New Religion on one side and hundreds of Catholics on the other, it looks like that's how it will be, it would be a shame if there were war between us, it would be a shame, madame, our common enemy is the Spaniard, that's what I think, too, we ought to get together but it is impossible, our people wouldn't stand for it, nor would ours, either, in King Arthur's times the differences were all resolved through a contest of two knights, that's called a duel, madame . . .

In under two hours Levasseur and Rebecca would come to an agreement. Before the Norman left, Rebecca would make him memorize the plan point by point, recommending that he write it down in all of its detail as soon as he got back to Port Boucan. If it seemed that d'Esnambuc would decline to participate in the project, Levasseur was to convince him that Crumber would attack him by land and sea; in the event that Poole should refuse to play, Crumber would threaten him with the noose; if the Caribs balked, Barbe was to convince them that the whites were planning their extermination. But it wasn't necessary to threaten anyone: Poole was fascinated by the possibility of being a captain and a founding member of the Brotherhood of the Coast; d'Esnambuc was happy to be rid of his undesirable subjects and to win a division of the island, and to the Caribs it seemed like a very good idea to embark in the big canoe with the whites toward Tortuga, for in the end they were seafaring people, and to row from one island to another was the only thing they'd ever done.

Once the commission had found Pentier's letter, a punitive expedition of both French and Englishmen was sent out urgently against the Carib village: the only thing they found was one of Poole's stockings, a shirt of Pentier's and the feather from the hat of Levasseur. Someone said the Caribs must have eaten them, and this grim version –

as one might expect – was the one posterity picked up.

Three days afterwards, in the shadow of the rubber tree and accompanied by the commission's members, Crumber and d'Esnambuc both signed the treaty by which the island would be happily divided.

That same night Rebecca wrote the following in her diary: "Man writes history down, but it is woman who makes it."

FULL MOON IN LE CAP

Time never dies.
The circle is not round.

Milcho Manchevski, *Before the Rain*

PART 1

Despaigne

Move that pot over here by the mattress, Claudette. There, that's it . . . Oh, God, nothing like a good piss. Wait, I'm not done. Ungh, there. Let's have a look. Bring it over here under the candle. *Merde*, my sight just gets worse! Now let's see. I thought there was more. Put it in a glass for Dr. Laporte. I don't see what the gout has to do with a person's kidneys, but that's for the doctors to worry about. What's for certain is that my leg doesn't hurt as badly any more. Those compresses with water of whatever it is have worked a miracle. Dr. Laporte says it's a confection of herbs they use for healing on the Spanish side of the island. Whatever they are, they've done me some good. No, don't read me anything tonight. I'm tired and I should get some sleep. Who knows what's happening tomorrow. Besides, I'm weary of hearing you read that novel. I thought it would be more interesting. Poor Madame Despaigne, God rest her soul, spent hours and hours reading it. How many dried flowers have you pulled out of it? A dozen, anyway. I don't know what she found in it. That Laclos couldn't possibly have strung together more foolish things than he did there. It puzzles me that Bonaparte promoted him to general. He must have had some bad advice. To me, you know, nothing beats the classics, and I mean stories about war and great men's lives, not a bunch of letters back and forth that tell you about immoralities and seductions. I'll take Homer, Caesar, Plutarch, Xenophon . . . Now, Claudette, see if you can turn my pillow over; I'm all hot and bathing in sweat. Wait a minute. There, that's good. I've never got used to this heat in Le Cap. The nights were cooler in Morne Rouge, weren't they? Yes, of course, you were just a little girl. But you'll see, we're going back there soon. Nobody plays with Napoleon Bonaparte. Of course, I'll have to build it all up again. Imagine what it's going to cost me to get La Gloire back up: the sugar mill, new iron crushers, new boiling pans, the purging room, the hardware, the warehouses and the stables, the new slave barracks, the overseer's and his workers' houses, then my house, which really is Emmanuel's. I've already signed the papers so that he'll succeed me while I'm still alive. He doesn't know it yet, but it's better for him not to know until I've got my affairs in shape again. My only wish is to make the ruins of La Gloire into the plantation that it used to be. After that, we'll see. We're going to take a trip, Claudette. We're going to Louisiana. La Gloire will be Emmanuel's. He can do whatever he wants with it, although it wouldn't make me happy if he sold it. I should have written that condition into the bill of succession. But no, I'm not changing a line. Emmanuel will never sell it. I know him. You know what he said to me when he left for Cuba? He told me he was going to come back with one of those new steam-powered machines. That's right. It's all going to work out. In fact, things are already working out. Fourteen ships of the line at the bay's mouth. Imagine, fourteen ships of the line, not even counting the transports. General Leclerc's troops are going to occupy Le Cap tomorrow, and in a couple of weeks Emmanuel comes back to Cuba with my money and the new machine. You saw what he said in his last letter. He's invested it all in the slave trade, the best business carried on there now. The changes that life brings. Our industry's ruin has caused the growth of theirs. They say Havana is now ringed with sugar mills. All right, it's their turn now. Although I think we'll challenge them before too long. I doubt that they've had time to build a lot of mills. It took my father, Colonel Despaigne, five years to build La Gloire, and I spent two more just to enlarge it and embellish it. I still cannot believe that paradise was brought down in one day. If they'd only spared the iron crushers and the boiling pans, I'd be selling some sugar now, but they pulled the workings quite apart. *Salauds!* Well, you can see I'm only growing bitter. Bring me a little water, Claudette . . . I'm thinking now, what if Emmanuel decides to stay there? After all, he's barely thirty, no, let's see, he's born in sixty-five, when the Dauphin died. *Merde,* my Emmanuel's going to be thirty-seven! That's right, he left six years ago. Six years. Well, now I fear for him all the more. A single man in the prime of life, still young and with my money, there in Havana with its pretty women and its many pleasures. Ah, Claudette, let's pray he doesn't marry on me and start sinking roots there. That's all I need now after what happened to Dou-Dou. Although I should tell you that Emmanuel is a man of great intelligence and depth, just the opposite is true of Dou-Dou, the silly one, who turned out to be like all the others in the family of Madame Despaigne. I was right to send him to study in Paris. Emmanuel has been taught everything there is. Well, you know that perfectly well. What? Yes, that's true, you weren't yet with me when he left. You scarcely know him. I was saying, oh, yes, Emmanuel knows the law, the sciences, and mathematics, geography, and politics, yes, politics above everything. It was he who talked me out of my royalist leanings. Just before he left he told me the republic would end up in the hands of its most gifted generals, and as you see he was a prophet. The coup came on 18th Brumaire and Bonaparte took power. First Consul. I'm telling you Claudette, I suddenly can't sleep anymore. A person starts to think and then the worries come. I'm not worried about the money. Emmanuel has a good head for business and he'll come back loaded. It's not my health, either. Death comes on when it will. It's true that I've been left alone now, but you're right here taking care of me and you help me pass the time, and both Kumina and Gustave are faithful servants. It could be that I'm not used to living under Toussaint's rule. A slave! You've got to see it to believe it! And losing La Gloire is also a thing I can accept. That's where my father put in all his energy, all his hope. Have I ever told you about my father? He was a Gascon. He fought in the war in Canada. Well, some other time. Of course, there's Dou-Dou as well. I'll tell you one thing, if it hadn't been for Dou-Dou and her problems I'd have gone to Cuba with Emmanuel. I'd be there now, living tranquilly in Havana, awaiting the changes that must occur here. But think of it, Dou-Dou would never have forgiven me. You know what she's like. Getting herself pregnant in these times! The fault lies with her aunt, that idle thing Madame Treveux, another reader of Laclos, I'll bet, who couldn't look after her. I sent Dou-Dou to spend some time at her house, and you see what happened. But I'm not sorry I took her out of Le Cap. No matter how bad things may have been in Port-au-Prince, they were worse here. But who would have thought she'd have dalliances with that royalist fop, that Chevalier de la Roche, that Valmont type, that seducer of ingenues? If you'd only seen how he looked at the wedding, a laughable Pierrot, face white with powder, three moles painted on it, lips and cheeks smeared with rouge. What can you expect from a man like that? Nothing. The child he gave Dou-Dou had neither arms nor legs, it's just as well he was born dead. God didn't want to give me a monster for a grandson. So now Dou-Dou writes to tell me that she needs money because the very noble and distinguished Chevalier de la Roche has decided to go to Jamaica. And what am I supposed to do, Claudette? All my sacrifices, what were they for? And where's the money I'm supposed to send? You know how tight things are for us. If Leclerc doesn't put down those goddamned *nègres* pretty soon, I don't know how I'll stay alive. I've sold the coach and horses, and you see how much they gave me for the silver candle holders, not a tenth of what they're worth. The doctors, even, behave like their damned leeches now. Laporte is charging me a silver spoon each time he makes a visit, and the price of meat and fish has . . . Hey! Did you hear that, Claudette? That was a pistol shot. Very close by. Stick your head out the window and tell me if there's someone in the street. See anything? Are you sure? There's a full moon, you ought to see something. No, don't leave it open. Every time I hear a noise I take a jump and it makes my leg hurt. Goddamned gout! Goddamned noises! I'm fed up with all these frights. There's not a night goes by that something doesn't happen in Le Cap. Some poor wretch who blows his brains out when he finds out that he's been ruined, or some thief, or some soldier drunk on *tafia* who decides to take a potshot at the moon. And as if that weren't enough, we've got that bastard Christophe arguing with General Leclerc, saying he'll burn down the city if the French troops come ashore. Ah, but this time it won't be the same, thank God. This time Le Cap will not burn down. Christophe knows quite well that if he does it Leclerc is going to chase him, trap him in the mountains, exterminate him with no quarter given. Now we've got here fourteen warships and a real army, troops that conquered Egypt, Italy, the Rhine. Don't you doubt it for a moment, Claudette, the French soldier is the best in the world when he's properly led, and at that there's no one better than General Leclerc, Bonaparte's brother-in-law. Tomorrow Christophe is changing sides, and after that Maurepas, and then Clerveaux, and finally Toussaint and Dessalines. No more monkeys wearing epaulettes! Know why I'm so sure of it? Because they fear the whip. They know Leclerc is not just any general, they know he's Bonaparte's right arm and that you don't play at war with Napoleon Bonaparte. In any case, go down and make sure all the doors and windows are locked. Then bring me a bowl of broth with some wine in it. Wait a moment, before you go, would you wet these plasters with some of that miracle water? Not too much, just spatter a little. That's it. Good. You're a good girl, Claudette. Don't think I don't know it. Ever since you were a little girl you've had a special way about you. That's why I had you taught with Dou-Dou. Don't take too long in the kitchen.

Justine

Please, don't give me away! Don't yell. Don't be afraid. Let go of that knife. I'm not a thief. Come here. Bring that light up here. See? Put the knife down on the table. Listen. I'm not going to hurt you. I need help. I haven't done anything bad. I'll explain. Wait. Wait a minute. I can hardly talk. My heart is pounding. Oh, my God! A little water. Please. Thank you. Thank you . . . I think I've seen you in the marketplace. What's your name? Whose house is this, Claudette? I know who it is. A *grand blanc*, a lame old man with pock marks. If he finds out I'm here, he'll give me away just to avoid any problems. He won't try to come down? Just as well. Listen, Claudette. Some soldiers are chasing me. They want to kill me. I'm not exaggerating. You understand? If they knock on the door, you'll say you haven't seen me. Swear it. Now make a cross with your fingers and kiss them. There, now I feel safer. No I don't. I'm done for. There's no place for me to go. They've just arrested my mother. Poor mother, how I made her suffer! My God, what's going to happen to me? I'd only need a place for a few days. After that they will forget about me. They say there's going to be a war. Don't you know any-body who can help me? Really? I'll be beholden to you all my life, Claudette. I can stay, then? Thank you, Lord, for putting this angel in my path! I would drink a bit of that wine. Thanks, Claudette. That isn't anything. It isn't bleeding any more. Take the knife and cut a strip from my dress. It doesn't matter; it's ripped up already. The garden wall has broken bottles on it. It could have been worse. There, that's good. Thanks, Claudette, I'm better now. But listen. In the street. It's them, Claudette. See the reflection of their torches? If they come here, try to get them not to search the house. Where will I be safer? What if I'm heard going up the stairs? Good idea. We'll go up together. Believe me, I haven't done anything bad. A problem with a colonel. An accident. A good man has been killed. It's very complicated. I'll tell you about it later. Should we go up now? I feel that God's protecting me. Right, you go first with the tray and the candle. Start with the left foot, my mother says it brings good luck.

Despaigne

What's taken you so long, Claudette? Did you make sure that all the windows had been shut? No, no. I want you to feed the broth to me. Rest the tray on your legs. That's right. Now bring the spoon over here. Mmm, that's good. Oh, mammy, that's good. What's wrong with you? You spilled it on my neck. Get a grip on the spoon. You've got blood on your finger. Did you cut yourself? That's why your hand is shaking. But who ever heard of uncorking a bottle with a knife? Why do they make corkscrews? Come on, feed the baby. He's been feeling bad. Poor little boy. That's right. Mmm. Mmm. Thank you, mammy. *Merde!* What's the matter with you, Claudette? Don't you realize I'm your little boy tonight? Don't you see that there's a full moon out tonight? I'm going to be mama's little boy all week. Come here, little mama, come. Wipe baby's mouth. Ah, mammy, baby wants some more. Baby wants to nurse. Give me your milk, mammy. Oh, yes, that tastes so good. Mmm. What are you doing? Take your nipples out again! The moon is full, and it's time for me to be your baby! What's that? How dare you? What do I care if you don't want to now? Come on, sit down on the bed. Sit down here and let me see them. Tomorrow? Not on your life; right now. I'm your father. Do you hear me? Your father and your master, too, in the eyes of God. You were born a slave and I engendered you. Do you see what I mean now? You have to do what I say. You're mine. You belong to me. Haven't I come through on my part of the contract? I freed your mother and your sister even before this damned revolution started. You're mine. You're my project. I educated you. I brought you up with my legal daughter Dou-Dou. I waited for you to grow up and become a woman. Years went by, Claudette. Years waiting for the fruit to ripen. You don't know how many times I fought off the temptation to take you. You don't know. You have no idea. I would watch you playing, running through the park at La Gloire, reciting your lessons, doing your piano exercises, learning to dance. And I didn't take you, as anyone else in my place would have done. I had the decency to wait until you had matured. But where does this sudden rebellion come from? I treat you like a queen. I please you any way I can. Almost every day you go to church, you go to the market, you go to see your mother. And you visit her at a place that I bought and paid for with my money. What happened? What is wrong with you today? What do you mean you don't know? Ah Claudette, my Claudette . . . All right, all right. I'm a reasonable man. It's late. We're all on edge. Tomorrow they may be fighting in the city. But remember everything I've done for you. Look at me, Claudette. What do you see? A good man. An old man, sick, alone, and ruined. When was it that I got the last letter from Emmanuel? Answer me, you owe me some respect! Yes, in fact it has been over a year. I can tell you exactly. I have kept track. It's been almost fifteen months. You think that I don't know what's happened? You think I don't know that Emmanuel has abandoned me, that he's taken all my money and will never come back from Cuba? But there's something more that you don't know about. Do you think I didn't go with him because of Dou-Dou's problems? I've never cared about her. Dou-Dou is a fool. I didn't go with Emmanuel because he asked me not to himself. I remember the moment. How could I forget? We were smoking on the veranda, and suddenly he pointed out to me the convenience of my staying in Le Cap. Just like that. No preambles. Of course Emmanuel gave me his reasons. If a person could call them reasons. While he went about making money in Cuba, I was to get close to whoever held power in Le Cap, so that when order was reestablished the name of Despaigne would be among the winners. Quite a plan. If I had followed it, I would have had to lick the behinds of Toussaint, Moyse, Christophe, and the devil himself. I saw quite soon what his real aims were. He sought an independent life, on my money, in a safe place. What can you do? He was my son, my hero. The only person I have ever loved. And so I stayed behind. I stayed here knowing he wouldn't return . . . Now leave, Claudette. Leave me alone. I've said enough. Too much. Go to bed. I pardon you this time. Don't put the candles out. We'll see tomorrow what the new day brings.

Bonjoux

It's her I should have killed and not the man. But just think about it, Mabillon, what a soldier's instincts are. Our job is killing men, not women. Besides, he was asking for it. Now it turns out that he's a *mulâttre* of importance. Well, I don't mind. But where is that bitch, that god-damned *sang-melée*? She couldn't be far off. I can't imagine how she got away from us. I saw her turn the corner and go up this street. When we got there, nothing, she had vanished. And there's even a full moon. You, sergeant, attention! What's your name? All right, Blaise, I want you to knock at that house and search it. No, you dolt, you can't take a torch along! Don't you see how you could set the house on fire? General Christophe hasn't given the order to burn down the city yet . . . You have your pistol ready, Mabillon? If she comes running from the house, don't waver. Remember, she's a rabbit. Dead, wounded, or alive, we've got to bring her to the colonel tonight. At least we got the mother. Another bitch. She was waiting for her outside, in her carriage. The colonel must be questioning her now. And you know what I mean by questioning. The business of the dead *mulâttre* doesn't worry me too much. In the end, no matter how important he may be, a civilian is a civilian and I'm a captain. Christophe needs me, same as you. The one I worry about is Colonel Trouville. A real animal. I know him. I'll have to watch out for his guards. Those four tigers give him blind obedience. The things I've seen them do! Of course, it won't last long. Because we understand each other, right? You know, what we talked over yesterday. Come closer. Going over to Leclerc. Good, I'm glad. Now, if Christophe burns down the city, he'll retire to the mountains and we'll have to follow him. Then we'll have to wait. I'm telling you this because it won't be easy. We can't let it disturb us. You agree? Watch out, the sergeant's coming. What? No one? You have to find her, Blaise! This is an order! She must be brought before Colonel Trouville. This very night. That bitch left him with one eye. Take a good look inside that other house. Search it up and down ... You saw it, Mabillon. She got him right in the eye with a fork. It wasn't my fault. As I told you, I wanted him to have a good time with the girl. Take her off my hands and do him a service. The *sang-melée*? She's fifteen. Yes, you're right, she looks older. Well, what do you want, I took her to my bed after Christophe's dance, and she stayed there. I swear I didn't force her to. You know the story well. It was all her idea. That bitch is insatiable. She doesn't know when to stop. These *sangs-melées* are hot as wild mares. Come over here, I'm going to tell you something. I feel sorry for Toussaint. I'm sure the battles that deplete him most are fought in bed. I've never served with him, but they say he has a real harem. Women of all colors. Incorrigible? Come on, my friend, you're a cultured man and you know that love and war have many things in common. *Merde*, she's not in that house either! All right, sergeant, this is where the street ends, a dead end. Let's go back. You know, Mabillon, I've got a feeling that she's hid in that house there, the big one on the right. Hey, you with the torch! Follow me! The wall has broken bottles on it, true, but it isn't a high wall. Come on, soldier, walk slowly and light up the wall. What did I tell you, Mabillon? Look at that cloth sticking to the glass. Come up here, Blaise. The bitch is in that house. What kind of a question is that? If they refuse to open you'll smash in the door with your rifle butts. Of course those are my orders. Yes, man, yes. The colonel said so. Dead or alive. Dead is better. It would be an act of mercy. If we don't kill her Colonel Trouville will have her quartered. Those were his very words.

Despaigne

Claudette! Claudette! What's that knocking? Claudette, go see what's happening! *Merde*! Maybe Christophe has already started burning down the city. No, if that were so the bells would be ringing like mad and there'd be cannon fire. Let's see if I can get out of bed. Oof. Ah, Claudette, you've come at last. Look out the window and see what's going on. Soldiers? Come on, help me walk. Lower your shoulder a little more. There. There. Hey, down there! This is Monsieur Despaigne! Come in? What for? There's no one here. My daughter and me. Nobody's come in here. General Christophe's orders? All right, that's enough knocking, you're going to break the door. I'm opening up now, Come on, Claudette, move. Go open the door. No need to make these swine wait. *Salauds*! But what's the matter with you now, woman? Why are you so pale? Go open up, I tell you! . . . Come in, come in. Pierre

Despaigne, your servant. How do you do, Captain Bonjoux, Lieutenant Mabillon. Of course I don't object, General Christophe is our protector. I have many things to thank him for. Search the whole house. But don't break anything. Go with these gentlemen, Claudette.

Blaise

Well, well, well! *Mon capitaine*, here we find a little pussy-cat! Let's see, come out of that wardrobe or I'll tickle you with my bayonet. Mademoiselle Despaigne, if you would be so kind. Step aside. Move, I tell you! Here she is, *mon capitaine*. Here's your pussycat. What? You want me to kill her? But she is just a child. My daughter is that age. No, I'm not killing her, even though I'll lose my stripes.

Claudette

Have mercy, Captain Bonjoux. Take pity on her. Don't kill her. Look at how she's crying. If you let her go, you can take me. Right here if you want to. Look at these breasts. People tell me that they're beautiful. They are yours. Touch them, touch them, Captain Bonjoux. You can do with me what you want, but don't kill her.

Despaigne

What a night, Claudette, what a night! The smell of blood is up to here. They could as easily have killed her in the street. As soon as Gustave and Kumina come, get them to clean up that blood. Poor girl. Unbelievable, her mother is Maryse Polidor, the one who bought the carriage from me! But what am I saying? She's no poor girl. She tried to murder Colonel Trouville. A vengeance. Someone must have put her up to it. Someone who hated Trouville. Fine, what do I care? It was a question between *nègres* and *mulâttres*. They must have put a spell on her to make her do it. If there's one thing in this world that scares me, it's the power of *vodoun*. I hope they don't get me involved in this. Who can get to sleep now? The sun is about to come up. Listen, Claudette, lie down beside me. I like to feel your body next to mine. Come here, girl. What's the matter with you today? Why are you looking at me like that? Why are you putting on your shawl? The market isn't open yet. Where are you going? You're crazy, Claudette. What are you going to live on? Don't be silly, you can't leave me. My God, Claudette! I'm your father! Come back here, you ungrateful bitch!

PART 2

Maryse

Thank you for receiving me, Jean-Charles. The guards at the door refused to show my card to you. If I hadn't started shouting out my name in my best soprano's voice . . . How did I know? In Le Cap there are no secrets. The more you want to hide something, the sooner it becomes public. Everyone knows you're here and what you've come for. Ah, you're always so genteel. But the mirror does not lie, *cher ami*. As a Spanish poet said, *sombra mía aun no soy*. You're all right. You have your old smile. Your same natural elegance. That mixture of sobriety and mischief. You are still quite handsome, Jean-Charles. Of course I'm not exaggerating. If you could read my mind, you'd see that the image of you I was keeping in my memory did not differ much from what I'm seeing now. And the gray temples become you. But what has brought you to Saint-Domingue, what's brought you after all these years? I'm not talking about the current situation. I told you, everyone knows you've brought a message from Leclerc. All right, you don't have to call it a message if you'd rather not, it isn't every message that gets written down. Fine, let's say then to meet with Christophe, or rather, I would say, to try to get him to turn against Toussaint. Am I wrong? If only I were. If only Leclerc and his twenty thousand men had come to put themselves at Toussaint's service. It would have been a fine gesture of Bonaparte's. We need young, strong arms. Not for fighting but to build this island up again. But of course you can speak with me. It's just that you forget . . . Come on, Jean-Charles, I'm not stupid. Tomorrow you'll speak with Christophe and you'll make an effort to sweeten up Leclerc's proclamation. Lebrun failed yesterday in the attempt, and today they're sending you, a more respectable citizen, as Leclerc would say, a founding member of *Les Amis des Noirs*, a distinguished member of the *gens de couleur*. But when I asked you why you'd come I was not referring to your interview with Christophe, but rather to next month or next summer, to the future. Oh, you needn't answer. The question was indiscreet. It's just that, as you've always been involved in politics, I thought that . . . A councilor in Leclerc's government? I presumed something like that. No, I'm not surprised. In truth, I'm not surprised by anything, Jean-Charles. But I confess to being curious about your reasons for accepting that commission. I know that you've kept up with all that's happened here. I've been reading in the newspapers about your life in politics. Still, it's not the same thing. I guess you must feel a bit of a stranger in your own land. You won't find many faces that you know in Saint-Domingue.

There's been a frightful slaughter. No, you can't have any idea. You'd have to have been here. Why have you come, Jean-Charles? Do you really think Leclerc can fix our situation? Ah, but what am I saying? Who am I to question your motives? An exile, a heedless singer whose imprudent head was almost guillotined. Now you see how even I have been infected by the brutishness unleashed here on the island. You must forgive me. Come on, now, say that you forgive me, be a gentleman. Ah, there's that sweet smile. Yes, of course. There's never too much wine, my friend. Tokay? Incredible! It's been ages since I've seen any. You brought it with you? Your health, your health. Delicious. Smooth as silk. Who would have guessed, the wine Marie Antoinette liked best. What happened to your republican austerity? Oh, I'm hopeless. But I don't mean anything bad. Well, *cher ami*, that is a question that you should put to no one in Le Cap. Here people get by as best they can. Everything is bought and sold. We all live and die intensely. Though I should tell you that the situation has gotten better in recent years to the degree that Toussaint has built his power up. You saw the American ships in the bay. They've come here to do business. Some of the abandoned plantations are producing again. Race hatred seems to be receding. Oh, no, I'm not painting an idyllic landscape for you. A gloomy air is blowing now through Saint-Domingue, an air of evil omen. It's something deep and hard to explain. A foreboding air, apocalyptic. I merely wished to say it's getting better here. Right here, in Le Cap, Christophe has rebuilt a good part of the city. Tomorrow you'll be able to see his house on la rue Royale. But now that Leclerc has got here, the bloodbath will begin again. No, Jean-Charles, I don't think it can be avoided. The cities of the coast will be levelled one by one and then there will be a battle for the hinterland. There

Toussaint will await Leclerc. No, I don't think you can convince Christophe. Don't take this badly, but I think that if he's chosen to receive you tomorrow it's in order to gain time. After all, the burning of a city requires preparation, and Christophe likes to do things right. But you asked me what I did to occupy myself. You're going to laugh. I organize banquets, parties, concerts, and literary soirees; I give dancing, singing, and acting lessons; I also serve as a marriage broker and, why not admit it, at times I recall my Paris days and sing a few things by Mozart. I'm the same as always? No, Jean-Charles, I am another Maryse. When you've seen a load of gunpowder shoved into a person's ass, it changes you. I've seen the dogs brought from Cuba gnawing children's bones. I've seen . . . Ah, Jean-Charles, I've seen what I should never have seen. In Saint-Domingue nobody is the same now. The *grand blanc* and the *petit blanc*, the Jacobin and the royalist, the *négre* and the *mulâttre*, all of them know they'll never again be what they were. Why do we enjoy ourselves? That's a good question. I'll tell you why. Remember the orgies that there were in Paris among the people sentenced to the guillotine? We held them in contempt. We wanted them to die with dignity, stoically, like the Roman martyrs. What idealists we were, *cher ami*. It never occurred to us to think that in their places we could do the same: go to our deaths with the taste of life in our mouths. Well, here we're almost all doing the same. If I were a priest I would help people to die piously; as I am a singer, I'm helping them to die happily. One of my clients, a conspirator from Limonade with an excellent voice, sang an aria from *Le Calife de Bagdad* while they were heating up the water they were going to boil him in. Yes, you're right. I already told you I had changed. Certainly, I'm not the Maryse Polidor you used to know. But I'd rather turn into a cynic than a hypocrite. *Touché*. Excellent phrase. I'll remember it: cynicism is the mask of one who suffers; hypocrisy is that of the unfeeling. Ah, Jean-Charles, how well you know me. But no, I don't think your coming here is the gesture of a hypocrite, nor of an opportunist, either. I know you well, too, you see? I know you think you can be useful here and now. And who knows? Maybe I'm wrong, maybe you can talk Leclerc into clemency. The rumor is going around that he has come to reinstall slavery and kill everyone who's borne arms. It would be a shame. The last thing we need here is a vengeful colonial policy. All right, I'll do what you want. I'll talk about something else. In fact, I'll tell you why I'm here tonight. Do you remember Justine? You don't have to apologize. I know your head is involved with other matters. Fifteen years old. In fact, when I left Paris she was six. Yes, I know. Yes, I'm very grateful to you. Jean-Charles, Jean-Charles, let me speak. I don't know how to beat around the bush. You know it. What I say will surprise you. Perhaps it will disgust you. Listen: Justine is your daughter. Let me speak, I beg you! Listen: she's your daughter and I want you to do something for her. All right, that's what I had to say. Now you can speak all you want. Yes, I told you that over there, but I was lying. The weeks we were apart I behaved like a nun. Quite simple. In those days the only important thing in your life was organizing *Les Amis des Noirs*. I saw you working day and night, writing articles for the *Mercure*, letters asking for contributions, pamphlets against the Club Massiac. I realized you would never be a father. And beyond that, I knew we wouldn't stay together because you weren't the man for me, nor was I the right woman for you. Nonetheless, Justine and I were going to live together many years. She would have suffered unnecessarily with our separation.

We are independent beings, Jean-Charles. Yes, it's true, we are capable of loving others, but what's truly important to our lives is the movement, knowing ourselves wrapped up in some activity, in work, ideas, books, discussion. You notice that none of us has ever married. Also, remember how you were about to go with Ogé on his unlucky voyage. Thank God it was decided you could be more useful in Paris. Afterwards there was the question of getting the National Assembly to confer rights on free *mulâttres*, which was your case exactly. And everything was like that, Jean-Charles. Between you and me there was always something important pulling us apart. In my case it was the theater, the public, the opera; in yours it was colonial policy. We made love hurriedly, between an editorial and a dress rehearsal. If we maintained a good relation for a few years, it was because you felt no responsibility toward Justine. If you had felt any, you would have resented me. Given the circumstances, I think I acted well. And who knows, maybe if that stupid Louise hadn't denounced me as an enemy of the people . . . What idiocy, how could anybody think someone can be an enemy of the people? But just the same, idiocy or not, I had to flee from France. I was alone in Paris. You had gone to London for a meeting of the Abolitionist Association. I couldn't wait for you. Why did I come here? Come now, Jean-Charles, was this something you didn't expect of me? That's it, *cher ami*, smile at me. With that smile you give me the reason. Saint-Domingue was your native land; Le Cap was your city; I was your woman. What man doesn't like to have his retreat secured? Here was where you'd preferred to have me, and here it was I came. I came and waited for you. I wrote you many letters. You only answered me once. Oh, Jean-Charles, I understand, I understand. I know you. Things are the way they are. Of course I don't doubt it. I know you missed me. But that's all over with. When Robespierre fell and you didn't come back, I knew that I no longer had any reason to keep on waiting for you, I knew you wouldn't come back. Oh no, dear, you have not come back, you have moved your office for a while from Paris to Le Cap. You've come here with Leclerc and you will leave with him. I hope you're right. I hope I'm wrong. But I don't know what's come over me tonight. Yes, of course I know. I'm nervous. I'm accusing you. I swore ten times I wouldn't do that, and here I am. All I need now are a few tears . . . What? Oh, thanks. That's enough. No more tears. Pour me another glass of Tokay. Let's talk about Justine. I should tell you, to begin with, that I think it's all my fault. But what was I supposed to do? To dress her and feed her I had to go to work, and what I do is the only thing I know how to. If I were to leave the house and have someone stay with her, anything could happen. And believe me, I've got good cause to say this. At some other time, I would have placed her as a boarding student with the nuns at Notre Dame. But I had no place to put her. So Justine grew up among balls and concerts, here, there and everywhere. Her school was music, waltzing, happiness. One night, almost two weeks ago, I saw her dancing with one of Christophe's dragoons. It was her first grand ball. I altered one of my old dresses for her and she was radiant. If you only could have seen her! She danced with the elegant indifference of a gull in flight. I could see she was a woman. On top of that, I saw she was a woman in love. All right, don't get impatient. You're right. Yes, that's right. Exactly. You guessed it. Justine has left me to go and live with that man. Yes, starting on that very night. Of course, I am no saint. You and I certainly never talked about matrimony. It's just that I have found out something about that officer, and he's a swine, Jean-Charles. Believe me, a perfect swine. I have indications that he beats her and he prostitutes her. When I came looking for her, he insulted me and flashed his saber at me. He shouted that if I were ever to return he'd cut off Justine's ear. I don't know if she's still in love with him or not, I just don't know. Maybe she won't come home because she thinks she's gone too far. My fear is that that scoundrel will take her away with the troop. Christophe is going to set fire to the city and retreat into the mountains. I know that I'll lose her there for good. What do I want from you? Christophe is a decent man. I'm sure that if you were to ask him to give me back Justine, he would seriously consider it. I had an appointment with him yesterday, but he canceled everything because the situation was so grave. He's called Bonjoux. Anton Bonjoux. He lives in la place Montarcher. Why did you ask me that? What has a man's race to do with his moral qualities? He's an evil man, no matter if his skin be black, white, or brown. What's happened to you Jean-Charles? Ah, but I'm reproaching you again. Don't be like that. Say something. Will you help her? Thank you. I expected that from you. She is your child as well. What ideas you have! To be frank with you, yes. She has your smile, and of course her skin is honey-colored. Very well, the last one. The farewell glass. Your health. And for old times. No, I don't think I'll go back to France. I would do it only for Justine's sake. Thank you, Jean-Charles. I'm truly grateful to you. We'll see. Later, perhaps. Yes, of course the situation worries me. Tomorrow, or the day after, Leclerc will disembark and the city will become a pyre. Don't worry, I know people all through the North. Yes, I have a carriage. That's where all my savings went. I bought it from Monsieur Despaigne, a *grand-blanc* who was ruined. My plan? I'll go to la place Montarcher. Bonjoux could well be mobilized at any time. If he takes Justine away with him, which I'm sure he will, I'll follow him as far as possible. If your intercession should bear fruit, Bonjoux will have to let me have her. Come with me? It's late, Jean-Charles. Really, it's not necessary. I'll be fine. Yes, it's true, she is your daughter. Well, whatever you want. Of course I'm happy. If things go well, Justine will be quite happy, too. But why can't everything go well?

Jean-Charles

Really, Le Cap is not bad. My city. I can't believe I'm here. Twenty years, Maryse. It's been exactly twenty years. What a beautiful night! Full moon. Look at those stone houses, how they shine. Stones brought from Nantes and from Angers. And you can see those roof tiles in Poitou or Normandy. Ah, here's la place d'Armes. There used to be a lot of pear trees there. Of course, the pears weren't any good; they were too puny and bitter, even; nobody would bite into them. Well, the house where I was born is gone. It was on the quai. It was big and very old. I almost can't remember it. My father sold it when I was a child, and later on they tore it down to build a warehouse. We lived on la rue Espagnole, almost in the outskirts. Just before you get to La Fosette. That might be gone, too. Someone told me that whole area burned down in the fire of ninety-three. So you see, Maryse, I've lost my roots. You know already that my parents drowned at sea. No, no, I don't think so. I had an uncle, my mother's older brother. I never found out anything about him. He must have died. You think so? Well, it's true. You're right. Roots stay with you always. That's why I asked you if you weren't going back to France. You know, I'm really happy to see you tonight. As soon as I stepped on solid ground I thought of you. But of course that's the truth. What do I gain by telling you a lie? I had thought about looking for you after meeting with Christophe. No. For some reason I knew you were alive, that you had survived this hurricane. Married? Well, look here, I never thought of it. No, I'm not conceited. It just never crossed my mind that . . . Maryse, I've just thought of something. Tomorrow, no matter what Christophe replies, I have no reason to reboard the ship. I'll just tell the men who brought me here. They're waiting in the launch. At the wharf. Not all of them are common seamen. There's a colonel of the engineers, a specialist in fortifications. Oh, Maryse, let's leave politics alone for now! Anyone in Leclerc's position would have done the same. Do you know what Lebrun said yesterday when he came back to the ship? That he was sure Toussaint went incognito to the meeting with Christophe. That's politics. I'm sure Christophe knows that there are engineers inside the launch. That's why he wouldn't let them disembark. But listen, I told you, nothing's keeping me from staying on here in Le Cap. If the troops should land and Christophe should burn the city, fine, we'll go away together. I've never been a soldier. I don't have to fight for one side or the other. I'll tell this to Christophe. I've come in order to negotiate an impasse, nothing more. When that is done, I'm just another citizen. That isn't possible? But why do I have to line up with one of the two sides? . . . Jesus! You took me by surprise. Where did that sudden kiss come from? Of course you still matter to me. What am I going to do? Leave you alone in the middle of a fire? Well then come along with me back to the boat. Listen to me, Maryse. Don't be stubborn. I admit it, I'm not doing this for you, I'm doing it for Justine. Ah, Maryse, you make everything so difficult! The world doesn't turn on principles, my love; it turns on vested interests, and you, Justine, and I, have just created one. Come here, come on. There. Your lips are cold. What do you think? How could I have stopped loving you? You'll see. One way or another everything will work out. Your driver is trying to say something. Yes, that's right, we're there. La place Montarcher. The theater used to be there. Which house is it? What floor does that man live on? He must be there. Look at those horses. No, you can forget that. I'm not going to wait passively. I'm going to look for him. No, Maryse. It would be worse if you went with me. This is a matter between men. His name is Anton Bonjoux, right? Of course I'm not armed, but nothing's going to happen. I'll introduce myself as who I am, Justine's father. Listen, dummy, nothing's going to happen. I'm protected by my credentials. Wait here, and relax. Give me a kiss. In a couple of minutes I'll be back here with Justine.

PART 3

Justine

I can't do it any more, Anton. You promised me. You promised me this morning. I know, I know, but I couldn't do it any more. Last night was horrible. I don't want to remember it! It hurts me, Anton, I hurt. It still hurts. But how can you doubt that I love you? I've given everything to you. You know it very well. I left my mother, my home. I ruined my reputation. I've asked for nothing. Just this, Anton. Don't make me do it any more. You want money? I'll work and I'll give everything to you. I can sing, I can dance. I'll earn some money. My mother always says that money comes and goes, that the important thing is . . . All right, all right, calm down. It hurts me to see you furious like this. I won't mention my mother again. Please, don't drink any more. You turn into a madman. I just can't do it, Anton. I told you it was the last time. What are you doing? Put down that pistol! What are you loading it for? Oh, Anton, watch out, that thing could go off, for God's sake! I know you're trying to scare me. I know you aren't going to kill yourself. Put the pistol down, Anton. No, don't do that! I can't bear to see you like this!

Bonjoux

Everything is set now, Colonel Trouville. The girl is waiting for you and dinner's on the table. Fish soup, grilled lobster, fricassee of goat. Everything with lots of pepper, like you wanted it. Make yourself at home. Don't worry about me. Lieutenant Mabillon lives downstairs. I'll be there if you need me. Her name is Justine. Fifteen. Two weeks ago she was a virgin. What? Oh, now I get it. She'll go at a gallop, sure. Whatever you want, Colonel Trouville. Gallop, trot, a Spanish gait, whatever you desire. The riding crop? Frankly, the colt is not too docile. I don't know, Colonel Trouville . . . All right. But be careful, she's hardly broken in. Yes, yes, you can come right in. I told you, I'm downstairs. At your service, *mon colonel*.

Jean-Charles

Good evening. I'm looking for Captain Anton Bonjoux. I've knocked at his door upstairs, but no one answers. Perhaps you could . . . Ah, it's you. My name is Jean-Charles Portelance. I'm looking for Justine. I'm her father. Monsieur, I'm telling you that I'm her father. That's right, she doesn't know me. But I repeat, I'm her father and I've come looking for her. Of course I can identify myself. Here are my credentials. I entreat you to let me in to clear this matter up. If it's money that you want, I am prepared to . . . What's that noise? What's going on upstairs? Let me up there! Move! Justine! What's happened to you? Come on down. Don't be afraid. I've come to get you. Your mother is waiting for you outside. Everything is all right. I'm . . . an old friend of your mother's. Put that pistol away, Captain Bonjoux. I've come in peace. I've come for Justine. Yours, captain? You're wrong. Justine belongs to her mother. She is a minor. Come on, Justine. Don't mind him. Give me your hand. Don't look back. He won't dare shoot.

Despaigne

Hey! Did you hear that, Claudette? That was a pistol shot. Very close by. Stick your head out the window and tell me if there's someone in the street. See anything? Are you sure? There's a full moon, you ought to see something. No, don't leave it open. Every time I hear a noise I take a jump and it makes my leg hurt. Goddamned gout! Goddamned noises! I'm fed up with all these frights. There's not a night goes by that something doesn't happen in Le Cap.

A VIEW FROM THE MANGROVE

To Pachín Marín and Nicolás Rojo

The heron, a white arrow, shoots down from the yagruma limb. As it hits the water's surface, it extends its wings, clamps its beak around one of the crabs on the mangrove's roots, and flies back up to the same branch. Then it tosses its head back, gives a quick shake from side to side, and swallows the crab.

From his hammock he has seen the heron repeat this feat about a dozen times, always with the indifferent regularity of a cuckoo clock. But nevertheless, and in spite of their methodical extermination, the crabs stay motionless, as if they were just empty shells or something growing from the exposed mangrove roots. He tries to explain these little crabs' stupidity to himself. Perhaps they're very young. At the moment he can't think of any better reason. After a while he concludes that they're not stupid. The crabs are following an instinct: the least movement of a leg or claw would draw the heron's immediate attention. There are thousands of crabs on the mangrove roots, and only one bird to prey on them. Statistics favor the individual who doesn't move.

The heron leaves its branch and starts to fly above the swamp. It disappears in the direction of the coast. The crabs begin to stir themselves, devouring the roots' tiny parasites. He feels a surge of nausea. Finally he falls asleep.

*

The hammock has been strung between two yagrumas, the only two trees growing on his tiny islet. His rifle, a Mauser, hangs from one of the branches overhead. The old man slung it from the stock and barrel, and now it dangles by his right cheek. The captain wanted to leave him with just a machete, with firearms scarce, and anyway, what use would a man have for a Mauser if he is dying of yellow fever? But someone said that to kill an alligator you have to have a rifle, and the general, already mounted on his horse, said: Leave the Mauser with that man and let's get the hell out of here! Leave him a bottle of my gin, too!

There are many little alligators all around the islet, but of the big ones he has only caught a look at two. They had arrived together. They came out of the black water and began to lumber toward the hammock. He grabbed the Mauser and aimed it at the first in line. He didn't have to shoot. On seeing him stir, both halted their advance. Then the trailing one bit into the other's tail and began to eat it, chewing with a desolate torpor, like a cow. The alligator that had been attacked stayed motionless for a long while. When it had lost a good part of its tail, it moved back slowly toward the water. The other followed nonchalantly.

There is a time of day at which the swamp's scenario shows some coloration. At noontime, when the sky is not cloudy, the sunlight washes away the carbonous coating that covers everything around. Then the twisted mangrove branches take on a rusty shade, and in their leaves one sees dark green, maroon, and yellow. Beyond, at a distance of two hundred feet from the islet, there is a clump of mahogany trees. Hidden among its highest branches there must be a parrots' nest; he has seen them fly by several times with worms in their beaks. At midday the gaudy pair always come out to enjoy the sun; they delouse each other and then approach the other's head as if about to kiss. Below, the water is still black, but in the fat, oily bubbles rising from the turbid depths there are all the colors of the rainbow. It is a beautiful moment. That is when he uncorks the bottle, takes a little sip of gin, and starts to read the English botanist's book in the vibrant clarity of the breeze that wafts in from the sea. Luckily the crazy old man who looks after him never comes by at this enchanted hour.

Look here, old man, my fiancée, what do you think?

I like those green eyes.

How'd you know they're green? They look gray in the photo.

Are you going to marry her?

Of course I am. As soon as the war ends. Her name is Julia. She works at the Cuban revolutionary junta in New York. How long do you think the war will last?

Wars last forever.

The general thinks this one will end in 1900. This war is not what I expected. It's shit. The things you do won't go away. But there's no choice, you have to keep on fighting. After the last shot is fired, I'm sailing to New York. We'll get married there and come back to live in Havana. I miss her. I can't show her letters to you because I left them with the general. You never know.

I'll see you tomorrow. The tide is going out and the rowboat will get stuck. It happened the other day.

The old man lives inland, at the edge of the swamp. He makes charcoal there out of mangrove wood. It isn't easy to make charcoal, the old man says. If a person doesn't know how to make an oven in the earth, the mangrove turns into ashes and all that work is lost.

Shortly before dawn, when the creatures in the swamp

are resting and the inland air blows strong, he can smell the smoke from the old man's ovens. He feels less lonely then, and starts thinking of the good things left for him to do.

What do you do with all that charcoal?

I stuff it into gunny sacks. Then I sew them up and sell them to a man who comes by in an oxcart. That man sells them to another man who has a big wagon with four mules. My charcoal gets to Havana, and from there they take it by boat to New York and London.

You're crazy.

I've been looking at the mangroves for too long.

To get to the islet, the old man has to set out two hours earlier in his little boat and open a path through the narrow channels of the mangrove swamp. A few days earlier, he had made this trip along with the old man, but he had the yellow fever then and he hardly remembers anything: just an atrocious headache and the certainty that he was going to die.

The general gave me money to take care of you. You'll be fine here. The enemy won't find you. I'll hitch the hammock to those two yagrumas. I'll work a herbal cure on you. You'll see, the old man says.

Here's *Ricinus communis* for your headache.

Hibiscus abelmoschus to sweat out the fever.

Pimpinela anisum to expel the gas.

Ammona squamosa to quiet the nerves.

Are you sure you're going to cure me?

Nothing is for sure. You have to survive a relapse. One morning you'll wake up feeling better and you'll think you're cured. But you won't be. The next day the relapse will strike. It always happens like that with yellow fever, the old man says.

I feel better this morning. I've only thrown up once.

That's a good sign. When you're stronger I'm going to arrange things so that you can go back home, the old man says.

I can't go back there. My town is occupied by a Spanish regiment. And besides, I don't have any family there.

Where do you want to go?

I'd like to go to New York. I'd like to see my fiancée. Even for just a few weeks. Sometimes I touch my face and I think my hands are hers. Afterwards, I'd come back to Cuba with any group that wants to fight.

I think I can arrange your trip, the old man says with assurance. Inexplicably, neither his face nor his hands have coal stains on them.

He lifts up his hand from the edge of the hammock and examines it, turning it over from one side to the other. His skin is still yellow.

It was the fever. It attacks the liver. But now you're over the fever. Only the memory of it is left. You're weak now, the old man says, as he feeds him cold rice and sardines. You'll have the relapse tomorrow. When it's over, you'll be out of danger and I'll take you in my boat.

How do you feel?

I didn't sleep too well, he says. He reaches out toward the tree with his yellow hand. A white owl had been perched there for a long time. The crabs, as well.

At night the mosquitoes don't bother him much. But the big crabs still climb up the tree trunks and get into his hammock. They don't bite. They like to wander over his body. That always wakes him. Then he takes his hat off his face and brushes them off.

Come on. It's time to go. I'll help you get to the boat. You can lean on your rifle.

The old man starts rowing at an incredible rate. The

mangroves pass by his eyes as though he saw them from a galloping horse. Who would have his horse now? Too fast. *Muntingia calabura* for dizziness.

On his arrival, he vomits a thick substance, black and congealed.

The house has a modest porch with two mahogany armchairs. The old man walks indecisively toward the door, stares at the iron ring that functions as a knocker, and turns around very slowly to face him: We'd better stay on the porch. The house is crammed with charcoal bags. If I leave them outside, they soak up rain and no one buys them. We'll wait here for the man with the wagon.

He slumps into one of the armchairs. The wound on his back starts burning and he squirms to the edge of the seat. I'm dead tired. Do you live alone?

I live with myself, the old man answers. The other me is inside.

If you hadn't taken care of me, I would have died. Where do you think the general is? He's a bad-tempered man, but he values me. He left me the Mauser and a bottle of his own gin. I'm on his general staff, he says, looking at the old man's worried eyes.

Nobody knows where he is. He had to retreat. The Spanish column brought artillery along. You asked them yourself to hide you in the swamp. You couldn't stay on your horse anymore.

I heard him say that he'd come back for me.

Don't worry. We've got to keep on going now. The swamp is full of Spanish soldiers and my house isn't safe.

He had thought he wouldn't be able to breathe inside the gunny sack. But he could. The old man put him in there, curled up like a fetus. He lay some charcoal over his hat and sewed it up.

What if the Spaniards stick their bayonets into the bags?

They never do, says the old man's friend. And he feels them loading him up into the wagon. Everything is set.

I'm coming with you on this trip. Don't think I'm doing it for the money.

Thanks, old man, he says from inside the sack. What about your work?

It doesn't matter. I've been crazy for a long time.

It isn't bad inside the sack. He feels a lot more protected there than in the hammock. He's not trembling any more. It's not as if the swamp was cold; the coldness was inside him. *Costos picatus* to warm up the stomach. The charcoal is protecting him as well. Why is that? It must retain the oven's heat. He sticks out his tongue and licks the charcoal. It is warm and tastes like toasted bread, with a crackling crust.

The oxen pulling on the cart move quickly. It feels as though he's going by train. It is all right, much better than the swamp.

The old man places his mouth on the sack and tells him in a quiet voice that they've arrived.

Where are we?

Nowhere.

The old man's crazy, he thinks.

Now the wagon will take you. When you get to Havana, tell the cook at the Hotel Inglaterra that I sent you. He'll let you know how you can travel to New York.

What's your name, old man?

I think my name is Eudelio.

What are you doing in there? Get out of that sack! We're going to hang you by the balls, says the Spanish sergeant, an energetic man with a thick, red face. The sergeant has ripped open the sack with a knife, and he emerges dusting off the charcoal soot with his hat. It's too bright there in the street. He looks around, squinting: a big avenue with trees, buildings, carriages, and Havana's walls as backdrop. The people who pass by stop to have a look at him. They inspect him from head to toe without saying anything, as if he were a circus attraction, the alligator man. One of the mules is peeing a thick stream of beer, good quality, with a head on it. Two soldiers help him get off the cart. They are blond and very young. They must be conscripts from Galicia or Catalonia. We're dying like flies, yellow fever, malaria, dysentery, typhoid, says one of them as he ties his hands behind his back, exactly where the wound is. You're going to die too. They're going to take you to Cabaña castle and they'll shoot you there this very night. They always shoot spies.

I'm not a spy. I'm a soldier.

If you're a soldier, where's your rifle? asks the other conscript.

They put him under guard in the pantry at the Hotel Inglaterra because the colonel is taking his siesta and can't be disturbed. The room is crowded with chickens and sacks of charcoal. The chickens are jammed inside some wire cages; they flap and cackle without end. They are gray and black, the colors of the swamp before the magic hour and just after. He doesn't like chickens, particularly their yellow, horny feet, there's something horribly human about them, the last thing he would eat, he thinks, is a chicken foot. The smell of chicken shit is nauseating him. He goes to a corner to vomit; he gags but nothing comes up. He sits down on a charcoal sack. Being below street level, he can pass the time watching the vertiginous feet of passersby through the basement window bars. After a while he feels queasy and stops looking at the anonymous feet. Below the window, by the wall, there is a crate with three guinea hens inside. They're not making any noise. They are not moving either. They look stuffed. The young roosters will be eaten first, he concludes.

The water of the swamp, at sunrise, is always covered with a whitish vapor, but it's not a big thing, it is as if down below the peat were burning quietly. At nine o'clock the black water stops smoking, and then it's possible to see the little alligators, as long as one's arm, eating crabs and conches among the mangrove roots. That day, nevertheless, the swamp was hidden under a persistent fog bank. When midday came, his hammock seemed to float in the resplendent vapors like a fantastic ship; for a moment he felt like a navigator of the mists, an astral being who crossed spaces not belonging to this world; for a moment the root of the universe seemed his and he felt close to God. Then, beyond the islet, the enchanted mist began to break apart in sections, and suddenly the sunlit heads of the mahoganies appeared. The parrots were right there, as always, picking lice from one another with their curving beaks and showing off their colors. There was something indecent in their disdain for the grandeur of the spectacle. Without thinking it over, he grabbed the Mauser, drew it up before his face, and fired. One of the parrots fell into the cloud bank. In the echoing of the rifle shot, he heard the alligators splashing. The other parrot did not move. It stayed there, rigid, perched on the branch like an unbearable, big, stuffed bird. When the old man arrived, there was hardly any fog left.

What's the matter? What are you brooding about?

I did something I shouldn't have. I don't know why I did it. You're old, you ought to know.

I've brought you some *Picramnia pentandra*. It helps you when your soul is sick.

Come on, old man. Don't play deaf. You ought to know.

Ask me some other time. Today I came here just to tell

you not to look at the mangrove trees too much. You can lose your sanity. Just look at me.

Late in the afternoon the pantry door opens, and he thinks they're going to shoot him now. It is the cook, an old man, short and thin. His moustache looks like the general's. The man pretends not to see him. He opens a cage, puts his arm in, and takes out one of the noisiest chickens. He has it by the neck. After examining it in the basement window light, he starts to whip it around like a windmill with his arm. The chicken drops a cloud of black feathers and stops its cackling. The man takes it by its feet with his other hand and walks toward the door. Are you the cook? he asks him. The man turns facing him and feigns surprise.

Who are you? What are you doing in my pantry?

I was sent here by Eudelio, the charcoal maker.

Come on with me. I owe a lot to him. How is he doing?

He's crazy.

The man smiles. He likes to play at being mad. But you seem in bad shape. I'm going to make you a good soup with this chicken's feet and head. I'll hide you in an empty room. There are a lot of them now because it's summer and there's a yellow fever epidemic.

I can't eat chicken feet.

That doesn't matter, you won't see them in the dish. Follow me confidently and don't close the door. The colonel will think you've run away into the street.

But the guards . . .?

What guards?

There were two of them.

Oh, those! They ran away. You look contagious.

The cook shows him an iron spiral staircase. It is very dark and he doesn't see the steps. He goes up falteringly, clinging to the handrail. It's for serving the guests who don't want to come down to the dining room, says the cook, raising his voice as if he were far away. You're really dirty and you smell terrible, he shouts. I'll tell one of the bellboys to bring you up some hot water. What country are you heading to?

There's something I have to do in New York.

That's no problem. I'll get the papers so they'll let you out of here and into there. I've got good connections.

Are we almost to the room? I'm out of breath. My heart is pounding.

Rivea corymbosa for heart palpitations.

Go slow. One more floor and we're there. The higher you get, the safer you'll be. I'm putting you with another one who's going to New York. So you'll have company. He's a Spanish soldier. A deserter like you.

I'm not a deserter. I had yellow fever and I'll come back to fight with another expedition. They organize the expeditions in New York. Haven't you heard of the New York revolutionary junta?

I don't care. They all say the same thing.

I'm ready to die for the cause.

You're a fool. Didn't the old man tell you that?

Of course I know you, the soldier says. He has just come out from underneath the bed. He is almost an adolescent. He has a tender blond moustache and a pimply nose.

You're mistaken. I've never seen you.

You seemed very sick this morning. Also, you didn't get a good look at my face. I was the one who tied your hands behind your back. My name is Pere. What's yours?

You're my enemy.

Forget that. I'm an anarchist like my father. My whole village is for Cuba's independence. This war is shit. We're dying like flies, malaria, typhoid, dysentery . . .

I'm really tired, he says, interrupting the soldier. He sits down on the bed.

What you are is really dirty. You shouldn't lie down in that bed.

I don't care if I get the sheets dirty.

That's not what I mean. The mattress is full of crab lice and bedbugs. I've already got the crabs. It itches like hell. I've got soldier's ointment in my pack. It's very good for the crabs, but I left it at the barracks. I don't even have a comb here.

Ask the cook for one.

I don't have a cent left. I gave everything to that man to get to New York. I've got an uncle there who has a bakery. He makes good money.

Let me get a little sleep. Wake me up when the hot water comes.

He lies down on his side to keep from aggravating his wound.

In the swamp it rains every day between two and three in the afternoon. When the first drops start falling on the leaves, he gets set to leave the hammock's sticky embrace and lie down on the grass with his eyes shut. The water is warm and very sweet. It does many things for him. Above all, it helps him to remember. But now he can't remember anything. It is as though his memories were no longer his. They are there, he knows, but they are outside of him. He imagines them as a deck of cards that someone shuffles in the rain. *Lepidium virginicum* to keep memory intact.

It is raining on his face, on his hammock and the white leaves of the yagruma, on the mangrove trees, on the swamp's black oily water, on mahoganies in the distance, a memory at last, New York, Chinatown, smell of sesame oil and ginger, and the man who's walking toward him.

He saw him from a distance. His pallid face emerged from among the open umbrellas of the passersby. He was talking to himself. People were avoiding him. But he hounded them. He stuck his palm under their umbrellas and asked for money. He carried a deep anger. He pushed some of them up into the shop doors, and others he shoved off the sidewalk. He had never seen a person ask for charity like that, so desperately. Suddenly the man was staring him in the face. He understood right away that it was a special, private look, just for him. He felt lifted above the people and the rain, and he realized that the two of them were alone in the street. He put his hand in his pocket and felt the coins' hard edges. He stopped and waited. He saw him come nearer dragging his clogs, his feet yellow and horny. He couldn't walk straight any more. He weaved from side to side as though carrying a great weight on his shoulders. His arms stopped beating on the umbrellas. Only his hand remained extended, his face a tightened knot of supplication. At first he couldn't explain to himself what he was feeling. He lowered his eyes. The man's open hand grazed a button on his coat. When he turned his head, the man had already disappeared behind the undulating black tide of the umbrellas. He thought of making his way among the crowd and catching up with him. But something kept him there, under his umbrella, outside the doors of the little Chinese restaurant. The rain stopped and the street looked different. He folded his umbrella and went in. He went up to the counter. He asked for a gin and a bowl of soup. The old woman at the counter shouted something that he didn't understand. He put his hand into his pocket and pulled out a fistful of coins. They were damp with sweat. He drank the gin down with one gulp and left all the coins on the counter.

What's wrong with you tonight? Julia asked him as they left the theater. It was raining again and he looked for the man among the umbrellas and the carriages.

I don't know. It must be the rain. I was thinking about Cuba.

Let's not talk about the war tonight. How about having dinner at Delmonico?

After the rain, in mid-afternoon, the low tide comes. The water retreats toward the coast, leaving behind an unbearable stink. The black mud that surrounds his islet then stretches out as far as he can see, giving up the secret of its genesis. Jutting from its puddle-ridden surface there are bones and carcasses of alligators, rats, amphibians, fish backbones. In this cemetery, everything is black, tarry, just this side of turning into peat. He can always get to sleep at this time of day. He wakes up when the bats begin to squeal.

Your hot water's here, he hears the soldier say. He takes off his hat, turns to face him, and sees him seated on the floor, scratching himself between his legs. He has taken off his boots and his stockings. His feet are horny and yellow. By the door there is a pewter bucket steaming faintly. Leave me a little water if you can, my feet are really rotten. My unit came from Sancti Spiritus on foot.

You can have it all. Spare me your feet and all your crabs for now, he says, pulling the hat down over his face. He'll sleep until the bats come out, he thinks.

Amelia patens for eczema and inflammations of the feet.

Are you sure you're crazy, old man?

Nothing is for sure.

Why do you think I couldn't give a quarter to the beggar in Chinatown?

I'm not here to answer that.

Don't play crazy now, he says, sitting up with difficulty in the hammock. You know the answer. Why did I keep my hand in my pocket? Why didn't I run after him? My money would never have saved him, but I would have given him something. Don't laugh. You don't get it. My quarter could have been a little match light, a shooting star, a firefly, something to grab on to in the darkness. What came over me, old man? Don't think I'm a bad person. I know you know the answer. I know you know.

I don't know anything about anything. Turn over on your front so the wound can keep improving. It's going well, there are worms in there already.

I told you. Don't bug me any more about your feet and your crabs.

They've brought the dinner. Aren't you hungry? I'm turning up the light, the soldier ventures timidly, as if he had to ask permission for his every move. He watches him approach the wall and move the switch on the gas lamp. The room fills up with pallid light.

What a shitty light!

The switch won't turn any farther, the soldier says. I wouldn't have thought that in this hotel they'd be so cheap. But after all it's named the Hotel Inglaterra.

What is there to eat?

I don't know. I haven't opened the door. Someone knocked for supper. I'm going to go look for it.

Chicken soup, the soldier announces from the door. There aren't any chairs or tables in here. I'll put the tray down on the floor.

What's in that bottle, water?

Smells like gin to me.

You can have all the soup. Pass me the bottle. He sits down on the bed and takes a big swallow. They haven't brought any spoons and the soldier drinks the soup directly from the bowl. He holds it with both hands and draws it slowly to his mouth in a respectful gesture. Before swallowing, he keeps it for a moment in his mouth, as if it were a sacred food. What did you say? the soldier asks.

Nothing.

I thought you were praying.

I asked you if the soup was any good.

A little cold, but nourishing, the soldier says, putting the bowl on the floor and scratching at his crotch lice.

No chicken feet in it?

How'd you know, the soldier asks, his eyes wide with surprise. I left them for the end. Now I'm going to chew on them.

Go to hell, he says. He takes another long drink from the bottle and stretches out again on the bed.

Salva officinalis for insomnia.

You know what, Eudelio? It's a pity juniper doesn't grow in tropical swamps. Instead of making charcoal, you could make a living by distilling gin. Imagine if all these mangrove trees were junipers weighed down with berries. You'd be a rich man.

I'm fine the way I am, the old man says as he covers the wound with a herb plaster.

Would you like a little gin? There's not much left in the bottle.

Keep it for yourself. I only drink *aloe vera* water. It's good for asthma and for liver ailments. Also for the kidneys.

How do you know so much about tropical plants?

I wrote the book you're reading.

You're crazy, Eudelio. The book was published in London.

You want to go to London?

No. I told you already. I have to go to New York. I want to see my fiancée. Afterwards, I'll come back with another expedition.

I'm happy for you. New York is very close. It's right there, below the mahoganies, where the parrot you shot landed.

The noise of the door makes him turn his head. The soldier is no longer in the room. He must have gone to wash his feet. The bucket of water has disappeared. There is nothing left on the floor but the soup bowl and the yellowish, half-chewed chicken feet. He thinks about the soldier with his tender blond moustache, a poor boy forced to fight in Cuba. They're dying like flies, the general had told him. Our strongest allies are the climate and the diseases, yellow fever, malaria, typhoid, dysentery . . .

Chrysobalanus icaco for dysentery.

One of the worst moments in the swamp comes at around midnight, the hour of the owls and the rats, of the nocturnal hunt. The owls sit perched above his hammock. They try to hide their plumage in the white leaves of the yagrumas. From there, with their specialized eyes, they scrutinize the mangroves. They hunt silently, solemnly, like exterminating angels; they hunt quite differently from the way the herons go about it, plunging head first without the least elegance; they hunt patiently, choosing their captives, lifting them upward in an open-winged glide, describing an arc in the night, to sit blandly back upon the branch. Over his hammock, they eat like pigs. They splatter him all over with the blood and bits of rat flesh.

Why don't the rats sit still, Eudelio? Maybe they wouldn't draw the owls' attention then.

They can't help it. Rats have lots of energy. They eat too much. They're just like chickens.

What would happen if they ate less?

In that case they would not be rats.

Which one am I, Eudelio, a white owl or a rat? Tell me. I know you have the answer.

You're an alligator. And stop calling me Eudelio, my name's Ezequiel. I've something for you here. *Rondoleta stellata*, very good for dog bites.

I haven't been bitten by a dog.

Of course you have. Don't you remember? They bit you at my house.

Shortly before dawn, when the creatures in the swamp are resting and the inland air blows strong, he can smell smoke from the old man's ovens. He feels less lonely then and starts to think of the good things left for him to do.

How do you feel?

I didn't sleep too well, he says. He reaches out toward the tree with his yellow hand. A white owl had been perched there for a long time. The crabs, as well. I've got to scare them with my hat. Do you think I've gotten past the relapse?

Of course you've gotten through it. Now you have to get through being dead.

You're crazy, old man. Leave me alone.

They say that you start seeing ghosts, and you've been seeing them already.

I haven't seen a thing.

A minute ago you said you had.

I don't recall talking to you about any ghosts. I don't recall anything. I just remember when it rains. Go to hell, old man.

It's raining now. Can't you hear the noise the rain makes on the mangrove?

That can't be true. There aren't any mangroves here. I'm

in Havana, in a room in the Hotel Inglaterra. Tomorrow I'm going on a trip. I want to go to New York. Lift my head out of this hammock and breathe city air, just for a few days even, a hot bath, a garden, piano music, something to get hold of. Afterwards, I'd come back.

You must have been dreaming.

No. You're my dream. When I wake up, you won't be here.

You're wrong. It's at this moment that I'm not here. The only things here now are the mangroves and the rain.

In the swamp it rains every day between two and three in the afternoon. The water is warm and very sweet. It does many things for him. Above all, it helps him to remember, to remember the houses in the town, in a line beside the road of red earth. That day his horse goes by. It's with the other horses in the general's retinue. The people recognize the general and they always have something for the troops, cheese, jerked meat, beans, rice, clothing, sometimes a little money. The people are for the revolution, for a free Cuba, and the general is popular. The girl is running alongside the horses, she is running barefoot and she catches up to the general's black horse, reaches out with her arm and grabs the stirrup: A Spaniard! There's a Spanish soldier in my house! The general turns his head around, looks at the girl and then looks back at him. He could have looked at someone else, but he looks at him and he guides his horse off the road and follows the girl. The house has a modest porch with two mahogany armchairs. It is surrounded by trees, avocados, mangoes, lemon trees, and behind there is a banana grove. He dismounts, takes his Mauser from the saddle and follows the girl to the door. He picks up and drops the iron ring three times and the man with close-cropped hair opens up for him. The whole family starts to shout at once, and he scarcely understands what they are saying, a Spanish soldier, the banana grove, the dogs. They push him down the corridor and exit with him through the far door. The black dogs begin barking, showing their fangs. If it weren't for their chains they would tear him to pieces. He knows their breed, there aren't many left, bloodhounds, years ago they hunted runaway slaves. Beyond the latrine, his back against a banana plant, is the Spanish soldier. He thinks that he must be seriously wounded. He's sitting in a pool of blood. He is almost an adolescent, a deserter. He has seen many others like him, barefoot, ragged, hiding in the canebrakes and in caves below the hills. At night they go marauding through the fields in search of something to eat, bananas, mangoes, melons. Almost all of them are conscripts from Catalonia, the last ones to arrive, village boys who scarcely know how to use a rifle. In the barracks they are dying like flies, dysentery, typhoid, yellow fever. They flee to the countryside to escape the epidemics. The general doesn't take them prisoner. Sometimes he takes pity on them and gives them a little food. Now the boy is raising his head toward the heavy bunch of bananas that hangs above his head. He knows he's being watched and he doesn't dare to look around him. His face is yellow with fever and with fright. He is clutching his genitals with both hands. Thick blood is seeping through his fingers. The dogs were let loose and they attacked him, the close-cropped man says, lying in self-justification. He's been there since daybreak. We knew the general was going to come, says an old woman, wringing her hands. Now he is your prisoner. Take charge of him, she adds imperatively. The boy's trousers are ripped and soaked in blood; his feet are horribly destroyed. He will never walk again. All of a sudden he feels the Mauser lifting up his arm. He watches how the barrel nears the boy's head. Don't kill me, *Cubanito*! A tender blond moustache, a pimpled nose. Looking to enkindle his compassion, the boy pulls apart his bloody hands, a thick and black coagulate. He fired without knowing why.

Ocinum sanctum for the soul in torment.

I think I'm dying, old man.

We're always dying. Once we're born.

The high tide hasn't come in yet. How did you get here? Look at the swamp. Nothing but tarry bones. Look at the mangrove roots, how long they are.

Mangroves are always mangroves. I already told you not to look at them too much. Get ready to travel. I'm taking you to New York to kiss the green-eyed girl.

Wait a bit, old man. I can't get out of the hammock. And I've been lying to you. The green-eyed girl no longer exists for me. I lost her.

I know. You told me. You've told me everything.

She's the only woman who's ever mattered to me. I'm not a bad person. Do you think I'll ever see her again? Sometimes I've thought your hands were hers.

I've got some chicken soup here for you. It will give you some energy.

Thank you.

Why are you pouring it out? It was a good soup, with the feet and head in it. I was thinking of making a fire to heat it up. It would have given you some strength for the trip.

Do me a favor, old man. Grab the Mauser and put it on top of me. I need to hold on to something hard.

I understand.

Now answer me. Why did I do the things I told you? I swear I won't ask you anything more. But answer me. Answer me if only this one time.

*

The general's adjutant entered the tent and came to attention, making his spurs resound.

The general lifted his head from the cot, wiped his eyes, and told his adjutant to be at ease.

We've found him, general.

Don't tell me he's still alive!

No, general, sir, the birds in the mangrove swamp had eaten him already. In the hammock there were only his bare bones with this Mauser on them.

The general sat down on the cot and took the rifle that his adjutant held out to him. He examined it carefully. He ascertained that it was loaded and he handed it back very slowly, holding it in the palms of his hands as though it were a sword of honor. That's how my men die, God damn it, with their rifle in their hands and ready to shoot! Give this Mauser to a brave man!

HEAVEN AND EARTH

Pedro Limón said good-bye to Pascasio and told him in Creole – so that he'd know that in spite of all the time between them he was still one of them – that it was good to see him working in the sugar refinery, taking apart the machines and reading engineering manuals. Then he put on his pack, and looking back every now and then, left, taking the new road that connected the compounds where the cane cutters lived.

Initially Pascasio hadn't recognized him, behind the face that'd been pasted together bit by bit in the hospital; the sad face that burned through to the bone on muggy nights and that, according to the doctor, had turned out all right but really should be touched up for the last time in a few months (it was always the last time). But straight off he asked Pascasio about Ti-Bois, and Pascasio let go of the ropes and smiled, extending his arm and shaking his hand, and Ti-Bois was fine, grumbling when he wasn't communicating with the greatest *vodoun* spirits, complaining that the young men from Guanamaca left to hang on the fine black women from Esmeralda, preaching to the old hags that Fidel Castro was crazy and had shaken up the whole island, taking for himself the land that the *bon Dieu* had given to the Cubans. He then had no choice to tell Pascasio about his life in the army, in the Sierra, in Havana; of the shrapnel that struck him in the face during the Bay of Pigs invasion, and later his discharge, the hospital, the teaching school; the things that he'd learned, the things that he'd done thinking about the people from Guanamaca – he was about to say "thinking about your brother Aristón," but didn't get it out – thinking of you and Ti-Bois and Aspirin and Julio Maní and of the rest, and of Léonie, of course. And now Pascasio had moved to the factory compound and was an assistant mechanic and was studying – he pointed to the book with boiler diagrams on the cover – and since we only received that one letter of yours, we thought they'd killed you in the Sierra. No, we never knew about your parents. Léonie? Léonie lives with me now, and we have a son. A six-year-old.

Yes, Pedro Limón, Léonie lives with Pascasio and just yesterday they moved to the factory compound; Julio Maní became a mason and he builds barracks for cane cutters in the south of the province; Aspirin married, quite legally, a widow from Esmeralda, and he went there to drive a cab, you know that he was always a good talker, anyway, and Pascasio laughed and then you understood that those whom you loved most will never return to Guanamaca, and only Ti-Bois remained; Ti-Bois the *houngan*, scaring the women and the kids, filling the afternoons of the old folks from the cabins with his stories – the sorcerer Ti-Bois, as the whites called him, Pascasio's and Aristón's grandfather, also your grandfather in some ways.

Pedro Limón stopped following the new road, climbed over the embankment, and walked on the old cross ties beneath the railroad tracks. He picked up a purple sugar cane that had slid off from some crate, took off his army boots and socks, and the timber was smooth and warm. He pulled his knife from the sheath and cut a section of cane. He carefully peeled it and bit into the soft, sweet stick, and suddenly he was a child again, a naive Haitian youngster, who killed the hunger with a shot of cane juice fought for tooth and nail, and he'd better get going because Mama and Papa, carrying baby Georgette, would already be at Adelaide Macombe's, Ti-Bois's oldest daughter, and surely they'd already sent Pascasio and Ariston to find him around the tracks, for the harvest was over and they were going to Oriente in the car of one of Adelaide's mulatto friends; they were going to the mountains near Guantanamo, to fill coffee cans on the land of Monsieur Bissy Porchette, honorary consul of the Haitian republic.

We walked to the highway with all our bundles under the strong sun. The driver was already at the roadside stand having a beer. Papa took a dime from his pocket and asked for a soda with plenty of ice. He didn't give me a single piece. The driver didn't care if we arrived late and had another beer. He started joking around with us until he finally offered a glass to Adelaide, who sweated a lot. He knew some Creole. Maybe that's why Papa unbuttoned his jacket, removed his old straw hat, and started to fan himself with it, and later used it to wave away the flies that surrounded Georgette's head. And he no longer looked as stiff as before, and he accepted a drink from the man and that time let me suck on some ice.

The driver put Adelaide's wooden suitcase in the trunk of the car and helped Papa to arrange our things on the roof, and he tied them with rope and he left the doors open to cool off the car. Finally we left, with me between Pascasio and Ariston, in the front seat. Every now and then you could see water at the end of the highway, but when we got closer it disappeared. We counted many imaginary puddles. Many.

Ariston slapped me awake and it's almost night and we

have to push. It could be that the battery is dead, surely with one little push it'll start, and Papa takes off his white linen jacket and folds it carefully over the back of the seat. Then everyone gets out and gives it everything they've got. I push next to Adelaide and I hear her puff and huff because she is too fat. The motor starts at the bottom of the hill and the car doesn't stop. We don't either. We run. We shout. Adelaide falls down. The car doesn't stop so we have to let it go. We shout again. Nothing. It's leaving. It has left with all our bundles and with all Papa's money, sewn into the lining of his jacket. Adelaide gets up and casts a spell on the driver that can't miss. She says Ti-Bois taught it to her, but Papa doesn't hear her because he is in the middle of the road with his arms outstretched. I have never seen him so quiet and so sad. He doesn't move. He looks like the *juif* that we burned last year during the carnival. Mama has stayed behind with Georgette, but I hear her cry. We slept in the sewer that night.

We're halfway there and Adelaide wants to keep going. Papa isn't sure. He looks at Mama and Georgette, shakes his head and looks at them again. He says that he only has twelve cents, that we'd have to walk for two days, that we're too many for any truck to take us. Mama gets on her feet and begins to walk with Georgette. Papa follows her, saying that it's insane, saying that he doesn't think that it's worth it because two days from now he isn't going to find work, nor Mama, nor Adelaide. Mama starts to sing. Adelaide starts to sing too, and she forces Pascasio and Aristón to sing along. Then I begin and later so does Papa.

We were still singing when the winds arrive and with the winds the dust, and Papa said that it's been a while since it rained and if we got jobs the work was going to be tough, and Adelaide removed the colored scarves from around her waist and we covered our faces as if we were bandits, and we continue to sing beneath the dust and the scarves and we arrived.

Monsieur Bissy Porchette didn't need more people. Papa said that the kids could help and the women will work for free. Monsieur Bissy Porchette said no. He kept saying no and Adelaide screamed into his face that he must have been lying to say he was a Haitian. We returned to Guanamaca on foot.

That summer we went hungry and my sister Georgette died.

Although I talked about the war against Batista's army, Pascasio didn't mention Aristón. He only said, "And since we only received that one letter of yours, we thought they'd killed you in the Sierra." And he said it almost smiling, without any resentment in his eyes, and who knows, maybe they don't hate me in Guanamaca after all; maybe they understood the letter, they understood that I did my duty. It's also possible that Pascasio doesn't know, that no one knows, that Maurice had kept it from them, Maurice, the most educated man in Guanamaca, my father's best friend.

Papa looked again at the twenty cents and put them in Ti-Bois's hand, and by the afternoon the money had been collected so that Maurice could run across the Biram Mountains and get to Santiago de Cuba to see the new consul. Because we didn't agree with the forced deportation, the law that the Cubans had created to throw us out of their country, so that we could no longer work for less pay and not take jobs away from anyone. But no. We didn't agree. No sir. We're ashamed to get off the boat and have the family and friends over there see us without clothes and without money after so many years. And we were still against it, although Maurice had returned within the week without having seen the consul and we already knew that it was useless.

"The ships have crossed the Windward Passage. They are in Santiago de Cuba's harbor. They are waiting for us," said the spirit of President Dessalines through Ti-Bois's mouth.

And the next day the rural police came with their long machetes in hand. Inside his hat the mulatto corporal carries a list of the families that must leave. Without dismounting, he goes from cabin to cabin shouting the names that the Cubans have given us, the names that appear on the plantation's payroll because the French surnames are too difficult, the names that complicated any transaction, José Codfish, Antonio Pepsicola, Juan First, Juan Second, Andrés Silent, Julio Papaya, Ambrosio Limón, Ambrosio Limón! Ambrosio Limón! And my father comes to the doorway laden with bundles and later my mother, dropping their eyes to the small garden of sweet potatoes and squash so that the corporal wouldn't see them cry. We're a proud race. We've a history. We're a race of warriors that defeated Napoleon's army and conquered Santo Domingo. But now something is wrong. They are crowding us into the center of the compound. They do a head count. They whip and herd us to the refinery train. The boats are waiting in Santiago de Cuba. The train leaves. It leaves, but I don't see it leaving Guanamaca. I don't leave with Papa and Mama. I fled three days ago and am far from the refinery. I'm staying here because I was born in Cuba and I love Léonie since I lay with her in the cane fields, and now she's not in the list and I don't want to look for more hunger in Haiti and I may end up there like a zombie without a name.

I live in Adelaide's shack, next to Ti-Bois's. My parent's shack was burned down by the rural police believing that

I was inside. I sleep with Pascasio and Aristón. They fall asleep right away. I don't. Through the cracks in the boards I hear Ti-Bois talking with the *loas* and the dead. Ti-Bois is a powerful *houngan* who even knows Cuban black magic. He also turns into a snake and eats the plantation manager's chickens. I respect him very much. Ti-Bois loves Aristón more than any of his grandchildren. He says that he'll make Aristón a *houngan*, that he'll teach him how to shed his skin and turn into an owl or a snake. That would frighten me. What I want to do is to work enough to be able to live with Léonie. Someday I'll dare to ask Ti-Bois for this.

That summer I go and make money from the coffee growers of Oriente and I buy two shirts, a pair of pants, and a hat. I bring Léonie a dark red dress, almost new. Julio Maní, a distant grandson of Ti-Bois, appears with a box of shoes. He calls everyone around to see them, he wants to amaze them, they are two-tone shoes, an American brand. Julio Maní is happy. Now he breaks the string and opens the box, but there are no shoes. They have cheated him and inside there is only a brick. Ti-Bois starts to hit him with his cane.

The rural police must have already forgotten about me, besides, you have grown and are as tall as a man, almost as tall as Aristón. But nonetheless I'm afraid to ask for a job in the cane fields. Adelaide pushes me because you owe me two years of room and board and you must make money.

And I go.

And nothing happens. Nothing bad.

They're going to pay me for lifting the cane that Aristón cuts.

I'm very pleased because I know that no one will cut more cane than he. And that's what happens: Ti-Bois has been preparing his arms with magical herbs and snake lard and now the blade is like lightning in his hand, and people look at him, and he has many friends and women. Once he argued with Splinter, a Jamaican who has killed two people. We agree to the duel. We went out into the plain and followed the narrow path that leads to the old locust tree. We scared away the cows and I sat in the round shade of the tree. Ti-Bois starts making signs with his cane and calls the spirits of the air and the earth. Splinter laughs. He is a black man who believes in the white's religion. He takes a gulp of rum and then spits it noisily, splashing Ti-Bois, and he takes out his machete and confronts Aristón. Splinter knows a lot. He continues to laugh and dodges Aristón's wild sweeps with the machete. He jumps around, making faces and mocking Aristón, and so the time passes. He has tried to tire Aristón, but it's he who is tired, and he no longer laughs. Aristón shouts and jumps him with rapid-fire blows that sound like a swarm of wasps. Splinter jumps back, but he arches away too late: Aristón has cut into his belly, and now he can only look into his ugly guts.

That night Ti-Bois assured us that Oggun Ferraille had entered Aristón, that he'd spoken with the *loa* and he was very pleased to have been able to move and fight inside the muscles of his grandson. We all thought this very fine. During those days Adelaide received many visitors, many gifts of rum, tobacco, codfish, lard, flour, and condensed milk. She gathered her friends around her, and it was funny to see her tell of the fight, playing the part of Splinter and of her son, jumping around, sweating and choking and shouting curses, but no one laughed. Finally, when she had to stop, she struck her chest and waved her arms speaking just like Aristón.

"I'll be a greater *houngan* than Ti-Bois. Oggun Ferraille

protects me, Oggun the Marshal, Oggun the Captain, Oggun of Iron, Oggun of War. I aaammm Oggunnn!"

Aristón was gone for a week, precisely the week when Adelaide Macombe was dying from a burst vein. He returned to the compound a day after the burial, a Sunday afternoon, with palm fronds on his shoulder. He walked like a god, very straight and tall, and stepped firmly on the red earth. The children ran after him, touching his powerful thighs and the case of his machete. He sighed when Pascasio told him about Adelaide. Then he turned solemn, put the palm fronds under the bed, ate half a bunch of bananas, and went to sleep. At dawn, before we left for work, he called me and Pascasio over and he pulled from the palm fronds a long machete and a khaki uniform, the kind that the rural police used to wear. Right there I dug a hole and buried the stuff wrapped in one of Adelaide's dresses. He didn't answer a single question, but in the cane fields we learned that the naked body of a sergeant had been found mutilated on the outskirts of Esmeralda. In the compound we all guessed who the killer was. And we were proud.

Before the carnival week I spoke with Léonie's parents. It turns out that I was too young, was in the country illegally, didn't have money from a steady job, and you must understand that we aren't going to give away Léonie just like that. I didn't insist, and that disturbed Léonie, but they really were right, anyway they can't keep me from seeing you, and I'll speak with Ti-Bois and he'll find me a good job, you'll see.

Aristón, Pascasio, and I joined the *bande rara* that Maurice organized every year. Maurice organized everything in Guanamaca. The whites called him "the Mayor." He could also read the newspaper and write letters in Spanish. Nicole, his wife, was the *reine* and we practised at night in the back of his house, lighting the place with kerosene lamps. Léonie played *princesse* and marched with Nicole. The *premier coutelas* was played by Ariston, and it was thrilling to see him do tricks with his machete. Pascasio was chosen as *premier bâton* but I wasn't skilled enough and only got the part of flag-bearer. We left on *mardi gras* after dinner, dressed in costumes that the women had made, singing and dancing with the whole compound following behind us. We returned on Saturday, tired from visiting the villages and all the compounds of the plain, tired already of so much rum, so much *merengue*, so much fun. We followed the ancient custom and burned the *juif*, and drank the ashes of the rags mixed in water and sugar. Of all my weeks, this was the happiest.

The happiest?

Yes. Because in some way (like they say in Havana) Guanamaca was, in spite of all the misery, my little piece of heaven, and I was never happier than during those nights with Léonie, next to Ti-Bois' bonfire, beneath the trees of the plain, listening to him tell stories of the old country, listening to him speak of the maimed Mackandal, of how he'd put three handkerchiefs in his glass and then removed them one by one, first the yellow one, then the white one, and finally the black one, the race that would reign in Port-au-Prince, and that is how it had been, and that is how it will be one day all over the world, and then I'd kiss Léonie and Maurice would start to play the harmonica and Pedro Maní would play the conch, and the dancing and singing would begin again until the new day would find us in another compound and we'd meet up with another *fiesta*.

"The happiest," I say, and now I sit on the train tracks and I put on my socks and my boots: I'm not going to go into Guanamaca barefoot; two kilometers and someone may see me.

I put down my backpack. It weighs more than usual. I'm carrying lots of things: presents for Ti-Bois and for the old men from the cabins, who are so influential. I also stop to have a cigarette, and suddenly I realize that I have brought these things because I'm afraid. Me, afraid. It infuriates me. I'm tough. A man of blood and fire. A Marxist-Leninist Haitian. A cadre of the revolution. Lies. All lies. I'm afraid of Guanamaca, afraid to inaugurate the school and have none show up, afraid of failure, that they won't want to see me because of the Aristón thing and that they'll throw the presents in my face. At this face of mine. Now I'm nothing more than a frightened school-teacher with the face of a zombie. Yes, I'm afraid. And it isn't only Guanamaca that I fear. I'm afraid of everything: afraid of having to fight again, afraid of captains and majors, of doctors and hospitals; I'm afraid of women, of children who stare at me, of having to face Léonie. I'm just like my father, a poor bastard of a Haitian not worth shit.

"If you don't come fight with me, I'll kill you," Aristón said to me one night, and I have also felt afraid. "Oggun says that I have to fight, to set the earth on fire, that I have to fight at your side, that you're my protection, and that the bullets won't do me no harm if you're there. They won't do you no harm too. Oggun told me, and he said the same to Ti-Bois. Fight or I kill you. Choose."

And because I was afraid I left Léonie and followed Aristón to the mountains of Oriente. This time we weren't going to pick coffee berries. We were going to war because Oggun had demanded it; we were going to fight against the tanks and cannons of Batista that rolled down the highway; against the airplanes, the ships, and the army, we, who hadn't meddled in the white's things for a long time, were fighting.

Aspirin, Maurice's son, knew the way. The people from the compound called him that because he was always begging for aspirins at the boss's drug store. His headache never went away – as a kid a horse had trampled him during the uproar over the deportation. In spite of this, he was a very bright guy, and Maurice has taught him to speak like the whites in the office of the refinery. He liked to get out of Guanamaca and roam around for days, and a man once told him, "Look in those hills over there, the rebels are holed up." And in order to fulfill Oggun's wishes, we had to join them.

I spent the entire afternoon with Léonie. We went to the fields but I could do nothing, nothing more than listen to her assure me that she'd wait for me all her life, and I was silent. We left at night. Ti-Bois said that Toussaint L'Ouverture's soul was with us and he gave us sweets to offer to Papa Legba, the Lord of the Roads. We said good-bye: "Good-by, Léonie. Good-bye, Pascasio. Good-bye, *houngan* Ti-Bois."

The sun rose when we'd already crossed the plains, and Aristón sang to the sun. Aristón would sing to the trees, to the rain, to everything. He knew lots of songs that Adelaide had made up, and he'd learned them unconsciously and would always sing them very loud.

We soon entered the hill plantations, at the foot of the Sierra, where the coffee is grown, and there were Batista's soldiers. Ariston was dressed in the uniform of the rural police; in addition, he had Adelaide's magic scarves hanging from his waist. I was afraid that they'd stop us. I told him to at least take off the hat, but he insisted that as long as I was at his side, misfortune couldn't catch up. "Don't be afraid, Pedro Limón, nothing can happen to us." And it was true: When the airplane saw us and Aristón pulled out his machete and shouted to it to come down if it dared, that he was going to cut off his wings; when it turned around and flew down low, firing many shots and I threw myself in the stream listening to Aristón's insults; when the plane flew by again and dropped a bomb and there were no sounds as they'd said there'd be, and I saw him crouching, trying to dig it up, then I realized that it was true, that Aristón and Ti-Bois were right, and then I was less afraid because certainly Oggun would also protect me.

Aspirin didn't show up, so it was difficult for us to find the rebels. At first they didn't want to accept us. But Aristón's arrival with the one-hundred-pound bomb counted for something.

Pedro Limón gets himself together and secures his pack. He looks at the smoke coming from the chimney of the refinery. He continues looking at it for some time. Now he turns his back to it, throws away his cigarette, takes the narrow path by the tracks, and begins to walk toward the island of palms in the middle of the cane fields. Behind those palms is Guanamaca, he thinks.

Pascasio wanted him to stop (if only a moment) to see Léonie (it'd make her so happy) as they passed by the offices of the refinery and had given him the address of the house (new and painted indigo blue). But he'd chosen the long way around, the old path that skirted the refinery compound (his face before Léonie's, his face, always his face, unsuccessfully repaired with blade and buttock skin, the look compassionate at best, the mistrust of the child, barely six years old, a six-year-old son, what do you think, Pedro Limón, oh how are we growing old, how quickly life flies away, yes).

"Ain't no one who can kill me," Aristón would say, charged by the spirit of Oggun, as we watched the passage of the tanks and the trucks full of soldiers. It was curious watching him fight. Just before the first gunshot, Oggun would take possession of him. He'd come into him silently as a snake. Aristón wouldn't notice. He'd let himself be swallowed up without moving, his skin scaly and cold and ashen, his eyes like those of dead oxen killed in the floods, the *loa* coming through his eyes and skin, Oggun Ferraille, the merciless god, the Lord of War.

Much later, when we stayed close to camp and I learned to read, the man from Havana closed the book, lit his cigar, and began to speak of the gods, of Aristón, of Haiti, of Guanamaca. He spoke of them as if he'd been there in the middle of our compound or in the mountains of the old country. That night we didn't sleep, we stayed practically out in the open, beneath the branches of a tree, and he, the Habanero, talking and talking while the stars moved across the sky, explaining everything in great detail and with much patience, like when he taught me to read, and I have never heard anyone explain things as well as he, no, no one put things together in quite that way to get them into another's head, and he told me that he was happy to know that I'd made my plans, and that after the war they'd need people like me, and it was then that he spoke of studying to become a teacher and I understood why he'd refused to write down all that had happened to Aristón.

But now we were only beginning the war, and I didn't dream of reading and the discipline was too severe and the leaders kept saying that morale must remain high. I didn't have any problems, because I remembered every single one of the captain's words about the regulations; Aristón did have problems. They'd promoted him three times and each time he was left without stripes. "It's a shame that he has no brain, a man so strong, a man who has balls," said the captain. Although Aristón really couldn't care less. All he cared about was fighting and killing.

That dawn the captain got me out of my hammock and later woke Aristón. It was still a while before daylight. We had coffee with some of the other men and we received our orders. There was word that they were preparing an attack upon us and it was necessary to make sure. If it was true we'd have to move the camp, go further up, to the misty summit of the Sierra. The captain divided us in two patrols. Aristón and I and Rubio, a student from Manzanillo, would explore the southern quadrant. I was leading: Aristón had a poor sense of direction and Rubio was pretty new to this. Soon it was daybreak and Aristón decided to sing and there was no way to shut him up. Rubio got nervous. He wanted to cover Aristón's mouth. I took a green mango from my pocket and gave it to Aristón. That shut him up. But he didn't finish eating it. He stood still, smelling the fibers stuck to the seed, and when he looked up it was no longer Aristón who looked at us, and I knew that Oggun had caught the scent not of the mango but of war, and suddenly a flash of light exploded over the boulders and struck down Rubio and infuriated Aristón.

The shots didn't last long, although we killed three men of their patrol. Aristón killed the last one with his machete because we ran out of ammunition. I crouched next to Rubio and he was dead, and suddenly shells began to fly and explode around us, and we had to leave Rubio and run into the hills.

We weren't fleeing. Rather, I was fleeing and he wasn't. Because Aristón didn't know what fleeing was. Oggun must have warned him that the fighting wasn't close enough, that he could no longer kill and that this type of war didn't interest him.

I *was* afraid, and I was fleeing. Should I flee now? It'll be so easy to take the bus back to Havana . . .

And now we return, sweating, through the weeds. To the camp.

And I look back and I don't see Aristón pushing back the branches that I've just parted: I only see the edge of the line of palms, dazzling in the afternoon, next to the broken cane field, the cane field that sweetens and embitters the air of Guanamaca. And in the distance there is an old man making magic signs with a cane, and behind Ti-Bois there are some women and children and dogs, and I can hear their bark. They wait for me, and it's going to be something like another war, but I'm no longer afraid.

When we returned to the camp, Aristón still walked with the *loa* inside of him, maybe because Oggun still wanted to fight. His feet came down hard, like children when they play soldier, very tall and dignified, carrying his machete on his shoulder and his rifle slung across the chest. I looked for the captain to tell him the news, that the attack was a sure thing. He was with some other man from the plains who came and went with messages for the camps.

"I didn't know what happened. I think we met up with an entire company of them. They carry mortars," I said, and told him about the shooting, the shower of shells, and what happened to Rubio.

There are people who shouldn't speak, who shouldn't open their mouths because all they do is offend. And the man from the plains was one of them.

"What happened is that you're a pair of asshole niggers, a pair of faggots who shit as soon as you hear a gunshot. If I'd anything to say about it I'd execute you right this minute . . ."

He couldn't continue talking: Aristón raised his machete and split his head in two with a single blow, right through the middle, from top to bottom, as if it'd been a papaya.

That's what the man from the plains died from. Immediately.

The trial was also quick.

That night we had to leave the campsite.

Aristón was there, standing in silence, surrounded by the troops.

The leaders were over there, sitting on the crates of rifles that'd arrived just the other week, all very stern and speaking softly.

Aristón didn't defend himself. He began moving his head, just like a horse, and began to say that he didn't remember anything, that he was sorry and that he wouldn't do it again, and no one could make him say more. And since the Habanero was the judge, it was me who had to answer his questions. It was me who had to tell them what happened and tell them about Aristón, Ti-Bois, and Oggun.

When the Habanero pronounced the sentence, he stalled a bit. Later he explained carefully, as they always did, why things had to happen that way. But no one wanted to be on the firing squad, no one.

Then Aristón raised his head, smiled, and asked permission to choose the men, and I was the first. "Pedro Limón," he said, and then he named the others.

"Don't worry," he said to me in Creole as they tied his hands. "If you're with me nothing can happen."

We walked along the trench toward the ceiba tree. Every three or four steps he turned his head and spoke to me of the scare they were going to have when Oggun performed the miracle.

Finally we reached the tree. He let himself be blindfolded and turned his back to the tree. The firing squad formed a line about twelve paces away from him.

"Ready!" yelled the captain and I cocked my Springfield. Aristón was, as usual, cheerful, with his rural police hat, the rim pinned up with the religious medals of the Virgin that he'd taken from the dead, placed sideways on his kinky hair, dirty with earth. I looked at him to imprint him in my memory, in case Oggun turned him into an owl or something. I saw that he wore two beaded necklaces, and I'd always thought that there'd been more, and the colors of Adelaide's scarves were yellow, white, and black, like Mackandal's handkerchiefs, and I had to look really hard as they were ripped and faded. I looked at his face again and it had already turned gray, and certainly the clicking sound of the rifles had brought Oggun down and now anything could happen.

"Aim!"

"I'm Oggun Ferraille! No one can kill me with Pedro Limón here!"

"Fire!"

He bounced against the tree. He made a sound like a cough and let out a mouthful of blood; he slipped slowly down the trunk; he sighed and sank into the thicket. The captain walked to the ceiba tree with his pistol in his hand. He bent down. I don't know what kind of snake it was, but immediately after the captain fired his pistol, an ashen wisp ran through his legs and lost itself up in the hill. It wasn't my imagination. We all remained looking up at the slope of the hill.

The next day, after settling down at a new campsite, I asked the Habanero to write a letter for me, to write to

Maurice so that they could know what happened to Aristón. I asked him to explain it clearly, as he knew how to say things. But the Habanero didn't want to say anything about the snake. He refused, he who explained everything in such detail. He looked at me directly, for a long time, and then began to write, and without looking up he told me to leave, to leave and to decide, because in life men have always had to decide between heaven and earth, and it was about time that I did so.

PART II

MARINA 1936

It was an old Cuban sloop, with mended sails and ruinous appearance . . . It seemed to make no progress, for it had to luff its course to push through the opposing current . . .

Alejo Carpentier, *Explosion in a Cathedral*

I

"Tin marín de dos pingüés, cúcara mácara títere fue," Lucianito would have said on that morning of a special year (what do you call the year when memories start falling into place?) as he'd have to choose between two fists that I had clenched and crossed. I'd be there with the rusty wingnut in one palm, leaning back above the star-board rail. I'd count to ten three times and listen as the clatter of bare feet and laughter spread out through the boat.

After noon had sounded, rung by mutinous Cisneros on the forward bell, Ana Zoila would appear at topside with her bilious long face, harried by the teasing wind inside her petticoat. She'd appear and start to hand out bumps and pinches, then she'd chase me weakly from the salt fish barrels piled up on the poopdeck over to the bow stays, moaning all the way that these damned nuisances that always held up lunch were inducing her nervous attacks, that she couldn't get the first idea of consideration through my skull, and that the whole thing came from playing as I did with rotten kids, as if it didn't matter what she had to do to keep the fishing business above water and on top of that to keep the company off her back.

In feigned exhaustion, I let her catch me by the coattails

and then pull me back into the cabin, under my friends' mocking faces, as they scrambled up the ratlines like a band of longtailed monkeys – Ana Zoila's name for them – illustrated somewhere in *The Book of Knowledge*.

The table was drawn up under the skylight with its leaded glass. On the tablecloth there would be spread a worn-out silver service, whose heavy, ashen pieces I could scarcely hold up. As soon as she had shaken out my knees and smoothed my cuffs, Ana Zoila would start tapping on the wall, and then Mama and Papa would emerge slowly from their game of ajolome that they'd been playing for years. Ambrosio, a courteous Negro with a tattered livery and a delicate tenor voice, would arrange the chairs for us deliberately, and stirring with his tongs inside a pot of murmuring brine above the cooking stove, he'd take out, for us to see, a steaming can of pork and beans or spaghetti with meatballs. The other dishes, except once a spoonful of syrupy fruit and maybe a bite of some fowl shot from our own crow's nest, were never products of the land: the basis of our sustenance was fish, and at dinner nothing else was ever tasted.

Our cabins took the best part of the upper deck, away from all the salting apparatus and the spinning drive wheels (not too present, actually, when the engine wasn't broken down we'd still be out of coal) stuck against the boat's ribs near the prow. The smartest cabin, which opened up below an overhanging roof, belonged at that time to Mama and Papa; in the others, situated at one end of the passageway, there slept, in the following order: Ana Zoila, a captain-elect (that year there were three), first officer Calleja, and I.

My cabin was the smallest, and its hatch opened to face the smokestack, which had been painted blue for luck. The furniture was just the following: a chest of drawers with bronze handles, a cracked mirror and – underneath the portrait of Don Fadrique Ocampo, my great-grandfather, oil oozing in the humid air, so faded that it showed nothing but a helmet with a greenish plume above one cloudy, persecuting eye – the rolltop desk, screwed like the chest into the floorboards; a Viennese chair, flexible and light as the albatross feathers that we sometimes found on deck in the morning; a basin, stuck to the wall by a rusted spiral stay, whose two inches of rainwater would be changed on alternate mornings by the decorous Ambrosio with bucket and sponge. Above and to the right, on the shelf that hung inside the berth, there stood in line a battery-powered radio (almost inaudible because it was a long-wave set and we sailed far offshore) and two ebony dolphins, their coiling tails holding up two school-books and a dozen novels. But no, all that was from another time, Padre Zacarías would not yet then have taken charge of my instruction and the mirror on the chest would not have cracked, and on the shelf, sitting sturdy and discolored, the picaroon Tribilín Cantore, and beside him the little Mickey Mouse pitcher and the brand new box of hussars and grenadiers, then the covered wagons, and the cannon that shot marbles and mothballs. And up on deck we'd play at hide-and-seek, and the forecastle was Bluebeard's. In time we'd storm it, having signed with Robin Hood or Captain Blood; later, sword clenched in his teeth, Lucianito would scale it, neither asking for nor giving quarter. But now we played hide-and-seek and seek-and-hide and had just begun a game of tag when George V died. Ana Zoila, on the verge of a nervous attack, ran through the deck to spread the news, heard over the two-banded RCA with the strong battery that the company had given her when she turned twenty.

Progress was a thing my parents measured by a radio's

sophistication, by the number of bands and tubes a set would have, by the effectiveness of contacts, circuits (specifications printed inside the Christmas catalogues that Company ships supplied to our first officer Calleja), resistors and condensers. Of course, only portables mattered to them. It would be awhile before we had electricity on board, and they'd die before it happened.

After supper we'd get together in the library to listen to the music of the whole wide world. Between the static squalls and the messages in Morse code, while Papa lit a Larrañaga and slid its fragrant ring onto my thumb, Mama, tossing back her wig with a movement quite her own, would fish for European capitals: Roman fifes and tarantellas, epic slavic violins, cymbals in Berlin, gay French songs, marches, ballads, turbulent *paso dobles*; an entire continent trickling down the antenna to spill out on the dusky sharkskin then in service as a rug; Europa, mythic name, a name that held its vowels together like a magic word, would find a passage every night through this resourceful cornucopia to storm us with ineffable froth, with sounds existing beyond good and evil, moving Papa to unroll old faded maps and scour geography books to find a more tangible reference, closer to our lonely, small, wandering reality. Where is Madrid?, here it is, that red star there is London, *Allemagne* means Germany, Russia is the great green bear, the wide blue space is the Atlantic, and Christopher Columbus sailed along that thin black line.

At other times, when the batteries were spent or the atmosphere too heavy, Ana Zoila organized the nightly concert. Ambrosio, mad with joy, helped her bring in the victrola and the record albums with Puccini's works (given by the company to recognize five years of service). All members of the family, including Ana Zoila, preferred the radio, its music and its necessary news reports, but Ambrosio, for some obscure reason or perhaps from pure presumption, preferred the opera disks. Standing beside the speaker, he memorized the words and music of *La Bohème*, *Madame Butterfly*, *Manon Lescaut*, amazing our visitors and his many friends on the second deck with his operatic talent.

When the concert was over, Ana Zoila carried me half asleep to my cabin. Seated in the Viennese chair, I watched her light the oil lamp on the shelf by holding up her candlestick. Then she urged devotion in my prayers, especially the last one, the one most likely to reduce my years in purgatory. Before withdrawing to the passageway, to leave me in the semi-darkness face to face with Don Fadrique Ocampo's rheumy eye, she'd run her finger through my hair as though trying to erase the bumps that she'd given me at noon.

One or two times a week, and always on Saturdays, the noises woke me up: a shuffle of hoofbeats, curses, thuds, and moans that beset my door and vanished down the corridor.

"That was the god Eshu himself, my child," Ambrosio would say, startled, pausing in the middle of a Puccini aria, signalizing with his sponge, spattering the mirror with a grayish dew that he wiped off quickly on his sleeve. He'd have to make him an *ebbó* with gills and guts so he'd eat by himself and not bother anyone.

"It's Satan riding with his devils," my sister would declare at breakfast time, crossing herself and bending her head down over her plate. "I heard them too this morning."

Mama and Papa never heard a thing. With the radio session over, daybreak found them still playing ajolome, moving the plugged Chinese coin through the encyclopedia's pages. And so they stayed there, lost in a reverie that only Ambrosio could break by bringing in their seaweed broth.

One night, when Ana Zoila had just stopped her finger's forehead-stroking rite, the awful racket came through early. After a parade of curses not loud but deep, a dazzling shadow fell down next to the half-opened door.

Ana Zoila, dismayed, put her hand over her fishlike mouth and told me to be silent.

Grabbing the candlestick, she dragged me out into the hallway.

Spread out there on the planks, wrapped in his spangled cape, lay first officer Calleja.

His eyes were shut and he had his head turned slightly toward the door; his braided, bicorned hat had fallen in the middle of the passageway. Escaping from his mouth there was a filament of vomit that ran down his beard.

Ana Zoila kneeled and pulled a handkerchief from her smock.

"Swear to me you won't tell anyone," she whispered, looking up. I leaned against the wall and nodded.

"Swear to God."

"I swear to God."

"Don't you dare say a thing, or your tongue will rot," she said, replacing the soiled handkerchief. "Now help me."

First officer Calleja was only as tall as a fifth grader, but girded in a heavy shell of straps and weapons. I by one leg, and Ana Zoila by the other, dragged him slowly toward his cabin door. He smelled heavily of rum.

"Empty his pockets," she said.

Next to the candleholder, then, I lay out a string of coins, matchboxes, poker decks, theater tickets, caramels, bullets, toothpicks, photographs of naked women, dice, cigarettes, holy images, colored pencils, amulets, chains, small bottles of Bacardí, brass knuckles, razor blades, keys . . .

"Stop," she said, when I had almost emptied out the pocket. And she picked up the keys, which she began trying in the door.

We put him inside. Reaching up, I lit a candle.

Ana Zoila, hunched next to him, reminded me of what could happen to my tongue. Then she ordered me to take the candlestick back to my bunk.

But when I shut the door I blew the candle out and peeped through the keyhole.

II

During the afternoon I was not allowed on deck. When the siesta was over, when Papa and Mama went back to their game of ajolome and Ana Zoila pursed her lips into the figure of a heart and recommenced her work, Ambrosio, unhooking the umbrella, went outside to find Columbia. I'd wait for her in my cabin, playing with the soldiers for effect, organizing them smartly on the floor. The little drummer, with his bandaged forehead and half-opened mouth, would lead the cavalry; his vivid beat would split the rows of grenadiers and spill, like dominoes, the four colonels and the defenders of the cannon and the flag. "He looks like you," Columbia had said at the time of my fall into the fishtank, my head wrapped up by Dr. Miñagorri. And now she'd come in, blushing, and approve my military operation with a wink, and taking her lined notebook and her primer from her bag, she'd admire her long, extremely red fingernails and then start fanning herself with her straw hat. "How hot it is, Julián Ocampo! What will it be like in August if we're barely into February now?"

And it's not as though Columbia was young, exactly ("Her pride has kept her all alone to dress up saints," said Mama), but there was a lively glow to her expression and she walked erectly, proudly, I don't know, in a very particular and captivating way. If I took too long to spell a word, she would interrupt the lesson and clutch me to her quilted bosom. "Learn all you can, Julián Ocampo; when you grow up I'll marry you." And her voice was low and broken, as if at any moment she could start to cry.

It was because of her that I met Isabel and Lucianito Goyanes.

"You're alone too much. I'm going to speak to your mother about bringing my niece and nephew over."

But if Mama had nothing against my playing with Isabel and Lucianito until nightfall – by late afternoon I was already getting bored with the tin soldiers and, enthralled by the spectacular forfeits that the rules of ajolome prescribed, I'd pull the Viennese chair over underneath the oxeye that opened on the library – Ana Zoila wasn't charmed at all to hear us running down the passageway.

"You're making me a nervous wreck," she'd screech out from her cabin, beating weakly on the wall.

Actually, she was already a wreck by the time she'd got back to her cabin, especially after inspecting the fishtank. Sometimes she hadn't even time to put down the lantern that she needed for going below, and one of her attacks would knock her out. "Get Miñagorri," she would say, piteously, poking her eel-like body out the door. But after she'd swallowed Dr. Miñagorri's silver-colored pills, Columbia smiling at her haughtily as she rubbed her legs, she'd lash out at us again, calling us the devil's minions, dark angels out to put an end to her.

Occasionally an auspicious cloud rose in the distance,

causing us to line up at the poop or down the beam. Then the mutinous Cisneros, alerted by the lookout's cries, would stop carving figures on the rail, stow his knife in the pocket of his mended jacket, and exhort a prayer from the entire crew – those were the Regulations – while mumbling obscenities. With the clapper's fervent ringing came a long exhalation of prayers and repentances that mounted up to heaven.

Ambrosio said that in earlier times, whenever a cruel drought would come, the prayers got so desperate they rose up through the airvents and condensed along the masts, to fall in thick drops that tasted like tears. When the lunatic knell had ended, the captain on duty and first officer Calleja came out on the bridge. While the latter peered through a spyglass and then set the course, Padre Zacarías availed himself of some nearby pious woman to count off names of penitents not yet on deck. By this time the Virgin, lowered from her altar, would appear, inspiriting and dolent on her dais, the hemp sandals of her bearers in plain view beneath the platform's flaring crepe. Those who bore colors and crosses, deaf to the accosting crowd, looked at each other laboriously through their cardboard hoods' ill-opened slits. By the smokestack, near the stands of grog and fritters, the members of the jazz band waited until the priest put up the Tent of Miracles to begin the hymn "Oh Lord, We Are Thirsty!", which had the surest beat for the nervous steps of marchers hoping to bring rain.

Seated on a velvet sofa that Ambrosio slid toward the forward balcony, immobilized between Mama and Ana Zoila, I looked out on Our Lady of Fresh Waters, her figure bronzed, escorted by three dozen penitents, with guards who held long machetes. I'd be envious of Bartolomé Bartolomé and Pepe Luis, who were hanging in the rigging, and Melitón, all trimmed up as an acolyte, clearing the way with his censer, and especially Lucianito, who was straddling a topsail and could oversee the bustling crewmen. Whenever a hymn ended, the penitents would lay down their insignias. Their stiff sailcloth robes, as if pulled down by the drum's somersaulting beat, came loose, and then on deck there was a penitential display of machete slaps, grunts, and ouches. "I never will get used to that," my papa grumbled, as Mama and Ana Zoila focused on the spectacle, rubbing their jet-black rosary beads in their fingers. After a while the priest, following the flash of Calleja's ceremonial sword, would lift up the Candle of Miracles. Trumpet and trombone would start in again, and so on until nightfall or up until the cloud might burst. Now and then the miracle would occur.

The Candle of Miracles had an unwritten history, and the events that led up to it lay so far in the past that one could only speak of them in the tones of sacred history. And so it seemed that the boat was Noah's ark, its animals having been eaten in the famines wrapped up in tradition. If descending from Noah gave us dignity, the shame of having stuffed ourselves with biblical animals meant that we'd sail on without glimpsing land until the Judgment Day. This grim version found simple and illiterate adherents: the old women who scrubbed the deck, we ourselves (at that time), and other characters like Ambrosio, whose simplicity would lead him to say, with his eyes spinning in his head, that Oshún of the Fresh Waters had yanked him from his hammock to show him, burned on one of the hold's planks, the tiny green brand that Noah placed there to prove for all time that he had built the boat.

"If that gibberish were true," argued Padre Zacarías from the pulpit, "no animal or person would be alive in the lands around the sea; which of course they are, as one can demonstrate by reading books and newspapers, or listening to the radio and staying on top of world events, or reflecting on the good things that the company brings us. Let's suppose, may God forgive me for suggesting this, that we're actually sailing in Noah's ark. If that's the case there never could have been a Flood."

Among the lovers, on the other hand, there was a firm suspicion that our ship belonged to the Flying Dutchman. "You're the Dutchman," I heard Ana Zoila tell Calleja as I listened through the keyhole. But weeks later, as we played hide-and-seek on deck, we saw an ancient ghost ship's burning sails cross through the air. Clustered on the bridge, we could see for an instant the renegade's silhouette, impassive and damned, like the face on a coin that had slipped into the waves.

One thing was certain: nobody could be sure exactly when and from where we had sailed, not even what the purpose of our trip was. Doctor Miñagorri would use yellowed compendia, zodiacs, and retorts to investigate the rear horizon. "Never let yourself be fooled, Julián; the rear's the thing. You know the course by looking at the wake." To which many businessmen and politicians answered: "The past is not worth looking into, because everyone knows that history repeats itself." It was all the same to Columbia: "Getting there or not, rags or riches, the only thing we know for sure, Julián Ocampo, is that we're born to die. So let's be dignified about it," and she'd let out a sigh before returning to her notebook. The priest would add that the reward was in the hereafter, and others of us figured that we weren't living, but rather dreaming, each one of us afloat in infinite and empty space. "You're all a bunch of egotists," the mutinous Cisneros would say meritoriously; the goal could be none other than to manage to plant a tree, ourselves, or have our children do it, or our children's children. And there were a lot of opinions.

All through her life, or through her death, as she preferred to call the short path from birth to extinction, Mama pronounced it "God's own writing" when a favorable or adverse happening came up, which did not keep her on troubled days – such as the one on which a bomb exploded in the offices of *El País*, one of the newspapers that we carried – from having her fate read to her by Aspasia, a cross-eyed medium from the second deck. Ana Zoila, for her part, swore to me that nothing mattered to her but first officer Calleja, not for his personal attainments, but because he was the Flying Dutchman incarnate and she'd wander at his side worlds without end. I'm pulling out these familial inconsistencies while leaving many others out. In general we all believed in everything, we were terribly loquacious, and we didn't know the first thing about anything.

In any event, it seems that in the times of my great-grandfather, Don Fadrique, things went worse. Sailing was then by astrolabe and log line, and the Inquisition still kept itself busy. Also there was the end of a massive mutiny which, after many deaths and tribulations, overthrew Don Fadrique Ocampo's absolute rule on board. "When the rebels' powder blew up," Padre Zacarías would recite to us in the catechism class, repeating more or less the same lapidary phrases that he'd heard from his predecessor as a child, "the bucket brigade could not decide which holds to bail with crocks and stewpots." Those who survived the explosion that sealed the triumph of the revolution, faced with a shipwreck that a mass set up quickly on the poopdeck held no promise of preventing, opted, perhaps deranged by desperation, to abandon prayer and start to sin adeptly. Padre Magdaleno, presiding at the maimed rite, stood up gallantly before the knot of sinners with crucifix and Latin exorcism . . . producing nothing but disaster. Dissolved in tears, begging a miracle that was plainly out of reach, Magdaleno thought himself the only one possessed by the devil, and seizing a candelabra from the altar, he set fire to the hem of his cassock, thus to burn out the demon that possessed him. As he knelt on deck, caramelizing from the bottom up, an inexhaustibly sweet melody burst out from deep within his beard. Tradition has it that the song went on for three days and three nights and that the mutineers, wrapped up in the celestial music, levitated, repentant, level with the crosstrees; it says that they descended calmly on a Sunday to discover, upright and inexplicable, a mound of silver-spattered ashes, the priest's immolating candle scarcely burnt; it says that from the center of the morning there came forth the prows of a white, majestic fleet that brought immediate help and order. "And that's the story, children, of the Candle of Miracles," Padre Zacarías muttered hoarsely just before dismissing the class and swallowing two fingers of brandy to clear his throat.

But sometimes the miracle recurred, it recurred or we would simulate its recurrence so that the farce could keep on happening and take us for the moment from that life of salt and scales. When the first drop plunked down on the cardboard hoods, the priest would leave the cover of the pallium to kneel before the old chunk of wax, making a real effort to work miracles, intoning a few bitter, out-of-tune psalms that nobody understood. Then the robes would be raised up a couple of inches by their tiptoeing wearers, and a good way farther up, on the rigging, the men, hanging from the hoisting lines, would describe pendulums and somersaults, swaying back and forth in a counterpoint of weird faces, jeers, and hallelujahs droned out with piping voices. Below, the Daughters of Fresh Water would collect the crosses, the standards, and the ornaments ratted out by salt's tooth. At the verge of the rainstorm, anticipating the *fiesta* with rapid, loving praise, they'd put the Virgin back below on her altar until another promising cloud might call her up.

The impermeable canvases would be hanging from the topmast and topgallants: they would fill up, pallid, almost translucent, rounded like the bellies of some beneficent flying monsters; aerostatic dinosaurs, floating, drowsy from the rain above the smokestack's hollow; timid hypogriffs and dragons who calmly rolled their deep zeppelin bellies below the stays that were decked with flags and pennants. On deck, everyone would have run off and then come back with their jars and a few hard, dry soap splinters rooted out from underwear and smelly socks; they were barely good enough for making puny suds. Singing, shouting, slipping naked on the slick, briny deck, the children moved about everywhere, jamming themselves into the ventilation tubes' open mouths, into the casks secured at the rail; they went hopping, noisy, stepping on the lump-footed fishermen, knocking down jugs, dinghys, inconveniencing the pencil pushers of the accounting office who were earnestly soaping their wives' buttocks above percale tunics with embroidered edges. And the music started on the quarterdeck. First there was a long *danzón* ("To get them shaking," Ambrosio would say) that put a gradual end to the enthusiasm of the bath. Forgotten, left there on the deck to do the ceremony, first kneeling and then crosslegged, the priest shivered beside the reliquary, with no other amusement but to sniffle and run down – with a wide gaze that later would flare out from behind the grill of his confessional – his congregation's venial and mortal sins. From the balcony on the forecastle, splashing about in one of the pewter sitz baths that Ambrosio had run up, I was following, between the handrail's arabesques, the march of the aldermen and khaki-wearing soldiers, my friends playing, and Columbia's dignified promenade as she pulled one Isabel Goyanes, who was naked, by the hand. They were traveling against the wind, toward an encounter with the sounds being pitched out by the Matamoros Trio and the Habanero Sextet. The couples, purple with scrubbing, squeezed up sneezing against the men who played the maracas and the donkey jaws, looking for the heat of "Papá Montero," "Echale salsita," "La mujer de Antonio," "Ay Mamá Inés," and "Frutas del Caney". Then came the jazz band's set – tentatively "Begin the Beguine," "Body and Soul," "El día que me quieras," "Pennies from Heaven," "Quiéreme mucho," "The Continental," and above all "Stormy Weather," the most popular of the foreign pieces. Then the rumba would come in with the *conjunto típico;* it followed a *conga,* the cowbell sweet as a willow reed. Most of the people circled the canvas awning, dancing, tripping on fish barrels, amid a stink that the sharpest breezes couldn't clear away; they danced with their faces to the sky, trembling, mouths up, sucking the tardy drizzle, in an intoxication beyond anything that grog distributed by Regulation might induce. In the hold there would be the dance of the Negroes. It began at nightfall, with a slow, mournful drum; there followed other beats, freer, rustic, crossing, impossible to scribble down on staff paper. Ambrosio would be down there, his service above deck now having ended, filling out the score of *Madame Butterfly* with syncopations, twisting like a conger eel, rocking, Puccini now forgotten, singing a song to his lost gods in an unexpectedly hoarse voice, greeting them with ancient formularies that had no official versions – honey-devouring gods who now had to settle for bones and wormy fish heads. And I went to sleep with all of this at hand, raving that I had to have been born into polite society, carefully reciting my three prayers, especially the last one in the hope that some day they would let me go down to the carnival of miracles.

III

There were mornings when we'd leap out from the marble boat and step on shore. The ship held back, her sails set, because back in Don Fadrique's time she had already lost her anchor. We rowed like madmen, under the flapping eagles and parrots, skirting violet reefs and green oyster beds, inferring the precise passage through a labyrinth of simmering pools, red whittles, and wedges at the surface, spirals of amber, seaweed, and jellyfish. The island was floating before us (it was always an island) walled in fog, mysterious, unmentioned in the charts that our captains and first officer Calleja scanned so often. We'd make our approach along the unbelievably narrow channel that would cut into a wall of breakers with the rumble of a lifting drawbridge. We rowed teetering above water flecked with scum, suspended, without railings, stuck to heavy bubbles of indigo blue. Crocodiles and long-tusked walruses were splashing on the banks; blinded in sunlight, they rooted in the sand. A stockade made of coconut and orange trees, royal palms, shore pines and breadfruit trees was growing in the resplendent dunes, enmeshed in heliotrope and jasmine vines. In a rocky inlet, hundreds of penguins were collecting dry branches to be thrown diligently into bonfires; others, clutching flint hatchets, cracked open tiny turtles. From the cities surfacing upon the lilac mountain there came music made by little bells and triangles that delicately stirred the sea. We jumped out.

"I claim this island in the name of Shirley Temple, Tarzan, Babe Ruth, and the Dionne quintuplets," said Bartolomé Bartolomé, kneeling and deepening his voice to sound like his uncle Calleja.

We straightened up and looked round our viceroyalty in silence.

"What's this?" asked Isabel, pointing to the smoke-stack.

"The Eiffel Tower," I replied.

"And that down there?"

"That's London's Big Ben."

"Over there?"

"New York."

"What about the forecastle? What about the mutinous Cisneros?"

"I don't see a forecastle," said Lucianito testily. "There isn't any forecastle and there's no Cisneros here."

"That's Bluebeard's castle," I explained. "The Abyssinians bring him virgins; when he's eaten one he'll notch it on the rail."

"What rail?"

"I mean the wall."

"Which ones are the Abyssinians?" inquired Pepe Luis.

"Those right there," I said.

"You said that they were penguins."

"They're Abyssinians," offered Lucianito in support. "Can't you see their spears? Don't you see the bows and arrows?"

"We've got to civilize them," said Bartolomé Bartolomé.

"And make them Christians," said Melitón, the pious one.

"And that, what is it?" Isabel went on, and I reached out above her arm, reducing the world to a manageable void, a bottomless space that came alive and made its presence felt through the power of my breathing: and the crows' nests were cities; and the lookouts up there were their mayors; and the rigging's ropes were docksides and the canvas awning was made of gold. And after Lucianito dispatched us inland on heroic missions we could never complete, when we'd grown tired of discovering huge toy stores interspersed with movie houses, zoos, soda fountains, and amusement parks, we'd gather up again beside the marble lifeboat and Bartolomé Bartolomé would then propose another game of hide-and-seek while I rubbed my finger on the mainmast and pronounced the magic word that Ambrosio had taught me. Then the contours of the mysterious island would fold up until some other morning and another call – like an intimate ghost – invoked it.

After a short while Ana Zoila would arrive to mete out blows and pinches.

IV

"So here you are, *muchacho*," yelled the mutinous Cisneros.

I hid my head and pressed against the foremast.

"I know you're there," he shouted again. "Come here, I won't eat you."

A month before, a company ship had carried off the fish and left us in exchange a load of Bayer products, muslins, Keds sneakers, Japanese parasols, and a player piano for the Shuffleboard Club. It left us the mumps as well, and I'd been the first to get them (sort of a cold, pain on swallowing, a fever, and suddenly a couple of swellings under the jaws like no hammerhead even) and now, convalescent, I was emerging with half-opened eyes in a heated-up, whitish wind, onto a deserted upper deck rent with the inconsolable shrieking of the gaff. Beyond the taffrail, the sea stretched out wrinkled and monotonous. None of our fishing boats was out. The smell of the fishtank, worse than ever, was nauseating, and I started walking toward the prow. Half-hidden by the foremast, I watched the mutinous Cisneros as he carved the rail. He carried a whetstone in the pocket of his jacket, and every now and then he'd take it out, spit on it, and slide the knife over it. I'd heard that harsh whisper of metal only a few times before: when we played too near the rail the old veteran came up to us gesticulating with his knife held high.

"Come on over here, *muchacho*," he yelled at me again. "You and I have got to have a talk."

I went up to him slowly. I pretended to be looking down the hole where the stairway went down to the second deck.

"Because you're Julián Ocampo, aren't you?" he said, examining the blade edge up against the light.

I nodded up and down and suddenly felt dizzy.

"Aren't you?"

I clutched the rail to stay up. It seemed the sky was flying.

"Sure, who else could you be?" he said, his eye still on the knife. "And you're bored. And pale. Now I see, you're dizzy. Because you've been ill, isn't that so? Eh?"

I breathed deeply and was able to make out the yellowish, unraveling weave of his palm hat, the thin rope he had around his waist, from which there hung a tin cup and a spoon, and the dull hollow worn into the heel of his right hand, calloused, beaten.

"All right, I think it's time now for you to open your mouth. Haven't they taught you any manners?"

The sawdust in my throat began to loosen up.

"Columbia says one of the workers died of the mumps, a great big loader," I said, stammering.

"Yes, they've almost all come down with it," he said, digging into the wood, tracing out a book-sized rectangle. All down the rail there was a row of rectangles with little figures in them.

"I didn't die, but Lucianito and Bartolomé Bartolomé might. Columbia says they've got a high fever."

"Columbia exaggerates. I told her once that she had a nice walk and she stopped speaking to me."

"That's like the stations on the *Via Crucis*," I said, pointing to some carvings on the rail.

Cisneros did not answer. His weatherbeaten, bony finger spread some spit over the whetstone. After a while he said:

"*Via Crucis*, ha, not bad. But that's not it, exactly." He started poking with his knifepoint on the rail.

"Are those stones from the mountains?"

"What do you know about mountains, boy?" he grumbled.

"They show them in the geography books," I said. "I see a mountain when we play discovery."

"I know. I've heard you."

"There are lots of mountains in *The Book of Knowledge*. There's Mount Vesuvius, the volcano. Mount Etna, too. Airplanes run into mountains all the time."

"How's this?" he asked, standing back from what he'd carved.

"It's a mountain," I answered, after edging toward the rail.

"Do you have any more mountains?"

"What do you know about mountains?"

"On my island there are mountains."

"You know what this one's called?"

"No."

"Then you don't know anything about mountains."

"Columbia is teaching me to read."

"That might be true, but no one's going to teach you what a mountain is. Come here," he said, getting up.

He walked toward the bowsprit.

The seat of his pants was ripped.

The carvings were hardly visible up there.

"See? These are the first."

"Mount Everest? Mount Olympus?"

"No. Those mountains are far away. I don't think they have much to do with you."

"The one on the island has to do with me. I'm the only one that sees it."

"Everybody has their own."

"I can't see it too well, though. Not with my eyes."

"It's hard to see. But everybody has a mountain."

"Are islands like that, too?"

"Same thing, almost. No island's any good without mountains," he said, and he pointed his finger at one of the carvings. "This one look like yours?"

I poked my face up next to the wood. There were little human figures fighting on a rocky slope; some had loin-cloths and arrows, others rode horses and had helmets like Don Fadrique's. "Those are Indians and conquistadors. There's a picture like this in the library, except they're not fighting."

"Does it look like yours?"

"No. Mine has music and flowers and birds like in *The Book of Nature's Kingdom*."

*

"Good. That's about right. That's your island. But this one here was everybody's. It still is."

"Everybody on the ship?"

Cisneros nodded.

"Now have another look. Take your time."

On one side of the battle there was a lush tree bearing flowers and fruits. A long-tailed bird, maybe a parrot, was visible on one branch. Up above, the sun, moons waning and full, stars, rainbows, and comets; in the distance the sea, with ships and canoes; in the left corner a cavern, with a river that splashed down in a frothy waterfall; at the foot of the mountain a meadow and a vapory bend in the river.

"Every one of those carvings has a bit of your island and mine too, and part of everybody else's islands," he said, smiling. "The one I just did is our ship's latest island."

"That's not so. The ship doesn't have an island. We sail and sail and never find one."

The mutinous Cisneros became grave and started breathing heavily. Suddenly, he grabbed me by the neck and made me follow the quick sweep of his left hand.

"What the hell do you think all this is?" he bellowed. "Can't you see the trees in the park, the church tower, and the houses, and the trolleys?"

"It's not an island," I said, stepping backward.

"Get out of here, *muchacho*," he snapped. "You don't have any common sense. Get out and leave old Cisneros alone. Go on. We've met now, and that's all for today."

"Columbia says I have the vision of an albatross. There's no . . ."

"Get lost!" he shouted. I could see deep into his eyes above his white moustache: it reminded me of Noah's green fire that Ambrosio had seen in a corner of the hold.

"Go split your head open right there, Julián Ocampo, and fill it up with some common sense," he said, holding his knife up, blocking my retreat toward the stern. "Then you'll never forget what I showed you this morning. We're going to meet again."

I ran toward the bowsprit. Without looking back, I jumped the "divide" and crossed over to the other rail. The clouds began to swirl again and the decks were heaving. I fell down in the shadow of a rusty intake tube.

The portside deck hardly resembled the starboard, and to us it may as well not have existed. The Regulation assured us that the ship was owned by no one, that floating space could not be anyone's property. But that clause was put in by the mutineers – Cisneros among them – in opposition to Don Fadrique, shortly before Padre Magdaleno's holocaust would humble them and pull the Company's ships over the horizon, and no one cared about those ancient precepts any more.

"Things are different now, Justino," Miñagorri told my father one afternoon as he sat recalling the smashing splendor of the Ocampos, the fierce battles with high-riding galleons and rich Saracen ships. "If only there were duels, at least," my mother sighed. "Boxing's not the same at all." Miñagorri finished wiping his monocle, left a box of silvery pills upon the table, and said, before he jammed on his pointed hat, a black hat that featured silvery zodiacs and constellations: "It's different now, Justino. The times have changed, señora." And they certainly had. A high official of the white fleet, after he'd provisioned the explosion's survivors with food and twelve gross of bailing buckets, had mediated between Don Fadrique and the rebel leaders. In the end, it turned out that neither of the two sides was right. The correct entities were Science, Industry, Commerce, Progress, that is, Democracy and Reason. And after dispensing multicolored almanacs that showed Phrygian caps, horns of plenty, gears, telegraphs, locomotives, theodolites, compasses, and other allegories, the elegant official unfolded an enormous plan before the wary eyes of Don Fadrique and the rebels. Then he began to tell about improvements, a lengthening of the freeboard, the whistling miracle of steam power, and the convenience of building a fish-salting industry amidship provided with a fishing fleet. Everyone was absolutely convinced that things were different, but when Don Fadrique, on signing the contract, learned that the company would not recognize the titles and the privileges conceded to the Ocampos throughout centuries of scimitars, Greek fire, and epic songs, he tried to run the official through with his sword. Tripped up unexpectedly in mid-thrust, he was hanged forthwith from one of the yardarms. His last words were: "I'll be in the history books." And he was.

Likewise it happened that, in time, certain planks began to dress up in an unexpected dignity. To the imaginary line that ran through them the name "divide" was commonly given, and it divided up the ship according to where the people lodged, also conferring certain ironclad rights and duties. Thus, to those who slept on the quarterdeck there fell responsibility for the ship's governance, the running of the fish business, and working out the trade agreement with the company's agents aboard ship; they could walk without safe-conduct passes through all the floating space. To those who slept in the forecastle fell the guarding, maintenance, and use, when the moment came, of the artillery and small arms, the lifejackets, the fire-fighting equipment, the grappling irons, poles, ropes, and lifeboats, the brig, and the store of emergency rations; they also took control of fighting off the hordes of vermin that would hit us every summer, issuing safe-conduct passes, and keeping an eye on everything, human and animal, because in a general way they looked after the security of the ship; they could go without a safe-conduct pass into any part of the floating space except the quarterdeck, with the sole exception of the effective boss (in those years it was first officer Calleja) who, according to the decision of the captain-elect, could or could not sleep there. To those who slept on the starboard side, there fell the directing of the extraction and/or collecting – later to be transformed, stored, transported, or consumed – of salt, seaweed for soup, species of marine fauna not to be processed through salting, drift objects, loose and apparently ownerless things proceeding from shipwrecks and beaches, and other floating objects; also the catching of rainwater and of migratory species of animal fauna, the construction and repair of workshops, markets, cubicles, storerooms, offices, and other sites intended for the promotion of industry, commerce, the family, health, culture, scientific research, art, the media of mass communication, sports, and leisure; also the good order and exercise of legislative, municipal, and public administration functions and, in general, any collection activities; they could go without a safe-conduct pass through the entire floating space, except for the quarterdeck and the forecastle. Those who slept on the port side had charge of the handling of tools, machines, apparatuses, instruments, rigging, and gear, as well as raw materials, products in the process of being manufactured and those already finished; they manned the bars, counters, and shops, performed paraprofessional duties and others not requiring the use of physical force, and still others where it was required; they could go without a safe-conduct pass throughout the entire floating space, except for the quarterdeck, the forecastle, and the starboard side with its corresponding rail and adjoining deck. Those who slept on the second deck had the job of catching fish, by hook or net, and the minor tasks related to the operation of the boat, the cleaning, the scullery work, and other physical labor of this sort. They had the run of all the ship, excepting the bridge, the forecastle and the deck itself. Those who lived in the hold and fish-tanks' nooks had the job of bailing – the company did not issue pumps for this – and they could go without a safe-conduct pass through the entire floating space, except the quarterdeck and the starboard side of the deck with its rail and adjoining deck and also the port side with its rail and deck; in general, one might say that they were kept from having any starlight fall upon their skin. In defer-ence to the memory of Padre Magdaleno, the clergy enjoyed the privilege of going, without safe-conduct passes, wherever they pleased, but the new Regulation prohibited them from living in the quarterdeck, because their power was no longer of this world.

This distribution of floating space was to be followed by many others within each sector. The "divide" had fallen over the works like the guides of a net, and it was now just a matter of splicing new footage to it, thus cut-ting the whole ship up into slices, parceling it out imagi-natively like the crossword puzzles that Columbia found in her fashion magazines. With its contours hardly to be grasped, suggested only by a brass nailhead or a small crack in the planking, the cubes, prisms, spheres, cylin-ders, cones, parallelepipeds, and pyramids into which the ship was broken down became the subjects of intermin-able litigations, alliances, and family squabbles, of fears, sins, fines, and punishments, and they lent themselves to the careful accounting of registry books, to a traffic in statements, jumbled proceedings, rubrics, wax seals and stamps, honoraria, legal briefs, taxes, and contributions that made a tangle out of everything.

The mutinous Cisneros struck ten blows with the clapper on the bell. The shadow of the intake tube had shortened, and the morning came up over my neck like a yellow sheet. I stood up. This deck was much older than the one to starboard; a compacted crust lay over the sunken and deserted planks. The quarterdeck and forecastle loomed up completely blind of hatches on that side, and the little cabins were unpainted. Papa and Mama only talked about the port side to remember the abominable crimes (later I would see one featuring the Organ Grinder and another one with Celia Mena, whose body they found in four separate, reeking packages), holdups, witcheries, disgusting practices, and horrible, suspicious diseases. "Once there was a little boy who ran off to the other side, and a small wart that he had began to grow and grow until he turned into one big wart and they had to throw him over the rail." I looked at my hands, held them in front of my face with the sleeve pulled back; the wart had not grown on me. I walked up to the rail. Next to one of the portholes there were strands of seaweed, and I thought about the big, strong worker – his name was Sotolongo – and about Columbia, too. "When I die, throw this flower into the sea and say an Our Father for me, Julián Ocampo, because you love me truly," she said one afternoon as the lesson ended, holding out a paper rose toward me. Ana Zoila's and Mama's flowers were white; Papa's was made of celluloid, a material that floated better. Nobody would throw them over into the ocean in their names after the priest's *Requiescat in pace*; they would have to go off like the poor dead worker with the mumps, under a bunch of prayers and modest seaweed garlands. But I am not ready to recall those sad times.

In any case, on the port side deck a staircase wound its way down a round hole.

Surely an entrance to the second deck.

A gust of rancid food and menthol wafted up to strike me in the face.

Long drawn-out moans were issuing from the iron spiral's depths.

I backed up.

"Fairy," Bartolomé Bartolomé had said to me when he saw me cry in sympathy with the flying fish he'd held crushed in his hands, spitting up pink froth.

"They'll never make a captain out of you if you act like that," Lucianito grumbled, frowning at my tears, snatching the tangle of trembling scales, and heaving it over the rail.

I called on the Virgin and shook off bad luck as Ambrosio had taught me, then lowered myself a little at a time down through the black hole.

The second deck's passageways were lit in sections by the mute, reddish glow of kerosene lamps anchored at the corners. Along them, people traveled on all fours because the ceilings were incredibly low. They moved along puffing and moaning. Most of them had strips of sailcloth wrapped around their heads, and their ears were hidden under menthol pomade poultices. "They've all come down with it below," Dr. Miñagorri had said confidently, taking the thermometer out of my mouth to hold up to his platinum-ringed monocle. Any other morning they'd all have been at work cleaning sea bass in the saltworks, harpooning tuna and bonito or shoveling coal into the boilers. Now, forced by the epidemic to be careful of the air, they wandered feverishly through the passageways, the hammocks occupied by those who were too sick.

I leaned against a bulkhead and made way for a fat youth on all fours whose tongue was rolling. Suddenly there was a creak of rotten planks, and underneath my feet the void: I was falling helplessly into the fishtank.

That night, when Dr. Miñagorri was assuring Mama that my head wound would not get infected, as Ana Zoila told me why things down below had to be the way they were – how could I describe the horror of the bailing, the people with water up to their waists who passed along the buckets in a chain of sighs, the pestilence scratched into people by the whiplashed fishtails, and the splashing of the ones who sank below, weakened by the bites? – I consoled myself by thinking that from then on I'd be captain and lead expeditions to the mysterious island. Then, alone in my berth, rocked by a sudden breeze, it occurred to me that the mutinous Cisneros was right; what I had seen that morning wouldn't ever leave me.

V

During those long Sunday breakfasts I never again mentioned the nocturnal noises. Whenever I opened my mouth, Ana Zoila, looking tired, would knock over the glass of precious water that Ambrosio had just filled, or perhaps she'd crack with one blow of her spoon the royal blue border of a china plate. I decided that I'd gulp my seaweed soup and run to the bathroom with a determined look on my face. From there I'd await the final call to eleven o'clock mass. Pacified by my silence, Ana Zoila would inform me from outside the door that if I didn't hurry the Kyrie would be half over when we got there. In the stairway leading amidships we'd run into first officer Calleja with his men. Papa and Mama would greet him frigidly, because everyone took it for granted that he hadn't made it to the quarterdeck without staining himself in blood. Sometimes we'd see the captain, and Papa, as he kept descending, talked about the recent law concerning women's suffrage, or the structure of the National Council on Tuberculosis, which Miñagorri would direct for several years.

The stairway opened to a spacious place, whose beams and bulkheads were dressed with posters, bills, and bulletins. A system of deft mirrors caught the light that came down from the deck and threw it, pacified and bluish, along the thirty-two possible paths marked out on a compass rose. At the left of this locale, beyond the portico adorned with clusters of trumpeting angels, the broad and majestic cathedral of Our Lady of Fresh Water would hide another clean, well-lighted space, with severe benches burnished to an orange glow by torches and candles. On the opposite side, beside the busy corridor that came from the communal and domestic installations, lay the Great Theater, set into the hull – admirable in its marquee of Chinese lanterns, its vestibule of damasks, marble, and coral, its spherical aquaria replete with jellyfish and seahorses – where twelve people standing and four more seated on a glorious couch of vermilion velvet would applaud, night after night, the songs of Ernesto Lecuona that came streaming out from Borja, the beautiful, and the incomparable Rita Montaner, who wiggled her hips like no one else. Facing the stairway, across the open space, there stood the threshold of the Labyrinth. Its high façade, pocked with faux windows in the shape of Latin capitals – you could read: LIBERTY–EQUALITY–FRATERNITY – and worked in bronze with dozens of lemmas and allegorical figures, scurried along the plaza's lateral framework to run, secret and officious, toward the far reaches of the ship. Above the roof there lay, like a sweaty eel, the gutter, whose intakes opened up on deck to pick up water dripping from the canvases that were stretched between the yardarms.

The chambers, halls, and offices would offer every day their beat-up stools and benches to the legion of men – there were very few women, because certain acts of violence were allowed – who lined up at the foot of the façade. The pavilion was scarcely four meters deep. At the end of a bare entrance hall, past a doorman who spouted gibberish as he hawked fried tidbits wrapped in brown paper, the elevator rose mechanically with its single passenger in a creak of cables, gears, and pulleys. To the right and left, facing the shaft's open sides, were two slow passageways, lit by a lantern chained to the apparatus. It was enough to twist one's body, pick a direction, and make a little jump to fall without much risk onto one of them. It would be something else again to go beyond the threshold's furtive penumbra and move ahead feeling the wall to find an entrance to a ministry, the mayor's office, the magistracy, the upper or lower house, while walking into the narrowed gale that knocked off hats no matter how stuck on they were, and the scalding jets of steam that hissed out from the elbows of the pipes, and the drippings from the aqueducts, intercut with the howling wind in a sweet, asphyxiating sprinkle, and trapdoors eating out the floorboards everywhere like hungry sharks. In order to be admitted in any of the public offices' halls, one had to proceed without a lantern, and above all, never let one's hat be blown off. But all that would have taken place on workdays, not on the Sundays when Ana Zoila, blushing beneath first officer Calleja's look, pulled me along the deck by my fingers.

VI

We played at discovering the island only on some mornings now. We'd meet at the poop taffrail by the little shrine that marked the Virgin's showing of herself to the Soyas brothers and to the dark Juan Joicos – in pictures they were always profiled kneeling in their fishing boat. There we'd yawn away our breakfast time with the wind at our backs until Bartolomé Bartolomé arrived, and then, with no clear idea of how to play the best games, we would look out at the bustle under the canvas awning through kegs of porgies, roe, and fishbellies. The workers waited until the big globe of fish, hoisted in a net by a winch from the fish tank, would spill out on the platform before moving in with their clubs; the women in their bloody skirts and bonnets would bend over the tables and apply themselves at cleaning fish and salting it, their big knives whirring dizzily.

We wouldn't take off our shoes to play then, as we would have done before: we'd be ashamed. Now we'd spread out over the whole ship, squeaking up a racket with our U.S. Keds, jumping over pools of sunlight written on the deck by wind and tackle, running first helter-skelter on the old planks but then describing circles, intersections, sketching S shapes and the other letters with our arms spread out like wings on the Company's airplane that pulled COCA-COLA through our upper sky. Sometimes we'd lie down on deck and use our hands as visors to explore the clouds, cut through the air more quickly looking for the China Clipper or the Hindenburg's resplendent panels, and we'd spend those mornings furrowing our eyebrows, with a painful bright spot somewhere in our eyes because – and that was what Cisneros shouted at us when he saw us there face up – there was nothing really worthwhile happening in our sky, far from it.

At other times we'd organize track and field contests to see who won the Olympics in Berlin. My favorite event was the one hundred meters, where I broke Jesse Owens' record, edging Bartolomé Bartolomé in a photo finish, the photo itself snapped by Isabel with the Kodak lent her by Columbia. The track was marked out between the sanctuary of the Virgin and the closest intake tube. When we reached the finish line we would be gasping and our legs would hurt. Not wanting then to keep on running, we'd imagine some more sedentary games.

Little by little we'd approach the marble boat – the boat that-couldn't-that-couldn't-that-couldn't-sail that Columbia had sung about to me a century earlier persuading me to swallow porridge from my little Mickey Mouse jar – it was hanging near the drive wheel from some chains that had been painted white. On a bronze plaque screwed to one of the davits a kind of epitaph was written. The pilot Ismael Sencillo, a beloved mutineer, a poet, had lowered starboard boat No. 5 during a spring squall, and armed with a compass and a dueling pistol, and with almost no farewell to anyone, had disappeared forever over the horizon. Ancient eyewitnesses had heard him shout: "I'll show you now, you sons of bitches!" as he rode out over the waves. But – as sometimes is the case with final words and drowned events – the phrase was *comme il faut* on the inscription. Since the reason for his departure was a mystery, or perhaps had not been examined in depth, some people – a minority – held that he had meant to find land all by himself at his own risk and then steer our ship toward it; others – also a minority – their opinions based on one or another of the contradictory papers that had been put together as his testament, were sure that he had glimpsed the infamous White Whale, the monster who had been stalking us since Genesis along the dark route, and that it would have to be destroyed if we were ever to reach land. But there also were those who never bothered with conjecture: the pilot's name might surface randomly at a birthday celebration or a christening, there to be associated with Matías Pérez, a talkative balloonist who one afternoon had launched himself toward Halley's Comet.

Except for me, everyone on the quarterdeck had seen Sencillo's ghost seated at the poopdeck of his marble monument. He made his appearances after midnight, when the taverns by the smokestack had all rolled down their metal curtains and only spirits stayed above the deck. Mama and Papa used to see him often on the hot nights when they left their game of ajolome and went out for air. Ana Zoila, returning from under the canvas awning on the laborious days of settling the accounts, would often hear him praying. Nonetheless, according to Ambrosio, who kept her company up to the door of the quarterdeck, the pilot's stationary shadow would quietly intone the ballad "great as the wide ocean, and as great the sorrow," his rowdy moustache quivering in the night air beneath the gleaming constellations.

We still pretended that we rowed the boat. But the mysterious island didn't come up quickly anymore, and along the route we'd try to reconstruct the color plates we'd seen inside a menacing book entitled *Storms and Shipwrecks* that Columbia used to read, in whose acted-out version Isabel would stuff herself, dying with laughter, with the choicest morsels of our arms and legs, which had been amputated by the dexterous Pepe Luis. Of course we knew already that the word *coño* had no magical properties anymore, not even if you laced your fingers together (Ambrosio's latest recommendation). For some reason its sonorous spell had worn itself out, and now, if I wanted to use it for something, it had to be written in the air in green fire, hung from the yards like a perforated shining curtain, and then, shutting eyes and teeth, I had to picture myself jumping a good distance through the center of the letters.

For several months I set out what we'd do on land, but in time my forehead's arrogant scar was fading, toasted by the sun of one day following another, and after a malevolent declaration made by Ana Zoila upon leaving church one Sunday, Bartolomé Bartolomé had blurted to my face that I had lied, I never had been in the fishtank. My friendship with the mutinous Cisneros, moreover, was not by then a sign of daring: his shabby figure, his notorious vagrancy, his link to the unruly rabble that, according to Mama and Papa, had disturbed the climate of normality that had ensued upon the opening of the university, plus the absurd visages and bows that he put on whenever anyone of quality passed by, had gradually undone the awe we had for him. One morning, when we acted out the *Treasure Island* episodes that radio brought us, we adopted without argument Isabel's suggestion that henceforward Cisneros's name would be Ben Gunn, the misshaped hermit who kept watch on Flint's unburied treasure. With things being as they were, the expeditions over land, which kept getting rarer, would be commanded by Lucianito or Bartolomé Bartolomé, though my role as the discoverer was still respected up until the morning when the mysterious island stopped appearing.

VII

But I haven't been entirely sincere in writing down these recollections. At the beginning of that year I was a protagonist in a strange scene which, perhaps from timidity or reserve, I first intended to pass over. However, I have decided to include it, now that time has passed and the ship and everything have changed so much.

We'd have been sailing across the Sargasso Sea in a winter of such heat and doldrums as to put the almanac in doubt. Columbia would come in flushed, accompanied in advance by the creaking ribs of the umbrella – always unwilling to fold up – which Ambrosio would hold. Tossing writing book and primer on my berth, she would admire her long, extremely red fingernails, fan herself with her smooth straw Leghorn hat, and say: "How hot it is, Julián Ocampo! What will it be like in August if we're barely into February now?" And on my berth now, with the door closed behind Ambrosio's good afternoon, she'd cast her glance over the knocked-down covered wagons, dead hussars and grenadiers that lay out on the planks, the artillery deployed to aid the soldiers' final charge, and then she'd open up the primer on her lap, seat me to her right, stiff, dignified, clutching in my hand the little drummer boy who had a bandaged forehead and half-opened mouth, repeating slowly P A, PA, P A, PA, PAPA, following the fingernail that traversed the page like a polished flame, M A, MA, M A, MA, MAMA, laying the drummer down beside the primer – impossible to stand him up, the folds, the pleats – to have her shove him when she underscored the last letter, send him falling from her thigh into the sheets, see her smile, and hear her say: "He looks like you," and then I'd raise my hand to touch the bandage Dr. Miñagorri had applied to me, try to adjust it, flushed with pride, make a mistake on N I, NI, Ñ O, ÑO, NIÑO, reading hurriedly NIÑA, actually not meaning to, thrown off by gratitude and pleasure because she also knew my blood was beating underneath the enamel and the lead, and slowly she would pass her arm behind my neck and press me to her quilted breast, hurting me a little, saying: "Learn all you can, Julián Ocampo, when you grow up I'll marry you," and she'd say it with a voice both soft and low, and broken, as if she were going to cry, and there we'd be, she complaining of the heat, murmuring that she couldn't breathe, that in Paris women went out on the streets not wearing corsets, and still squeezing me, she'd tell me that perhaps she'd give hers up that very afternoon, at least until the weather freshened up, for she was suffocating, couldn't take it any longer, and leaning forward with the buttons on her blouse undone, she'd ask me to let go of her and keep going on the lesson, but beforehand I should bolt the door and shut the curtains, and I'd stick the soldier in my pocket, carry out the mission, and then go back to my berth to confront an intricacy of flesh, hems, and laces soaked in sweat, she urging me, explaining how one had to pull the cords so that the silver arrow would go through the eyelets, then her back appeared, much whiter than you'd think, the skin indented by her seams and stays, crisscrossed by reddish stringlines, a little like the penitents whipped to a drumroll on the deck, and she herself, now standing, would unhitch the last buttons of her blouse, and turned around to face the curtains she'd remove her corset with the pale silk ribbons sliding on her shoulders, to let it drop while twisting windward, there being almost no transition, her skirt eddying, her eyes lost in the upheaval, her breasts whipped back like canvas in the wind, and haughty and enigmatic she'd navigate back toward my berth, her ankle nudging aside the long siege cannon Ana Zoila gave to me, knocking it against the grenadier who lunged out madly with his bayonet, I watching as she neared, stopped, snatched up the primer from the berth and then sat beside me murmuring that we would resume the lesson now, and naturally the class resumed, but now beneath a different emblem, different flag, perhaps the one that flew upon the island I discovered every morning

after I'd erased the ship with the magic word, and it
would be so easy now to jump above the N I, NI, Ñ O,
ÑO, NIÑO, fix my vision on the letters' center, and pro-
nounce C O, CO, Ñ O, ÑO, COÑO, the enchanted sound
Ambrosio used to lower the drawbridge resting on the
edges of all things, and she'd embrace me once again, listening surely also to the little bells whose music gleamed
onshore, and I'd take out the soldier from my pocket,
make him march carefully between the dunes and pen-
guin bonfires, then inch by inch he'd climb up to the jasmine fence, I'd order him to sink his forehead in the
brown and almost lilac-colored crown of the great mountain which a profoundly sweet and submerged voice
would pose as J U A, JUA, N A, NA, JUANA – the other
one, the one trembling in my half-opened mouth, would
be in an instant "her sister," although just as tender, soft,
and fragrant as the pillow stuffed with albatross down
that Ana Zoila rested on whenever she was suffering from
headache – and there we'd be, she loosening my pigtail,
smoothing out my hair above the gauze, conjecturing,
after a sigh, that when the summer came the heat would
kill us, and I, attentive, silent, scared to open up my eyes,
my face sepulchred in the languid scent of talcum powder
and cologne, the soldier's head sepulchred likewise in the
other mountain's peak, more yet, the epaulettes, the torso,
the hand that hung above the drumstick, drum beating on
his thigh, stiff blue coattail that rolled up when gaiters
pushed against it, she muttering that her skirt was boiling
as though on a stove, and I would be the one who felt
around her waist to find the buttons, pull her ruffles, making them roll to her feet in a crackle of stretched seams,
she saying nothing to me, her body arched, letting her
salmon-colored bloomers slide above the hollow curves,
so I'd take them, with her stockings and her skirt, out

from between her ankle boots, I on my knees, stretching out my hand now with the soldier in it, fingering the lead nub over his left thigh – the right leg would be suspended midstride – moving his bare head toward the fleecy mystery that rested on the sheets, moving it gently over the hairy wound, its opening now dribbling a little, she moving her hips more and more, and then a mouthful of foamy spittle, and suddenly she'd jump up from the berth howling and fall on hands and knees on the floor, spoiling the deployment of a lancer squadron, and then she'd start to tremble and moan as though grieving, shaking her head from side to side in desperation, and I would see now she was suffering but I wouldn't know why, maybe some painful illness no one knew about, and I'd give her a long look, as if I'd seen the queen in chains brought low in an engraving printed in *The Book of Heroic Deeds*, the ax blade to her neck, and suddenly the urge to get it over with, to cut the wailing and the tears, rescue her forever from that misery of distressing, cloudy liquids, and I'd reach behind the cannon, aim its mouth, and load it with a green glass bomb, and snap the spring to shoot and make it burst against her flank, then reload with a fat, yellow bomb to stagger the more conspicuous of her breasts, and dip my hand into the box again to find a red bomb, and then another that had purple veins, and another one, especially malign, rolled up with spit and scraps of newsprint, she moaning at each impact, lifting at intervals her startled head, inflamed, her lips all chewed and her eyes all whipped, in shock, and finally, after a mothball's lethal impact, she'd collapse, plugged full of holes, grave, stiff, and she would have to wriggle on her spine like a covered wagon blown down by the cannonade, its canvas shredded, horses gone, axles broken, and I'd start crawling toward her, smell the secret wetness of her wound, and without knowing why, I'd run my tongue along her thighs to dry them off before I left her to the soldiers and ran up on the deck to find a disconcerting scene of trees and trollies, and Cisneros laughing, dressed in immaculate white linen and a Panama hat, smoking a cigar while seated on a park bench, telling me to wipe that scared look off my face, that soon enough there'd be an end to Columbia's letter books and primers, Ana Zoila's noontime persecutions, and the vision of the mysterious island; that there'd be an end to many things and others would begin, because I'd neared the age of common sense, which – and he'd say this just before disappearing – was the least common of the senses.

ff

Faber Caribbean Series

The aim of this series, edited by Caryl Phillips, is to publish the finest work being produced in the Caribbean and the Caribbean diaspora, in the four major languages of the region. It contains original work, including classic texts some of which are published for the first time in English.

Gabriel García Márquez
The Fragrance of Guava
Conversations with by Plinio Apuleyo Mendoza

In these conversations with a friend and contemporary Márquez speaks movingly, revealingly and unaffectedly about his family background, his early travels and struggles as a writer, his literary antecedents and his artistic concerns in Paris in the sixties.

Maryse Condé
Windward Heights

A brilliantly imaginative transportation of *Wuthering Heights* to a Caribbean context. Heathcliff is re-incarnated in the character Razyé; and Cuba and Guadeloupe in the last quarter of the nineteenth century form the backdrop to the murderous passion which binds him to Cathy.

Wilson Harris
Palace of the Peacock

The compelling adventure story of a doomed crew beating their way up-river through the jungle of Guyana. First published in 1960, Wilson Harris's novel reveals a poetic vision of hallucinatory vividness and uncompromising energy.

ff

order form

Please send me:

THE FRAGRANCE OF GUAVA (0 571 19326 9)		£7.99
Gabriel García Márquez		
PALACE OF THE PEACOCK (0 571 19323 4)		£7.99
Wilson Harris		
WINDWARD HEIGHTS (0 571 19324 2)		£7.99
Maryse Condé		
EXTRAVAGANT STRANGERS (0 571 19240 8)		£8.99
Caryl Phillips, ed.		
THE NATURE OF BLOOD (0 571 19205 x)		£6.99
Caryl Phillips		

Total including free postage and packing   £ _____

I enclose a cheque for £ _____ made payable to Faber and Faber Ltd.

Please charge my ⌐ Access ⌐ Visa ⌐ Amex ⌐ Diner's Club ⌐ Eurocard

Cardholder _____ Expiry Date _____

Account No ⌐ ⌐ ⌐ ⌐ ⌐ ⌐ ⌐ ⌐ ⌐ ⌐ ⌐ ⌐ ⌐ ⌐ ⌐ ⌐ ⌐ ⌐

Name _____

Address _____

Signed _____ Date _____

Send to: Marketing Dept, Faber and Faber Ltd, 3 Queen Square, London WC1N 3AU
TEL 071 465 0045   FAX 071 465 0034